CHARLIE CALLING

COLIN P. CAHOON

Caja Negra Enterprises
Dallas, TX

Charlie Calling
By Colin P. Cahoon

Copyright 2019 by Colin P. Cahoon. All rights reserved.

Cover Design by Bonnie Cahoon and Joshua Manley. All rights reserved.

ISBN 978-0-578-53508-1
Published by Caja Negra Enterprises
Dallas, Texas

Printed in the United States of America

No part of this publication may be reproduced by any means without the express, written permission of the author.

This book is dedicated to Claire, Paul, and Mary.
May you never look into the box.

CHARLIE
CALLING

CHAPTER 1
BLACK BOX

Lieutenant Archibald Turner of the Royal Navy contemplated his options. Trafalgar Square lay dead ahead and on route for the shortest distance to his destination. He need only cross the square and turn left on Whitehall. His destination, Admiralty House, was but a short distance further on.

The mob was the complication. Thousands of men, working-class men with smudged faces glaring out from under rough and worn caps, milled about shoulder-to-shoulder, filling the square and spilling out into every adjoining street. In fact, Turner encountered the beginnings of the demonstration a quarter of a mile up the Strand as he approached Trafalgar Square.

He mounted a short wall to get a better look at the crowd. Placards hammered to ominously stout boards sprouted up from the sea of humanity. Nervous-looking Bobbies in their dark blue coats and tall helmets stood in pairs thinly interspersed about the periphery of the square. If he hugged that periphery he'd make better time than attempting to penetrate the middle of the mob.

Turner slid down from his vantage point and patted the left breast pocket on his jacket. The documents were still there. He glanced at his pocket watch. There was no choice. The First Lord of the Admiralty was expecting him, and to detour now would put him past his time. He'd press on.

As he worked his way through the mass, keeping his eyes down and ignoring the occasional sharp elbow jab, he mentally rehearsed the presentation he would give. The message must be conveyed perfectly. The plans in his pocket could change the path of history, putting the Royal Navy years ahead of the persistent Germans and saving countless British lives if His Majesty's Navy was ever put to the test. It all made perfect sense to him, but the First Lord must be convinced, and that would not be easy.

A disgusting smell caught his attention, something between burning sulfur, raw sewage, and a rotting dead animal. He reached for his handkerchief to cover his nose. Someone pushed him from behind. He staggered forward, tripping on a foot. As he extended his arm grasping for something to break his fall, a strong grip on his forearm pulled him back upright.

"Why, what 'av we 'ere?" the source of the strong grip inquired as he released Turner's arm and began to brush and straighten the lieutenant's jacket with one hand.

Turner turned to face the stranger and pushed his grubby fingers away.

"Now look here..." Turner's protestations were cut short when he inhaled the putrid rotten-egg-smelling breath of his would-be savior. The smell came from a mouth full of brown, broken, jagged teeth framed by a flabby, unshaven face. The stranger grinned at him as he straightened Turner's cap and continued his random tugging at Turner's jacket.

"Why, it be a gentleman in distress, I believe. Now, 'av no fear, I be 'ere now to help you, sir."

Turner pulled away, placing the handkerchief back over his nose. He took a harder look at the man. The stranger's right eye was covered with a grey film, and his left eye drooped. He wore a dingy jacket that was too long for his arms, a battered and greasy cap, and trousers with rips over repaired rips. The man fussed about Turner's person with one hand, but his other hand cradled something under the dingy jacket.

"Now look here, I don't need your assistance. Be gone with you before I have a policeman take you in for theft and vagrancy. Go!"

"'Theft and vagrancy,' you say? Humph. Think I'm a ruffian, do yer? Humph. No good deed goes unpunished." The smelly stranger straightened himself, placed his free hand on his hip, and, hurling a last smelly "humph" in Turner's direction, slipped into the morass.

Gagging and coughing, the lieutenant turned away in search of fresh air. He took a moment to get his bearing and instinctively patted his left breast pocket.

"No, that can't be!" he exclaimed aloud. He felt the inside of the pocket. Instead of finding his papers, he pulled out a small card imprinted with a single word, a man's first name. It made no sense. His mind raced. "No…the vagrant!"

Turner searched the crowd in the general direction the stranger had gone. He glimpsed a greasy cap headed for a side street. Turner pushed through the mob trying to reach him.

His movements were no longer polite as he jabbed, pushed, and fought his way forward. He ignored the shouts and curses from the men he shoved about. Someone poked him in the ribs with a hard object. His cap was knocked from his head. He kept moving forward, not bothering to stop to retrieve it.

As he worked his way down the side street, the crowd thinned somewhat. The rotten smell returned, lingering along his path. The man Turner was following turned suddenly off the street into a mews. A gap opened in the crowd, and he sprinted forward.

Arriving at the mews, he stopped and peered ahead. The contrast between the packed street and the empty mews was unsettling. There was no one to be seen along the mews' entire length, just a spot of sunlight at the other side where the mews constricted to a narrow alley. The same stench hung thick in air. His man was somewhere in there, and so were his documents.

"Come out and make this easy on yourself," the lieutenant shouted down the shadowy passage. "Those documents are of no use to you, but they are of great value to me. I'll do you great harm to get them back."

There was no answer. The disgusting smell seemed to build in waves. Turner put his handkerchief back up to this nose and entered the mews.

It took a moment for his eyes to adjust to the lack of sunlight. To make matters worse, they began to water and sting. He spit into his handkerchief and applied the wetted portion to his nose. As he crept forward he methodically searched to his left and right, pausing every few steps to listen for any movement.

"This is your last warning…"

A shadow leapt toward him. A raised knife gleamed above the form. Turner reached up with both hands grasping toward the knife. The form grabbed the hair on top of his scalp. Turner held tight with both hands to an arm holding the knife before his face. In an instant his head jerked forward and the knife lurched at his throat.

The searing pain was fleeting. He heard a thud and crack against his neck. The world pitched downward until his eyes looked up at the sky. He felt nothing; he couldn't move.

A black, square object with a small hole in the middle advanced toward his face. His eye was drawn to the hole as it went from red, to purple, to white. A blinding flash filled his brain.

He blinked and looked around. He sat in a bubble of light surrounded by a shroud of pitch black. He felt his neck, smooth and normal, only a bit of beard stubble made any impression. There was silence all around. Where was this place? A dark cave of some sort?

The bubble grew, gradually expanding to illuminate objects, no—claws, no—creatures that appeared from the gloom. On the bubble expanded until all was light.

The creatures encircled him, standing shoulder-to-shoulder, in rings perhaps a dozen or so deep extended outwardly as far as the light of the bubble extended. There must be hundreds of them, cat-like with faces a mixture of animal and human features. They appeared to stand about four-feet tall, but slightly stooped on skinny legs, as if they were dogs that learned to walk upright. Behind them they trailed tails, mostly hairless but for a bushy end. Their bodies were nearly hairless too, except for a line of rough bristly stuff that started on the base of their tails, followed their spines, and ran to the tops of their heads.

Their faces were round and almost childish looking. Each had a generous mouth that revealed pointed white teeth when opened, and open them they did. Chomping ensued, each creature making a clicking sound as their jaws closed. At first they stood still except for the odd chomping. Then each one began to twitch. Drool dripped from their mouths. The encircling mass began to quiver and jerk. The clicking grew to a deafening continuous thunder.

Hundreds of shrieks pierced his ears. The creatures lurched toward him, hopping forward on hind legs while using clawed hands to help propel them in monkey fashion. Soon those claws were scratching and pulling at him. Pain erupted from the puncture of sharp teeth, his flesh ripped by the mouthful from his limbs and torso. He tried to scream but heard nothing over the frenzied screeching of the creatures.

All went red, then black, then silent.

***

Inspector Edmund Jenkins of Scotland Yard reached under his mattress for his pistol, sat up in his bed, and listened intently. The first creaking noise, the one that abruptly woke him, would be from the third step from the bottom of the stairs that led to the landing outside his bedroom door. He counted in his head to the rhythm of the ticking clock coming from a corner in his dark room, "One, two, three."

The next sound should be the creak from the seventh stair, which was almost halfway up the flight. There was no reason for someone to be on the stairs. He locked the front door before going to bed, and the door was the only access to the stairs.

"Four, five, six, seven." The anticipated creak came, the unmistakable more muted sound of the seventh stair. Whoever was on the stairs was moving slowly, stealthily toward his bedroom door.

He continued to count the seconds while making a calculation of the expected arrival time at the landing, given the elapsed time between the two squeaks. He sat rigidly still with the gun pointed

5

at the outline of the bedroom door, barely perceptible in the blackness of his room, but visually anchored by a soft glow underneath coming from the electric lamp left on in the entry hall below. He breathed deeply, pushing back the thumping in his head as his heart pounded his body to alertness.

When his math and counting told him that the intruder should have arrived at the door, he held his breath and listened. Nothing. What was the intruder waiting for? Maybe taking aim?

The glow from under the door went out. Jenkins didn't hesitate. His pistol banged concussively as he fired two shots at the door. He strained to hear over the ringing in his ears for any sound confirming that he'd hit his target on the other side, a groan, or the sound of a body hitting the floor, but again, there was nothing.

Pitch black followed the flash from his pistol. He groped for his bedside table, felt for a match, and lit an oil lamp that flickered a yellow hue upon the door, revealing two bullet holes.

Jenkins got up from bed and retrieved a jacket, an umbrella, and his bob hat from a coat stand. Laying the jacket open on the bed, he placed the umbrella along the length of the jacket with the crook end sticking above the collar. Next came the pillow, placed inside the jacket on top of the umbrella. He buttoned the jacket and placed the hat on the crook end of the umbrella such that the hat rested above the neck opening to the jacket.

He picked up the bundle and approached the door, standing next to it near the handle. With his pistol in his right hand and the jacket bundle cradled in his right arm, Jenkins turned the handle and swung open the door. Out he tossed the bundle, hat side pointed up, toward the landing at about chest height.

The eruption from the bottom of the stairs was deafening, the sound of three guns exploding away several times in short succession. The jacket, pillow, umbrella, and hat all blew back into his bedroom. Feathers from the pillow floated crazily about the doorway intermingling with the gun smoke that wafted up from below.

Jenkins dove for the floor of the landing. He poked his pistol over the top of the landing, pointed it toward the ground floor, and fired three times. He stopped firing, saving his last bullet of his six-shot revolver.

This time he'd made contact. A loud scream was followed by several more shots from below, all of which sailed over him to strike the bedroom doorframe.

He heard shuffling and then the sound of the front door opening. The inspector peered over the edge of the landing. There was nothing below, just an open door to the dark street.

Jenkins got up and bolted down the stairs. He emerged from his apartment as a horse-drawn carriage sped away down the empty street outside. A man was being pulled into the coach. What was under his arm? Jenkins caught a glimpse before the man disappeared into the passenger compartment. Jenkins raised his arm and fired his last shot at the back of the carriage to no apparent effect. The carriage accelerated and was soon down the street and around a corner.

Had he really seen what he thought he'd seen under the man's arm? It was dark, and the man and carriage were moving fast. Surely not. He'd not seen or heard about a black box in over a year. Doctor Cunningham and Jim Talbot had destroyed dozens. Had one box escaped notice all this time?

Back inside, gunpowder smoke hung in the air. His feet slipped on the entryway. He reached down and felt blood thick along the floor. He switched on the electric lamp and clicked the receiver on the telephone mounted on the entry hall wall.

"This is Inspector Edmund Jenkins of Scotland Yard," he barked into the mouthpiece. "Put me through to the night watch at the Yard."

A series of clicks was followed by the answer of the officer on watch.

"This is Inspector Jenkins. I've been attacked at my home on Wandsworth Road by gunmen. Send out an alert noting that at least three gunmen have fled my residence last seen headed south on Southville Road in a carriage sporting a bullet hole in the center of the back window. At least one of the gunmen is wounded and bleeding. Instruct all London hospitals to be on the lookout for him." He quickly dismissed the idea of reporting a possible sighting of a black box. It was just a glimpse, after all. No need to start panicked rumors. "Did you get all that?"

The officer on the line dutifully repeated the report back and inquired as to the inspector's wellbeing.

"Yes, I'm fine. Also dispatch a detective to my home to assist with the collection of evidence. Oh, and ask him to bring me the extra bob hat and jacket I keep in my office. The ones I wore home this evening will need replacing."

Jenkins set the mouthpiece back on the receiver, walked up the stairs, and reloaded his revolver.

***

"Inspector Jenkins, I'm pleased to see you this afternoon," announced the coroner as Jenkins entered the examination room. "I heard you experienced a rather frightful night. Nasty thing…a Scotland Yard Inspector attacked by armed gunmen in his own home. I pray you escaped any harm."

Jenkins flashed an angry glare at the police sergeant standing on the other side of the body from the coroner. "Word travels quickly. I'm quite well, thank you. I understand we have another knife victim?"

"No surprises here, Inspector, similar to the others." The coroner removed the thick linen sheet to reveal the bloated naked body. "The knife was found buried to the hilt in the front of the throat. Here, you can see the bruise marks around the entry point indicating the severe force exerted. Despite the blade being slightly shorter in length than the distance from the front of the neck to the back, it left a half-inch exit wound on the back of the neck. The tip of the blade was not protruding through the back when the body was found. The neck had been flattened by the initial force at entry, but flexed somewhat back round over time. The trachea was crushed, you can see, as I pull open this entry wound. Yes, there it is just above my finger. The spinal cord was severed. Death would have been almost instantaneous."

The coroner wiped his hands on the butcher's apron he wore around his suit and looked expectantly at Jenkins.

Jenkins rolled an unlit cigar from one side of his mouth to the other with his tongue. "Yet, the eyes are still wide open. You have the knife?"

The coroner nodded turning to an assistant, likewise clad in a butcher's apron, who retrieved the knife from a shelf across the room and handed it to Jenkins.

"You'll note the lack of imprint on the top of the handle," the coroner offered.

Jenkins gnawed on the cigar as he examined the weapon.

"You said no surprises here. I assume there was a calling card?"

"In the left, interior jacket pocket."

Jenkins turned to the uniformed sergeant standing casually on the other side of the body. "Who was he?"

"Archibald Turner, Lieutenant, Royal Navy."

"Never heard of him."

"Top of his class at the Royal Naval College, Dartmouth," continued the sergeant. "Reported to be bright, hardworking, and quite capable. Despite his modest family connections, most saw him as an up and coming officer destined for great things. He did seem to have quite the imagination."

"Imagination?"

"We searched his lodgings. In going through his personal effects we happened upon a paper he drafted last year to the Admiralty. He hypothesized that the greatest threat to our nation is not surface ships, but submarines, small craft that attack from under the waves. He proposed the immediate investment in research on the use of land and, eventually, ship-based aero planes to counter this supposed threat."

The coroner chuckled. "Quite an imagination indeed, I can only imagine the Admiralty's reaction to the suggestion that such cowardly underwater milk-bottles could so much as scratch the paint on a British dreadnought."

Jenkins kept his gaze on the sergeant. "How did we find him?"

"A child was playing in Regent's Park in bushes near the boating lake when she stumbled upon the body."

"Any witness to his death?"

"None, nor to him being placed in the bushes."

"Placed?"

"There was a tremendous loss of blood," the coroner interjected. "You can see evidence on his jacket and shirt. When I inquired about blood in the shrubbery, your sergeant told me there was none to be found, nothing on the ground, nothing on dry leaves and so forth. He must have been placed in the bushes at least several hours after he was killed."

"How long has he been dead?"

The coroner paused and looked over the body again. "Three to four days."

"Which corresponds with his last known movements." The sergeant drifted closer to the body, as if trying to urge some concurrence from the stiff body. "The lieutenant was last seen on his way to a meeting at Admiralty House three days ago, a meeting with the First Lord, no less."

"About? Wait, don't tell me." Jenkins raised his hand high, still holding the murder weapon and pointing it at the ceiling. "'Top secret, not to be shared with Scotland Yard'."

The sergeant cleared his throat and issued a nervous cough. "I was instructed by the First Lord's Secretary not to inquire."

"Of course." Jenkins shook his head, bringing the knife back down to his side.

The inspector approached the body, focusing on the glassy eyes staring upward.

"Let me summarize." Jenkins removed the cigar stub from his mouth, holding both the stub and the knife in one hand. "We have now examined six bodies with similar wounds in the past three weeks. All found with knives buried in the neck, entering either from the front or back. All these victims were stabbed with such force that the knife traveled in one side of the neck and out the other, severing the spines. All were found with their eyes open. None exhibit evidence of a struggle or other injuries."

He returned the cigar to his mouth, bit down and rolled it toward his cheek with his tongue before continuing.

"All victims were found fully clothed with a calling card having an identical single word typed thereon found somewhere on their person. Three of the knives had a distinctive "X" stamped on the top of the hilt, whilst three did not, the knife involved in this case being the third of the latter category.

"All the victims were seemingly healthy males of various ages from various professions and various backgrounds. We have no witnesses, no motive, and no clues other than what are provided by their corpses."

Jenkins looked about the room, at the coroner, his assistant, and the sergeant, all of whom were staring at the corpse.

Jenkins removed the cigar stub again, setting it on the examination table.

"May I see the calling card?"

The coroner's assistant obliged, handing the small rectangular card to the inspector.

Jenkins turned it over in his hand. "A single word in black print, 'Charlie.' What does it mean?"

He brought the card close to his face, looking hard at the print. Wait, that smell. He brought the card to his nose and inhaled. There it was, a slight sulfurous note, distinct from the smell of the dead body. He sniffed at the knife handle...the same rotten egg smell.

"Could it be?" Jenkins murmured.

"I beg your pardon, Inspector," the sergeant meekly inquired.

Jenkins ran the variables through his head. The smell, the calling card marked "Charlie," a possible black box sighting, the pieces in the puzzle began to fit, and the picture was...

Jenkins dropped the knife and card onto the corpse. He grabbed the sergeant by the arm and pulled him toward the door.

"Quickly, sergeant, follow me and listen very carefully."

The two men flew from the room and into a corridor, the inspector out front and the sergeant trailing slightly off his shoulder as they both sprinted down the hall.

"Where is Jim Talbot?"

"I'm not certain, sir. I've not seen him since last week when he informed us his father had died."

"Item one, find Jim Talbot immediately. I want him under escort and inside this building within the hour. Item two, get word to my man, Mick. Tell him he must fetch our colleague in Manchester without delay. He's in grave danger. Item three...are you getting this?"

"Yes, Inspector, find Talbot, Mick to Manchester."

"Item three, turn off at the next hallway ahead." Jenkins pointed at an approaching entrance. "Find the cryptologist. Bring him to my office straightaway."

"Yes, Inspector," the sergeant replied as he made the turn down the hall.

Jenkins ran on until reaching his office. He drew a key from his vest pocket and unlocked a filing cabinet. Rifling through the drawer, he selectively pulled two sheets of paper from a manila folder.

"He's right behind me, Inspector." The sergeant stood at the door, breathing heavily with sweat rolling off his brow.

"Thank you. Now be off and attend to the first two items."

"Yes, Inspector."

The sergeant had no sooner cleared the doorway than the cryptologist appeared.

"You called for me, Inspector?"

"Yes, here, take these." Jenkins handed him the papers he had pulled from the cabinet. "These are the coding protocols for Doctor Cunningham in Dallas, Texas, and Mrs. Bell in New Mexico. You'll see them so labeled on their respective pages. Write this down."

Jenkins handed him a notepad and a pen.

"The coded message to be sent to Cunningham is as follows: 'Proceed now to ranch and await instructions.'"

The cryptologist scribbled away on the notepad.

"The coded message to be sent to Mrs. Bell is as follows: 'Molly in grave danger; hold her at ranch until further instructed.' Read them back."

The cryptologist obliged, reading each message back to the inspector's satisfaction.

"But sir, it's late evening now in America. At the earliest they'll get these messages tomorrow morning."

"It's the best we can do. See to it."

***

Jim Talbot stared down the road, the road that led to his father's house. He still couldn't do it—go back. A week had gone by, but he still couldn't do it. The image of his father, lying stiffly on his back, eyes wide open, dead—push it away.

And the smell, he'd never forget the smell. It was unnerving. His father hadn't been dead for more than a few hours, but the house harbored an awful smell, a familiar smell, sulfurous and putrid. It scared him. The last time he smelled that stench was two and half years ago in the cellar when confronted by the man with the black box.

What a terrible nightmare, living with those awful creatures, always urging him to eat while he starved away.

"Eat, eat," they screamed.

"I will not eat people!"

Thank God, Molly Bell brought him back. He'd never met her, but Inspector Jenkins said she was hidden away somewhere "at the end of the earth" where no one would ever find her.

Inspector Jenkins...he must be wondering about his whereabouts by now. Jim doubted anyone knew where he'd been the last week, wandering the streets of London, thinking, trying to resolve in his head his father's death stare, the stench, and the terrible memories it all brought back. The memory of that smell still lingered, or was it wafting up the street now? He snorted hard hoping to expel the smell or thought of it, whichever it was.

He couldn't return, not yet. Even the thought of his father's horse and their hansom cab, the former needing daily attention, wasn't enough to overcome the fear. Surely someone was feeding the poor horse. He turned away from the street heading home, and trudged in the opposite direction.

He meandered, lost in thought. Images of creatures, little monsters they were, kept popping into his head. How many black boxes had he looked into, praying never to see those monsters again? They clawed and pulled on him as he pushed to the light. The more boxes he looked into, the harder it became to reach the light. His faith in coming back out diminished with each box he entered.

The black boxes must be all gone now. Jenkins hadn't asked him to explode one in a while, at least a year. A blessing and a curse it was. He was blessed to be alive, away from the monsters. He was blessed with the power to save others and destroy the infernal black boxes. He was cursed to be one of the few who could do it, and he wasn't sure he could do it anymore.

Did Molly Bell feel the same way? Did she dread looking into the next box, pulling away from the monsters, fighting for the light? Was it harder with every new box for her? Thank God they were all gone.

He wandered on without caring where he was going, sometimes going straight, sometimes turning this way or that.

Where was Molly Bell? Did she have the dreams, the nightmares? He hoped not. He saw his father dead, glassy eyes wide open, before he actually saw his dead father. It was a dream, and then it wasn't.

Jim was roused by the sudden sense that something wasn't right. A shiver ran up his spine. Jim Talbot had done enough following in his short life to tell when he was being followed, and that was exactly what he sensed. What had he heard? He focused on the sound and his memory of it.

It started with the clicking of a worn heel. Every other step of someone behind him clicked. Then the clicking stopped, but the footsteps from behind continued. The same footsteps were joined by others, how many he couldn't tell.

To look back might provoke a confrontation, but how else to gauge the odds? What would Inspector Jenkins advise? The late afternoon sun sliced between the passing London buildings behind his right shoulder. If he made a left turn at the next street, he should see his pursuers' shadows entering the junction before they made the turn.

Quickening his pace as he approached the next street, he spun to his left at the earliest opportunity. Soon the sound of footsteps grew louder. He glanced back to his right. Three shadows stretched across the road—three men pursuing one seventeen-year-old boy who now sorely missed his hansom cab.

Jim looked ahead to see he'd made a mistake. The sidewalk was empty to the next mews. The relative safety of a busy street was gone. He couldn't risk being confronted with no one else around, and so he ran.

The noise of pursuing feet spattered behind him as the shadows responded to his flight. Perhaps if he got back into a crowd, they'd stop? Jim pushed hard to the next intersection and headed for the busiest nearby spot he could think of, the Battersea Bridge.

The approach of spectators didn't seem to deter his pursuers. Jim pressed on harder and harder trying to increase the distance between them. His heart pounded up through his neck. Looking back would cost him distance, so he focused on the iron bridge ahead as it slowly hove into view.

He was dodging pedestrians now, but the sound of clattering shoes seemed as close on him as ever. He made another turn and now had the bridge directly in front of him. It was crowded indeed—a few motor cars, some horse carts, and lots of pedestrians. He commanded his legs to keep churning toward the crowd on the bridge. His side ached; his head pounded.

As he turned onto the bridge his forward progress slowed while he picked his way around the human obstacles. The gap between him and his pursuers might close, but at least they would be equally slowed by the mob. Jim was a dodger, though, and he pinned his chance of escape on extending enough of a lead through the crowded bridge that he might lose himself on the other side.

On he pressed, often going more lateral than straight ahead in order to find the quickest route. The commotion grew behind him as pedestrians protested first his rude darting about and then being more roughly handled by the pursuing lot.

A shot rang out. The people ahead on the bridge instinctively stopped and crouched. Jim was exposed. He turned for the railing. A hot, sharp blow smacked the back of his right arm as the sound of another shot reverberated across the bridge.

The pain in his arm brought time to a halt. Motion, sound, his heartbeat—all stopped. Was it a dream? Was he a dead man? If he wasn't, he had to get over the railing before another shot found its mark, but only his mind seemed to move.

Then the world sped back into focus. Over the edge he leapt. As he accelerated toward the brown swirling water he clasped his throbbing right arm with his left hand, held his breath, and braced for the impact.

CHAPTER 2
BAD DREAMS

Downward, ever downward, the mass of miserable creatures trudged, thousands upon thousands of naked figures crammed shoulder-to-shoulder. They all looked the same, small hairless bodies with stubby arms and stubby legs attached to a thin torso supporting an oversized bald head, each small mouth contorted in agony. This form didn't allow them teeth. This form didn't allow them to feed on flesh. This form—their new form, their redeemed form, their eternal form.

Their feet burned on the hot, steeply sloping surface that dragged them inexorably forward. Their pink skin glistened with sweat which added to their torture due to the bone-chilling, sulfurous-smelling headwind that swirled and roared around them. Each one sensed others nearby, but it gave them no comfort, only fear. For they had no eyes to see, only ears to hear the howl of the foul, putrid wind. They tried to cry out, but they lacked voices. Each was alone in a sea of desperation. They were the wretched refugees of the broken boxes. All had surrendered redemption for eternity.

Molly Bell shivered herself awake. She blinked up at the star-filled New Mexico sky. Another bad dream. When would they stop?

She focused on the happy stars in an attempt to push the image of the tortured souls out of her mind. She sucked in a deep breath of the crisp, dry air tinged with smoke. The evening fire was down to an orange glow but still popped and crackled with little yellow sparks sputtering in random directions and then floating upward, only to die out well short of their remote, sparkling cousins. She closed her eyes and imagined the sparks floating higher, and higher still, until they too sat in the heavens blinking down on her. A sky filled with white and yellow twinkling stars…how beautiful.

Why the bad dreams? Three years of them now. Ever since she awoke from that awful experience with that man with the black box in New York she had the dreams. With every box she stared into the dreams became more foreboding, prophetic, real. No, they weren't bad dreams. They were nightmares. What did they mean?

She'd had tonight's nightmare many times before. She hated seeing her old friends reduced to such a state, like tortured babies. They were awful before, that is true, eating people and all. But she forgave them long ago. Mother was right. We must always forgive, or we can't get on with life. So, she forgave them. But now to see them in such agony in those new forms...why? Was it real? Who was doing that to them? Was it her fault for breaking their box? She wondered about that often. What could she do now to help them? She wondered about that a lot too.

She sat up from the bedding that kept the cold ground at bay and stared into the darkness and then at the glowing embers. The three sleeping cowboys were still there forming a rough ring around her bedding and the fire pit. Raspy snoring from one of the cowboys played a steady rhythm against the otherwise random desert symphony of crickets and coyotes. The horses were all tethered nearby, including the paint they kept saddled "just in case." Good old Pluck, he was always ready to go. Somewhere outside her view, she knew, the fourth cowboy was standing his lonely night watch.

She loved working with the cowboys. And with her childhood asthma long since cured, Molly took advantage of every opportunity to ride the range since turning twelve. That was a year ago, and her worried mother still fretted about her back at the ranch. The cowboys took her under their wings and taught her how to be one of them, how to ride, rope, shoot, sleep on the ground, and, most importantly, to not be afraid. They said she had to "be a man" to ride with them, and she set out to be just that.

The cowboys were good men, too. They kept at her education with patience, cheer, and humor. She missed New York and all her friends there. Living in the high desert outside Alamogordo, New Mexico, as the lone child among hardened men was bewildering at times, but she was never happier than with them and their "dogies."

At least Father came to see her at the ranch from time to time. Molly wished he didn't travel so much.

"I do it for you and your mother, my dear Molly." His voice in her head calmed her. Father was so strong. He never cried like Mother. Once a cowboy told her that Mother had cried the whole time she was out riding the range. Mother denied it. She sure hugged hard, though, whenever Molly got back.

She'd be home soon. Tonight they were on the far eastern edge of the range. Tomorrow they'd look for more strays, count heads, and confirm brands. How long had they been away, seven nights?

She missed Doctor Cunningham, too. Where was he tonight? Mrs. Cunningham must be with him, as she left the ranch more than a year ago when all the black boxes were gone. She loved Mrs. Cunningham. She had a musical laugh and the quickest smile. The cowboys adored her, and always went out of their way to lend her a hand. She remembered how Doctor Cunningham's eyes sparkled whenever he looked at his pretty wife. Maybe someday a man's eyes would sparkle at Molly like that.

Then there was Mick. Of all her friends, Molly missed him the most. His red hair and broad smile made her laugh. Her "protector," that's what he said he was. He talked with that funny Irish accent. Sometimes the cowboys would scratch their heads in confusion. They dared not tease him, though. Mick seemed twice the size of any three of them, and had impressed them enough to think the better of it.

One time a ranch hand was pinned under his horse. The horse had broken its leg in a rattlesnake hole and rolled on its side trapping the rider's leg underneath. Mick ran over, bent down, and single-handedly rolled the horse off the man's leg. The cowboys said they'd never seen anything like it. She was sorry Mick had to go back to England. Sure, she didn't need his protection anymore, but it still felt better when he was around.

Something pulled her away from her thoughts. The crickets had stopped.

"Who's that!" a voice rang out from the darkness. "Get up, boys!" the same voice cried out again.

The other three cowboys sprang to their feet, grabbing rifles and pulling pistols from holsters. A shot rang out, then another. Several men rushed in from the darkness and a melee broke out around the fire pit. Molly watched in stunned silence, standing now, a spectator to the violence breaking out all around her.

The world seemed to slow down as bodies struggled in the glow of the dying fire. The figures moved like large ants wrestling in molasses. The cowboys were forcing the action away from Molly, but they were badly outnumbered. "Go, Molly, go!" shouted one of them as he clung desperately to two men while trying to fight off a third with his leg.

Molly grabbed the wire cage she kept near her bedding and ran for Pluck. The world sped up again as she regained her focus and sprinted at the darkness. She was on in an instant and off they flew into the black desert abyss, leaving the sound of more gunfire behind.

***

Sam Cunningham struggled to wake up. It *must* be a dream. A puppet master in filthy, ragged clothes grinned broadly showing jagged yellow teeth against an unshaven face with a droopy left eye. He commanded his puppet, a gentleman with an indistinguishable face, to dance while engulfed in flames. As the puppet burned, the puppet master laughed, letting out a sulfurous stench.

Sam turned to run. Out a window he fell, impaling himself on rose bushes covered with a glistening, sticky liquid. The rose thorns burned in his skin. He felt uncontrollable anger welling inside him. He was screaming and thrashing about, an animal, no longer man.

The smell of smoke grew stronger. He forced open his eyes. It was a dream, a bad dream. But the smoke, he could still smell it. The smoke was real!

He threw back his bedsheet and stood in bewilderment trying to focus in the dark bedroom, trying to focus on the reality around him. Yes, he was in his home—his new anonymous home in Dallas, Texas, and the smoke was burning his eyes.

"Mary, wake up! The house is on fire!" The form of his wife stirred next to him. He ran to the bedroom window and threw open the curtains looking for an escape route from the second floor via a nearby oak tree. Outside a red glow and hot flames licked up the exterior of the house and engulfed the tree. The window was not an option.

"What's happening, Sam?"

"The house is on fire! It looks like it's coming from the yard on this side."

"The fire's coming up the stairs," Mary yelled from the doorway of their bedroom.

"We'll have to jump. The guestroom, quick!" Sam instinctively pulled the shotgun from under the bed and ran after Mary as they retreated to the guestroom around the corner.

Mary had the window of the guestroom open in a flash and put one leg out as she looked back at Sam. "The rose bushes will break our fall. Don't wait for me to get out of the way!"

Mary had both legs out the window about to push off when Sam grabbed her by her nightgown. He poked his head through the window and peered at the rose bushes below. They glistened in the moonlight. Something deep inside him screamed for an immediate course correction. He pulled Mary back into the room.

"We can't go that way. No time to explain," Sam shouted, picking Mary up from the floor.

"Then where? There're no other windows."

"No, but there used to be. The storage room."

Sam pulled Mary along with one hand while holding the shotgun in the other, now realizing its purpose. They fumbled their way into the storage room, lit partially from a faint glow flickering through the entry door behind them. Sam let go of Mary and blindly ran at a dark corner holding the shotgun upright with the butt leading the way. The gun slammed into the wooden surface giving Sam enough warning to stop before his body made contact.

He felt around the wall until he found a square area of different texture, the now boarded-up window. He stepped back, pointed the shotgun at the center of the square, and pulled both triggers. A flash and bang opened a jagged hole in the wall. Moonlight streamed through it back into the storeroom. Sam smashed away at the edges of the hole with the butt of the shotgun and a strength he didn't know he had, enlarging the opening in the wall as pieces of wood gave way with each blow.

Poking his torso outside the hole he faced a sturdy elm branch reaching out toward him, well within his grasp. He threw the spent shotgun turned sledgehammer to the yard below.

"You first, Mary. Here, I'll help you out."

Soon they were both outside, breathing in chilly night air tinged with smoke coming from the front of the house. They scaled down the big elm and fell to the ground.

Sam looked back at the house, now half engulfed in flames. The bedroom would be an inferno by now. He looked back at Mary as she lifted herself off the ground. "You all right?"

Mary nodded and stood, gaping at the flames.

Getting back on his own feet he retrieved the shotgun from the yard.

"Where are you going?"

"To the rose bush. I must know something before it burns."

Sam sprinted around the corner to the rose bushes below the guest bedroom window. Using the shotgun barrel like a hatchet he hacked off a long stem from one of the plants. He ripped a strip of cloth from his night shirt, wrapped it around his hand, and gently picked up the prickly stem. As he examined it, a sticky liquid covering the entire stem and every thorn glistened in the light of the fire.

***

Fred Miller reached for a nearby lamppost to break his fall, but succeeded only partially. He kept his face from hitting the street, but his knees stung from the impact.

"Fine way to treat a patron!" he yelled over his shoulder at a closing pub door. "Fine way to treat a patron," he mumbled at the wet road in front of him.

He straightened himself and looked about, trying to get his bearing. This normally lively part of Manchester was now dark and quiet with only some muffled laughter spilling out of the establishment that had ejected him. "Hmm, where else in this fine city can an old boy go for a drink?" He pondered for a while, holding himself up by the lamppost. Then a sign across the street came into focus. "The Grey Horse Inn, ah, they love me there, don't they."

Off he stumbled, tacking left and right of his intended course, but always homing in on the sign that came clearer into view with every purposeful step—first the heel then the toe. After what seemed like quite a long trek that ended abruptly, he mounted the steps with a wobble, opened the door, and leaned in.

The tiny room looked bigger than usual, with only two white-haired men hunkered over the bar. The few tables in the place sat empty. A hulking barman looked up from wiping the bar to see who had opened the door.

"Fred Miller, what do you want at this hour?" asked the barman.

"Why, a pint, of course. You do love me, don't you, John?"

"It's Phillip, not John, and your credit's no good here anymore. You know that, Mr. Miller."

"Phillip, yes, you're right. You do love me, don't you, Phillip?"

"Mr. Miller, I suggest you turn around and go on home. You've had enough to drink tonight."

"Hogwash, one can never have *too* much to drink. Come now, John, just one wee, wee beer for your old friend Fred. Just one—" Fred took his hand off the door frame to illustrate a wee beer, but lost his balance and had to grip it again to stay upright.

He'd no sooner steadied himself when he felt the hands of the barman on his shirt collar. This time there was no lamppost to cling to. Backwards out the pub he went, back to the street he fell.

"Mr. Miller, until you pay your outstanding bill, you're not welcome at the Grey Horse Inn. I told you that three nights ago, and two nights before that. Next time I see your face in my door I'll not be so gentle."

Fred sat up and started to answer, but the door was already closed and the barman nowhere in sight. "Fine way to treat a friend," he mumbled. "Why, you and I were mates before I left for school, or was that Phillip?" He put his head back down on the street and closed his eyes.

When he awoke it was to the strangest sensation. He was moving, that was sure, but how? The sky slowly strolled by, and his rump slid along something. Then he felt the pull at the top of his jacket. Someone or something was dragging him. He leaned his head back to see who or what it was, but it wasn't yet light enough. All he made out was the rough outline of a stooped form. He reached up and felt two hands gripped firmly on his jacket.

"What do you want? I'll get up. Let go of me."

"Shut up," came a low, gravelly command.

Along he slid. Fred blinked several times and tried to focus, gathering his wits as he looked around at the slowly moving scenery. Fear soon jolted him awake and began to clear his head. The walls of a narrow alley came into focus on either side.

"I don't have any money. What do you want?"

A shadow flickered by followed by the pull of two more hands on his jacket. The night sky strolled by a little quicker.

"Look, you best let me go. I warn you, you can't hurt me. No one ever can. Trust me, I've even tried to let them, but it just doesn't work."

"Shut up, I said."

"No, truly, I'm in earnest. You might get hurt, better if you let me be. You see, something always intervenes, like a bad dream that never ends."

"Not this time, Mr. Miller. Apparently your usefulness is no longer useful."

"How do you know my name? Who are you? Let me go!"

"If we bash him now," came a second hushed voice, "he won't sing out when we go to slit his throat."

Fred felt a sharp pain across the crown of his head, and then everything went black.

CHAPTER 3
A RED PACKET

The walk from his London club to the British Foreign Office was one Sir Charles Hardinge, the Permanent Assistant Undersecretary of State for Foreign Affairs, had made a thousand times before, but rarely at the noon hour on an empty stomach. It couldn't be helped. The note from the Foreign Secretary, Sir Edward Grey, urgently summoning him back to work, arrived before the first course hit the table, and now his stomach growled as he retraced the route he'd taken but twenty minutes earlier. Damned inconvenient, it was. It certainly must be urgent, given that they were already scheduled to meet in a few hours.

"Sir Charles," came a stiff salutation from a young gentleman at the main entrance. "Follow me if you will, please. Sir Edward is waiting for you."

Down the corridors Hardinge followed the young gentleman until they came to a door marked "Map Room A." Must be something to do with Europe, he surmised, knowing well the stock of maps found inside. As he entered the room the lanky Sir Edward Grey held open an unrolled map on a large table, hands spread wide apart and neck bent downward, looking like a stork staring in the water for fish, which, when he thought about it, was a pastime with which said stork was certainly well acquainted.

"I came as fast as I could, Edward. What's afoot?"

Sir Edward tilted his neck and gave Hardinge a worried look. "Bosnia." He rapped his knuckles on the map and turned to the young gentleman. "That will be all, thank you."

The door closed, leaving Grey and Hardinge alone.

"Bosnia? What now?"

"Yes, Bosnia." Again his knuckles hit the table. "Thank you for coming so quickly, Charles. I hope I haven't spoiled your luncheon."

"No bother at all. Bosnia? Have the Serbs been agitating again? They're so fixated on this pan-Serbian idea of some Serbian nationalist empire."

"No, not the Serbs." Grey motioned with his head for Hardinge to join him at the map as he continued to hold it open. "Amazing, isn't it? Such a small, insignificant former chunk of the Ottoman Empire, and yet such a large irritation to the rest of the world. I'm afraid they may have done it this time, the Austro-Hungarians, that is."

"Done what?" Hardinge sidled next to Grey at the map.

"Brought us all to the brink. Silly, stupid thing to do, really. I received a red packet just within the hour. I've come to loath those infernal crimson harbingers of doom—anarchist assassinations, border flare ups, political crisis after political crisis. Here, read it yourself. See what the harbinger brings this time."

Grey handed him a sheet of paper, from which Hardinge felt obliged to read aloud.

"Six October, 1908, Foreign Minister Aehrenthal of Austria-Hungary announced today the annexation of Bosnia-Herzegovina. Aehrenthal asserting consent and cooperation of the Russian government, but this assertion cannot be verified and has thus far been denied by the Russian government." Hardinge stopped reading and scanned quickly ahead for more details. The Germans confessed no advance knowledge, but were assumed to be supportive of the Austrians. The French were thus far non-committal. The Turkish government had strongly condemned the annexation of a province over which they technically claimed sovereignty. The Serbians had likewise issued a scathing denouncement that hinted of war to protect the next-door Serbian population of Bosnia. There was no news at all from Italy, Serbia's most likely ally in the region.

Hardinge looked up from the dispatch at Grey's anxious face. "Terrible timing with the announcement yesterday that Prince

Ferdinand of Bulgaria had declared the independence of Bulgaria from Turkey."

"Do you think it's a coincidence?" Grey asked earnestly.

"Perhaps, but the Young Turk movement has no doubt pushed these two events into our laps. Either the Turkish government is going to fall with civil war the result, or the Young Turks, a fresh powerful element, will take Turkey over from the Sultan. If the former, Bulgaria and Austria will want to get ahead of the collapse to claim the spoils. If the latter, all the more reason for the competing interests to act now before it becomes more difficult to pull the Turkish Empire apart."

"Fools, all of them, fools." Sir Edward rapped his fist on the table in conjunction with the repeated word. "I received a report this morning that Ferdinand has declared himself a Tsar. When announcing Bulgaria's independence from Turkey he actually appeared in robes of a Byzantine Emperor made for him by a theatrical costume supplier. Fools." He smacked the table again.

Hardinge pondered the Armageddon that was certainly at the forefront of Sir Edward's concern. Serbia may push toward war with Austria for annexing their next-door neighbor. If so, Russia would come to smaller Serbia's aid. That would pull Germany into the fray on Austria's side. The Germans were wed to the Austrians after only Austria supported Germany in the recent Moroccan affair. The French would certainly join Russia against their mutual enemy, Germany. French involvement could lead to Britain being sucked in on her side. What Italy and Turkey might do was anyone's guess.

"What do you propose in response, Edward?"

Grey didn't answer, seemingly lost in his thoughts. He combed back his hair with the fingers of his right hand and let out a sigh. His fingers were long and elegant, the sight of which made Hardinge wonder why Grey didn't play the piano. Such hands were perfectly suited to the task.

"Russia and Germany, they're the real concern here. Russia," Grey held up his right hand and stared at it, "will side with Serbia. They have no choice. They hold themselves out as the guardian of the Slavic peoples. And Germany." He held out his left hand changing his gaze in that direction. "Germany will stand by Austria. They have no choice. Austria-Hungary was their only reliable ally during the Moroccan crisis. When Serbia and Austria go to war..." He clapped his hands together focusing on the collision. "They drag the rest of us in—a world at war."

Again Grey seemed lost in his thoughts. "A response, yes." He finally looked up at Hardinge. "That's what I was going to ask you."

Hardinge rubbed his chin, working the possibilities through his head. "We do need to be careful. There's so much combustible material about. But we also need to make clear our position. Misunderstandings at this stage can be deadly."

"Yes, careful, I agree completely. Did you hear what one of the backbenchers asserted in Parliament yesterday? He claimed to have hard evidence that German agents were concealing 50,000 rifles and 7 million rounds of ammunition in a secret location in London to support their coming invasion. Absurd! Why inflame the situation with such nonsense?"

"I quite agree. I've not seen such agitation toward war since the Moroccan affair. But to my last point—"

"We mustn't be hasty," interrupted Grey as began pacing about the room. "No need to stampede the herd, as the Americans like to say." Grey let out a long sigh. "These are such troubling times...labor riots in the streets of London, crowds agitating for war all over Great Britain." He stopped his pacing and with a jolt looked at Hardinge. "Oh heavens, how rude of me. Would you like something to drink?"

"No, thank you." Hardinge paused, noticing that Sir Edward was fishing for something from his jacket pocket.

"I was so distracted…ah, here it is. I was thinking about issuing a statement to this effect." Grey unfolded a small piece of paper. "Recent developments in the Balkans, a region outside the immediate sphere of influence of the British Empire, are being monitored with keen interest while His Majesty's Government is in continued and constructive dialogue with all interested parties. It is His Majesty's Government's desire and wish that the status quo between all parties with a direct interest in the region be maintained while allowing for flexibility in recognizing regional differences and the evolving aspirations of the many peoples involved."

Sir Edward looked up quizzically at Hardinge who, spurred on by his empty stomach, was half inclined to respond with "what the bloody hell does that mean," but thought the better of it. His lack of enthusiasm for the communiqué must have been apparent as Grey suddenly frowned at him.

"I take it you don't approve?"

"Edward, the point I was about to make…"

Grey interrupted again, this time beginning with an agitated wave of the hand. "I don't care to be lectured today about clarity of intentions. One must hold one's cards close to the chest and keep options open. I suppose you think I should say 'we are mad as hell and expect the Austrians to revoke their annexation before we do something drastic in conjunction with the Turkish government, and your friends the Germans be damned!'"

"Not exactly, but it does make a point." Grey was clearly not amused, Hardinge noted before continuing more cautiously. "If in conjunction with your communiqué we were to dispatch additional warships to the Mediterranean, the Austrians would understand our displeasure and perhaps then be more amenable to some compromise."

Grey grasped the bridge of his nose and shook his head. "No, that would be even more provocative than the most direct of words. Besides, then I'd be lectured by the Admiralty about how thinly they're stretched and how dangerous it is to further deplete the Home Fleet when the Germans are furiously building battleships. No, you know I've supported the naval building program publicly over strenuous objections from my Liberal colleagues, but I don't want to pour any more fuel on this destructive arms race."

Grey put his hands out, palms up. "They build two, we build three," he said as he looked alternately at his left then his right hand. "They build three, we build five." Each hand raised slightly with the increasing tally. "I understand that we can't tolerate anywhere near equality in strength, but this naval arms race is spending us into penury. I suppose we'll keep building battleships until there's no more room for them in the sea. Then our armies can walk from ship to ship to get at each other."

He stopped as if pondering the last proposition and then looked up at Hardinge. "I'm sorry, Charles. I mustn't ramble on like a madman. You know what we're faced with better than I. What puzzles me most is why we didn't see this coming. We normally have such reliable intelligence from the Austrian court."

"We should at a minimum dispatch a fleet to the Adriatic. Might I suggest we leave it to the Admiralty whether the Mediterranean Fleet should thereafter be reinforced? We need a presence on the scene to emphasize whatever message we decide to send."

Sir Edward slumped his shoulders and look down again at his hands. Then he let out a sigh and looked back up at Hardinge.

"Perhaps you're right. We can always recall them to station. Best to get them started. You didn't answer my question, Charles. Surely something this momentous should have been picked up by our agents?"

"Interesting you should inquire about that point. Just this morning I received news about our primary contact in Vienna. I had an appointment to discuss it with you this afternoon. He was found three days ago, washed up on the shores of the Danube a few miles downstream from where he was last seen having dinner."

"Drowned? Yes, sorry about calling you here early, but I thought it important. I *do* fear I've interrupted your lunch. You say our agent drowned in the Danube?"

"Not exactly. He had a dagger embedded in his throat. It had apparently been thrust with tremendous force. The dagger entered the front of the neck and exited the rear, severing the spine en route. He was most certainly dead before he was wet."

Grey turned away, tilting his head toward the ceiling. His narrow shoulders turned inward. He cleared his throat and took a drink. "What else?" he asked with his back still to Hardinge.

"If you mean the calling card, yes, it was in his waistcoat pocket, just like our agents in Berlin and Saint Petersburg."

"Who is he and why is he taunting us? And what does it mean? 'Charlie,' what the devil does that mean?"

Grey turned now to face him, but having no answer, Hardinge could only shake his head.

Grey sighed again. "Very well, draft a communique more forcefully reflecting our displeasure. I'll consider your tone and make edits to satisfy my concerns."

"I'll attend to it immediately after lunch, if that will suffice."

"But of course, I'm sorry. I did interrupt lunch then? Here." Grey handed him the piece of paper. "Take this with you as a starting point. Shall we say a first draft three hours hence?"

"Yes, more than adequate time, thank you." Hardinge started to leave, but then paused. "As long as I'm here, shall I give you a preview of the matter I wished to discuss at our appointment? I don't mind delaying lunch a little longer. This may take a moment to explain, though. It can wait until later if that would be more convenient."

"By all means, please have a seat." Grey motioned toward a small table with two chairs in the corner of the room.

Once seated and joined by Grey, Hardinge took a deep breath and mentally reviewed the main points of his difficult message.

"You hesitate, Charles." Grey gave him a bird-like stare.

"Hmm, I'm afraid I do." Hardinge sucked in another full breath. "Are you acquainted with Special Department B at Scotland Yard?"

"Top secret, hush-hush, that's all I know. My understanding is I'm to refer all inquiries into such matters to the Prime Minister." Grey waved in the general direction of 10 Downing Street.

"I have been authorized to fully brief you."

"Have you, now?" Grey sat back in his chair and crossed his arms.

"Edward, please understand that my involvement in Special Department B stems from my personal relationship with the facts I am about to relate, and have little to do with my official position."

Grey stared back blankly, still crossing his arms and seemingly in no mood to do anything but listen.

"In 1905 at the beginning of the Moroccan crisis, this office was losing agents around the world at an alarming rate, reminiscent of our current experience but with different facts. There were numerous sightings of a mysterious man with a black box somehow linked to the deaths of these agents as well as to the deaths of other British subjects unrelated to the Foreign Office. As with our present situation, the Foreign Office was dealing with the mysterious deaths of agents while simultaneously struggling to avert a world war.

"I, in consultation with your predecessor, Lord Lansdowne, decided to reach outside the Foreign Office for assistance. I retained a certain Inspector Edmund Jenkins of the Yard to look into the matter. He came personally recommended by a close friend of mine in the Admiralty."

"Yes, yes," interjected Grey with a still irritated tone. "The police detective who chased after the mysterious man with the black box. I read all about it in the papers, truly fantastic stories."

"Precisely. Jenkins had been on the trail of such a man for months. This mysterious assassin seemed linked to the instant death of adults and to children falling into comas and their eventual deaths, all related somehow to his black box. Because several of our dead agents had been seen in the company of this mysterious man and his black box, Jenkins was well positioned and eager to assist.

"After we retained his services, Jenkins chased his quarry to New York, where he met an American doctor, Cunningham, I believe, and his patient, a young girl named Molly who had looked into the man's black box and gone into a coma. Cunningham later looked into the box as well.

"Somehow this doctor and his patient escaped the consequences of looking into the box and became immune to its powers. Not only immune, but gifted with a useful and inexplicable power of their own."

"This all sounds inexplicable to me. 'Consequences'? 'Powers'?"

"I'm sorry. I know it all seems incredibly fanciful, but if I may continue. More black boxes were found and examined. It was never determined how the black boxes killed when someone looked into them, but they did. And we never found an explanation for what they were made of. They were indestructible to all but a select few. Dynamite that would bring a building down left not a scratch on a black box. Yet, when either Molly or Cunningham would peer inside such a box, they did not die. Instead, the box would explode and be rendered harmless."

Grey shook his head and frowned, but kept silent.

"Their power over black boxes left both Cunningham and Molly targets for assassination by the man with the black box and his accomplices. Jenkins moved Molly to safety and brought Cunningham to London. Only one other person is known to be immune to the power of the black box, a young London hansom driver named Talbot, whom Jenkins later employed as well."

"I don't follow."

"Yes, I suppose it gets more confusing as we go along. You see, the man with the black box was eventually cornered back in London by the inspector and his men. The evil assassin lit himself on fire rather than risk capture. He did so before a single witness of his choosing, a gentleman from Manchester, a patent agent, named Fred Miller. But, duplicates of his deadly black box remained in the hands of his accomplices.

"A secret joint effort between Scotland Yard and this office was formed to hunt down these accomplices and destroy the deadly black boxes. It was named Special Department B. Only those three previously mentioned, Cunningham, Molly, and Talbot, have the ability with their immunity to destroy the boxes when found. They look into one end of the box, and it explodes."

"Ridiculous," interjected Grey. "You surely must be in jest."

"No, I'm afraid not." Hardinge looked straight into Grey's eyes before continuing. "Over the period of two years Cunningham and Talbot destroyed many boxes, with Molly destroying a few as well. Once all the boxes that could be found were destroyed, Cunningham was sent back to America under an alias to live with his wife in Texas. His young patient, Molly, remains in protective custody at a secluded ranch in New Mexico. With the inspector's box-busting reserves thus hidden in the southwestern part the United States, Jenkins keeps Talbot on the job in London, a canary in a coal mine, so to speak. Meanwhile…"

"Special Department B? Exploding boxes?" interrupted Grey with a sour look.

"Edward, please understand that the nature of this problem required that as few in the government know the details as possible. Many lives were at risk and the stakes high."

"And what is the function of this Special Department B now, still hunting for black boxes? What has this to do with His Majesty's Government? Black boxes?" Grey raised one eyebrow with the exaggerated utterance of the last two words.

"That...and to protect certain known or suspected targets of the accomplices with the black boxes. Some of those targets are members of this very government."

"Am I such a target?"

"Not that we can tell, no."

"You said all the boxes had been destroyed. Why would anyone be in danger?"

"The sighting of black boxes did fade over time. I don't believe a new black box has been found in almost a year. But now dead men are popping up with knives in their throats and an identical calling card in their pockets."

Grey shook his head and frowned. "Then why are you telling me about Department B now?"

Hardinge reached into his waistcoat pocket and produced his own square piece of paper. "This," he said as he unfolded the paper and handed it to Grey.

Grey read the document and looked at Hardinge with even more confusion written on his face. "It's only a letter, a letter from an uncle to his niece."

"That *is* what it appears, but actually it's a letter to me from our now deceased contact in Vienna. He was also a very highly placed agent in Special Department B and, in such capacity, reported directly to Inspector Jenkins by a channel to which I have access. The letter, apparently written within days, if not hours, of his death, has a coded message, a coded message that answers your question. May I direct you to the third paragraph?"

Grey looked back down at the paper and began reading aloud. "The funniest thing happened at lunch today. I had no sooner put jam on my bread than a bee made an appearance. To thwart this industrious bug from alighting on my jam, in which it showed great interest, I held my bread with the jam side down while I ate it. This bee was of no ordinary talent, however. The next thing I know, the bee is flying upside down, thus defeating my strange table manners. Clara, we all got quite a chuckle from the spectacle. Imagine, a bee flying upside down!"

Grey again looked at Hardinge, seemingly more confused. "Is it coded? I don't understand?"

"The operative phrase is 'the bee is flying upside down.' This agent is a former naval officer. The 'bee' he is referring to is in fact Special Department B."

"I still don't follow, Charles. I'm afraid you must come to the point to have any hope of eating anytime soon."

"When a ship is in distress, it flies its color upside down. This *is* a coded phrase, albeit written in plain sight, signifying that Special Department B is in distress, or, under assault. Everyone associated with the department is in grave danger. Because the security of Special Department B has been compromised, it is now imperative that the leading members of the cabinet be briefed on the existence of the operation. It may take the full force of His Majesty's Government to avert the disaster of this critical operation being snuffed out completely."

"Forgive me for seeming incredulous. But…"

"Edward, please, I understand." Hardinge placed both hands on the table and leaned forward. "It *is* quite a fantastic tale. I have in my office a file that I intended to give you this afternoon. It is critical that you review this file and become acquainted with Special Department B and the history of the case of the man with the black box. There is much we still don't know, but it is clear that the peace and security of this nation, if not the entire world, are at risk. It will all make more sense once you review the file, including a list of past targets of the black box assassinations."

"All right." Grey put his hands on his knees and stood. "I'll reserve judgment until I've reviewed this file. In the meantime, I urge you not to lose sight of the immediate crisis. I need your assistance in calming the waters. We are on the verge of a world war today because of this Bosnian folly. We need to tread carefully. We need to buy time."

Hardinge rose and faced Grey. "I'll have a draft of our official response to you shortly."

"Excellent. Now, do return to lunch first, though. One should never embark on an important task on an empty stomach."

The two men exchanged nods and Hardinge turned to leave.

"Charles." Grey paused and raised his hand with his index finger extended, placing said finger momentarily on his chin. "One thought does occur to me. When last this office was mysteriously losing agents, Inspector Jenkins was contacted to come to our aid. Now, you say the inspector's entire operation is under siege. Who shall we call this time for help as we find ourselves in the valley of the shadow of death?"

"Good point, Edward. Calling on the Good Shepherd may, indeed, be our best course."

***

"Mr. President."

Theodore Roosevelt rolled onto his side.

"Mr. President."

He heard it again, knocking and someone calling from beyond the bedroom door. It wasn't a dream.

"Teddy, there's someone at the door." His wife, Edith, gently prodded him in the shoulder.

"Just a moment," he called to the offending door. "Excuse me, dear, I'll be back momentarily." He gave her a peck on the cheek and smiled as she rolled away from him while hugging an overstuffed pillow.

His feet found his slippers below the bed, and he pulled his robe off a nearby valet stand. Quietly making his way, he gingerly turned the handle, opening the door barely enough to extricate himself from his bedroom and into the brightly lit hallway. Roosevelt placed his right pointer finger to his lips and softly closed the door behind him. A young secret service agent acknowledged with a nod and motioned for the president to follow.

The two men walked silently down a hall and into an anteroom.

"What the devil is this all about? It's two in the morning!"

"I'm sorry, Mr. President. It's Secretary of State Root. He's on the line for you." The agent pointed at a telephone with the earpiece off the receiver, sitting on a table.

Roosevelt picked up the telephone and gave the agent a stern look. Taking the hint, the agent left the room, closing the door behind him.

"Yes, Elihu, what is it? You do know what time it is?"

"Theodore," came the familiar voice of Elihu Root from the earpiece, "I'm quite sorry. I've received an urgent message from the British government. The newspapers will have the full story shortly, and I thought it prudent to brief you immediately."

"Yes, go on."

"The Austrians have annexed Bosnia. The Serbian government has issued a strong objection and has canceled all military leave. King Peter has called for a meeting of his cabinet to discuss war, and an office has been established in the central city square in Belgrade for the enlistment of volunteers to the army. They may be mobilizing, although that isn't yet clear."

"Bosnia, you say? And the Russians?"

"The Austrians claim the Russians were consulted in advance, but the Russians deny it. No sign of Russian mobilization yet, nor mobilization by the Germans. The Turks have demanded an immediate retraction, but their reaction seems muted to me."

"I'm not surprised. First the Bulgarians declare independence from the Turks and now this. His empire is falling apart, but I'm not sure there's much the Sultan can do about it. And what do the French and British intend?"

"The British have placed their Mediterranean Fleet on alert, but the Home Fleet status has not yet changed. The French have been strangely silent."

"Fleets? Yes, Bosnia is accessible from the Adriatic. What else?"

"We also haven't heard from the Italians yet."

"No doubt, they're in a bit of a pickle. I'm sure the head says stick with the Germans, but the heart says kill the Austrians. Where is the fleet?"

"The fleet?"

"Yes, where is my fleet? Has it left Manila yet?"

"Ah...the Great White Fleet. Yes, they're leaving Manila today for Japan."

"When are they scheduled to be in the Mediterranean Sea?"

"Uh, let me see. A moment, please, Theodore. Yes, they are scheduled to reach the Suez Canal first of next year, in about three months. Shall we change their itinerary? We could reroute them. The coaling schedule would be the hard part, but I'm sure we could get them to the Adriatic by the end of the month."

"Elihu, you sound like Taft! Edith wouldn't approve of that. She says Taft and I think too much alike. She thinks I need a calming influence. She's probably right. Reroute the fleet?"

"Theodore, we could have fifteen modern battleships on station in a matter of weeks if we turned them around now."

"No, too provocative. Besides, the British, French and Italians will get there well before we can. It might get a little awkward, don't you think, all those battleships crowded into such a small pond? No, this isn't our fight, yet. Let that big stick trundle on. I want a meeting with you and Secretary of War Wright as soon as it can be arranged."

"I'll call him next."

"Where is Taft? We'll need to brief him so he's not blindsided on the campaign trail. Is he in Ohio?"

"I believe Illinois, but I'll check and get word to him."

"Yes, and tell him to stop being so defensive about my executive orders. He'll see when he's President, it's the only way you get anything done around here. What's our ambassador in Vienna's name? By devil, I'm not quite awake yet."

"Rives."

"That's right, Rives. You get Mr. Rives by the ear and find out what the Sam Hill is going on with the Austrians. Now, may I return to bed?"

"One more thing."

"Yes?"

"I'm not sure what to make of this, but I was asked to communicate something verbatim without question or alteration and with the utmost secrecy."

"Go on."

"It's hunting season on bees."

Roosevelt paused and digested the message. "I see. Thank you. Goodnight, Secretary Root."

***

Molly crawled to the top of the rise and slithered under a creosote bush. As she parted the thin branches she saw the same thing as the last time she stopped, a dust cloud in the distance. Whoever it was, they had followed her now for two days. She had kept the paint moving, resting a little during the day and plodding on through the night. But there they were, closer than yesterday.

They must have surprised her camp that night with spent horses. The paint was rested, and Molly was light. Initially she put a lot of sand between them, but they'd been making it up since. She was too easy to follow on this desert floor.

She pushed back and slid down to the lower ground and her waiting horse. "Well, Pluck, what do we do now?"

The paint looked back at Molly quizzically, but made no reply.

Molly walked over to an ant hill and retrieved the wire cage she had set there. "Joshua, what do you think? We can't keep running forever." The horned toad licked in a stray ant off the straw in the bottom of his cage, but likewise made no response.

"I wish Mick was here. I'd feel a lot better about all this if he hadn't gone back to England." Molly looked hopefully out to the desert imagining the familiar image of the redheaded Irishman riding toward her in the distance.

"What would a cowboy do; that's the question, isn't it boys?" Molly strapped the cage on her saddle and mounted Pluck. "Isn't that the question? A cowboy would head for higher ground instead of doubling back to get around them. That's what he'd do. We need rocks and streams and stuff to lose these bandits."

Pluck let out a whinny and wobbled his head.

"I know, that would be north, away from the ranch, but those men keep putting themselves between us and the ranch. We don't have much more food and finding water out here is hard work when you're being chased." Molly dropped her head and allowed a tear to run down her cheek. "Why are they following me? I just want to be left alone. It's not right."

A soft breeze blew across her cheek drying her skin. She rubbed her eyes and snorted. "You've never seen me cry, Joshua, sorry about that. I need to be brave. 'Keep your wits,' that's what the cowboys say.

"Let's think on this. We can get behind the Sacramento Mountains and head up to Mayhill. From there we'll wander upstream the Rio Peñasco until we throw them off. They'd never expect us to cut north to Cloudcroft after that with the ranch in the other direction. We can hole up there for a couple of days and then make a beeline for the ranch."

She flicked the reins, urging the paint forward. As they plodded on, Molly bit her lip. Salty tears slid down her face, but she sat up straight as an arrow in the saddle.

CHAPTER 4
ON THE MARCH

"Top of the mornin', Inspector. You sent for me?"

Inspector Edmund Jenkins plucked the unlit cigar from his mouth and looked up from his desk to see the familiar round face of the burly Irishman, whose hulking body filled the doorway.

"Good morning to you, Mick. Please, have a seat. Tea?"

"Why, bless you, sir. You might be addin' some scotch to that tea, then?"

"As is my practice. I have Irish whiskey if you prefer."

"Bless you, very kind indeed. Then I'll save you the trouble, sir, and you can pour just the whiskey." Mick grinned and planted himself firmly in a chair before the inspector's desk.

Jenkins smiled, stood and retrieved a bottle and two glasses. Mick would never accept drinking alone.

"Now, sir, what you be need'n Mick for this time?"

"How was Manchester?" Jenkins poured the amber liquid into each glass.

"All in order now, sir, retrieved and delivered. We cut that one close, now, didn't we?"

"Indeed. I sent you on that errand based on an educated guess. Regrettably, what you encountered and subsequent events have now confirmed my guess as reality. I'm afraid I'll need to steer you in a different direction based on this new reality."

The inspector handed Mick a glass, which he cheerfully grasped with one of his enormous hands.

"Do you remember Jim Talbot?" The inspector moved back to his desk chair, taking the bottle with him.

"The lad who drove the hansom cab and then got stuck in one of them infernal black boxes before Molly Bell saved his life?"

"To your health."

"Aye, and to yours as well, Inspector. Best while you have it use your breath. There's no drinkin' after death." Mick took a swig, closed his eyes for a moment, and then let out a satisfied sigh.

"Yes, well he works for me now, for the Yard."

Mick took another longer sip, raising his bushy auburn eyebrows as if to say "does he now?"

"Talbot gained the same special talent that Molly and Cunningham gained once he recovered from his coma. The lad has been our principal black box buster in London going on two years. Now he's missing, which is why I called you back to London."

"And all this time I thought you wanted to see me and have some tea."

Jenkins capacity for much more frivolity was wearing thin, and this time he ignored Mick's grin.

"Jim Talbot was last seen being chased by a group of men. They followed him to the Battersea Bridge and, in broad daylight, fired two shots at him from a distance of thirty yards. It's believed that at least one of those bullets found its mark. Witnesses say Jim's arm was bloody as he leapt from the bridge into the Thames. Three men then ran to the spot from which he jumped and starting firing revolvers into the river. After a few moments of peering over the side, they disappeared into the crowd."

"And what makes you think he might be alive?"

"I don't think that, but until we find his body we must assume he is. He has no family. His father died suddenly a fortnight ago. The cause of death has yet to be determined, but he was found with his eyes wide open."

Mick sat up straight and leaned in slightly.

"If Jim Talbot is alive, he's smart enough not to go home."

"Where would he go, then?" The Irishman took another long swig from his glass and a deep breath with his nose hanging over the rim.

"What's the verdict?" Jenkins pointed at the glass.

"Oh, the whiskey." Mick took his cue and drank again, holding the liquid briefly in his mouth before letting it slide down his throat. "Quite good, but I 'aven't the discerning nose for it like you, sir. Whiskey and women, never met one of either I didn't like, particularly of the Irish variety." Mick grinned again and took another drink, tilting the glass up to demonstrate unmistakably that he had drained the last drop. "They both do leave you wantin' more now, though."

Jenkins poured more of the whiskey into the glass which Mick had deposited on his desk. He waited for Mick to pick it up before continuing.

"Jim Talbot would come here if he could. That's easily deduced. Which is why you need to find him before he tries. He'd be a dead man before he knocked on the front door."

Jenkins detected a sense of slight from the hurt look on the big man's face. "What was I thinking? To leave you drinking alone…how incredibly rude of me. Please accept my apologies, Mick." Jenkins quickly picked up his glass and took a drink of his own.

Mick's face beamed. "'Tis only a stepmother would blame you, sir."

Jenkins raised his cup toward the Irishman and took another sip. "There's more you need to know."

Mick placed his glass down and shifted in his chair, causing it to creak in protest of the man's enormous weight.

"We're under siege. In addition to what you've seen and what I've just told you, I'm afraid news is coming in daily about agents and associates being attacked, many have been killed. Some of these attacks involve people you know."

Mick's countenance changed in an instant from jovial to concerned. "Anarchists?"

"Someone tried to kill Doctor and Mrs. Cunningham."

"The Cunninghams? But why? All the black boxes have been found."

"My educated guess, the one that sent you to Manchester, was based on a different assumption."

Mick looked about the room, as if in search of something familiar that was no longer there.

"No, don't tell me, sir."

"A bounty has been placed on Molly Bell's head, and no one knows where she is. Her cowboy bodyguards were killed in a night ambush, but they apparently bought enough time for her to get away."

Mick rose, his face flush and fists raised. "Inspector, I'm needed in New Mexico. I can't stay here talkin' about a dead boy, bless his soul. Miss Molly needs me."

"Mick, calm yourself. It would take nearly two weeks for you to get to the ranch. Molly does need help, but she needs help now. I'll take care of that end. An urgent plea has already been sent to the highest levels of the American government. But we're spread thin here. I need you—" Jenkins thrust his pointer finger to his desktop—"here. I need you to find Jim Talbot before they do."

"Please, Inspector, she's but a young lass." Mick's fists opened and he clutched his hands at his chest, the picture of a schoolboy pleading of the headmaster not to hit his friend again for the schoolboy's own misdeed.

"Mick, sit down."

The stern command seemed to bring the Irishman around as he meekly complied.

Jenkins reached into a desk drawer and pulled out a large envelope. He set it on his desk and pushed it toward Mick. "This is a file on Jim Talbot. The sooner you find him the sooner we can consider sending you to the ends of the earth and Molly Bell."

Mick stood up and reached for the envelope. "I'll be leavin' now, sir, unless you 'ave more for me. I've got a lad to find."

"One more thing, Mick. You must be very careful. There's an assassin about who has taken a special interest in our men. He leaves a knife through the throat and a calling card on the body."

"A calling card?"

"Yes, 'Charlie' is all it says."

"So there's a Charlie calling." The big man shrugged. "May I take my leave now, sir?"

Jenkins nodded his head, and Mick hurried out, leaving a glass full of Irish whiskey on the inspector's desk.

***

Molly opened the front door to the Cloudcroft Lodge and peered cautiously inside. There was no one in the reception area, not even at the front desk. She turned around to look back to the front porch, but saw only her paint tied to the railing. She had timed it just right. The whole area seemed so busy for the last hour or so that she had been watching. Now she was alone.

She quietly closed the front door and turned back around surprised to see a young woman with long, red hair staring at her from behind the reception desk. She was hauntingly beautiful in a purple dress with white trim. A large white brooch in the shape of a heart was pinned above her left breast. Her hair rose like flames against her pearl-white skin.

"May I help you?"

"Yes, sorry, you startled me. May I inquire about a room for the night?" replied Molly, trying to sound as grown up as possible.

"Oh, I'm sorry, we're all filled up tonight on account of the big bounty news."

"I'm sorry? A bounty?"

"Where have you been, out on the range for a month? It's all the news from El Paso to Santa Fe. Somebody's put up a huge bounty on some ranch girl from outside Alamogordo, dead or alive. Every gunman and bandito in the whole territory is swarming in to join the hunt. They say some of them ambushed her party and she's on the run. They found a bunch of dead cowboys out in the desert day before yesterday. Must've been a heck of a gun fight, but nobody's claimed to have the girl yet. You haven't heard about it?"

Molly shook her head. "What's her name?"

"Molly something, Bell or Beal, I think. Heard of her?"

Molly shivered at the sound of her name. The room seemed to dim. She blinked a few times and wiped her eyes. Gathering herself she looked straight into the face of the redheaded woman. "Can't say that I have. Why do they want her? What has she done?"

The lady shrugged her shoulders. "Poor child, she's probably scared to death, not a friend in the world and the whole of New Mexico hunting her down like some animal to be shot and skinned. Groups of bounty hunters have been stopping by here all day, bunch of smelly brutes. I don't care what she did. The whole thing makes me sick."

Molly stared harder at the woman. Was she leading her on? Who could she trust? Suddenly she felt exhausted. Days without sleep weighed her down. She rubbed away the beginning of some watery tears and struggled to keep her mouth from frowning.

"You know, I could let you have the little maid's quarters in the back. The chambermaid who stayed there went missing a while back. No one'll stay there anymore. They say she haunts the place. I think it's all nonsense. You don't believe in ghosts, do you? Ashtrays moving around, that sort of stuff? Seems like nonsense to me."

Molly looked harder still. She had to decide, could she trust her? She was so tired, now barely able to keep her eyes open. "I know where that girl is. The one they're looking for. Molly."

The young woman frowned and shook her head. "Well keep it to yourself, then. I want no part in it."

"I'll take it, the room. How much?"

"Oh, I can't hardly charge you for it. Like I said, no one will stay there."

"Why not?"

"Like I said, they think it's haunted." The young woman leaned toward Molly, letting her red hair hang down along the sides of her face. "See, there was this young gal who worked here, cleaning rooms and such. She was beautiful, they say, boys coming round as thick as flies to a sorghum mill. She had a beau, a gentle cowboy from down by Carlsbad way who came to call whenever he found the time. They were to be married, so they say.

"One night he comes to see her and finds her in that little room with another man. That gentle cowboy must have gone mad, or maybe the other man objected to the interruption. No one knows but her beau. He killed the other man, right in that same little room. They think he killed his gal, too, or maybe she was shot by accident, but they never found her body and he ain't sayin'.

"They say she never left, her soul, that is. She still haunts that little room to this day." The young woman leaned away from Molly and smiled with a look of satisfaction. "That's why no one stays there. You sure you want it?"

"I said I'll take it."

"Fair enough, you take your horse down to the stable and then meet me around back. We'll settle up in the morning after you've had a good breakfast."

"You're so kind. What's your name?"

"Rebecca." The young woman paused as if waiting on something. "You can call me Becky. And what's yours?"

"Anne, Anne Smith."

***

Dr. Sam Cunningham, known to the Dallas locals as Dr. Sam Westcott, looked up from his notes and poked the lab rat with his pencil. It was sleeping nicely. The chloroform was doing its job. He exchanged the pencil for a slender paintbrush lying on the lab bench. He dipped it in a nearby bottle and hastily painted a red 'X' on the fur of rat's back. That should keep it identified.

He rolled the rat on its side and inspected it one last time. "All white, male adult rat with red markings on its back," he entered into his notes. He next picked up the glass beaker he had kept warming on an iron plate. He'd determined that the oily substance on the rosebushes near his house was somewhat soluble in a warm water and ethanol solution. If sufficiently agitated by mixing, the combination formed a low viscosity emulsion.

He swirled the liquid in the beaker. The stirring had done the trick, and the sticky residue from the rosebushes was now dissolved sufficiently to be injectable. The concoction shimmered in the laboratory's electric lights as it circled around in the glass container. The added ethanol should do nothing but give the rat some happy dreams and, he hoped, not otherwise interfere with the experiment.

He retrieved a syringe equipped with a needle from a drawer under the table and inserted the needle in the beaker. He gradually pulled back on the syringe, drawing in the mostly clear liquid. He turned the syringe upright and, while tapping it, expelled a drop of the liquid. He poked the rat again with his finger. Seeing no reaction, he held the rat down firmly with one hand while injecting it with the other. There was again no reaction.

He took one last look at the sleeping rat. "What's in store for you, my furry friend? I guess time will tell." With that, he scooped up the rat and put it in a wire cage through a small door at the top of the cage. He retrieved a pair of heavy leather gloves he had left on the table and, placing them on his hands, carried the cage to the other side of the laboratory. There, from another wire cage, he selected another lab rat, this one fully awake and expressing its desire not to be handled with a futile and ineffective bite on the glove of Dr. Cunningham's right hand. He placed the squirming rat in the cage with the sleeping, marked rat, and secured the cage's door with heavy wire.

"Well, boys, I guess I'll have to take you with me if I'm to observe what happens next." The awake rat sniffed at the sleeping one, but made no other notice of his remark.

He wrapped the wire cage in paper sheet secured with string, leaving a loop in the string at the top of the bundle to act as a handle. Donning his coat, he picked up the wrapped cage by the string handle and left the lab for the short walk to his temporary home at the Oriental Hotel in downtown Dallas.

He hadn't gotten far down the street before he heard a familiar voice from behind.

"Doctor Westcott!"

He turned to see an unfamiliar man with a black beard wearing a long coat close behind him. The man wore a driver's cap over thick black hair and carried a peculiar cane. The cane had a short horizontal handle at one end, which the stranger held with his right hand, attached to a single straight shaft. What was peculiar was the other end of the shaft, though, the end in contact with the ground. At about six or seven inches from the ground the straight shaft was connected to an upside down "U" giving the cane the appearance that someone had welded a large horseshoe to the ground end of the shaft. Perhaps for added stability, he thought.

Sam had no sooner turned around than the stranger with the peculiar cane turned into an intersecting alley and disappeared.

"Doctor Westcott, a word with you, please!"

Sam looked further down the street recognizing Dr. Carter, one of his colleagues from the hospital and the source of the familiar hail that had caused him to turn around in the first place. His fellow doctor puffed on a bent pipe as he briskly closed on him.

"Doctor Carter, good to see you."

"Sam." Dr. Carter removed the calabash with his left hand and extended his right for a hardy shake. "Good to see you too. May I walk with you?"

"Please, I was just headed to the Oriental."

"Yes, I was distressed to hear about your house burning down. I'm told you lost nearly everything?"

"I'm afraid that's true. We didn't have much to move into the hotel."

"Dreadfully sorry. The Oriental—nice place. How long will you be living there?" Carter puffed away between sentences, removing the pipe just long enough to communicate his thoughts before returning to the habit.

"Until we can find a suitable house. We'll start looking tomorrow. I'm not fond of living in a hotel. I prefer to have my own walls. Oh, and if you could keep our temporary locale to yourself, please. My wife is very sensitive about our privacy. I wouldn't have mentioned it to anyone but you."

"Your secret is safe with me. Dreadfully sorry about your predicament. What was the cause of the fire?"

"That's not clear. The firemen told me it was started outside the house below our bedroom window and simultaneously inside the house at the base of the stairs."

"Started in two places? How can that be?"

"Assuming they are correct, I can only conclude that it was purposeful."

"Purposeful? How dreadful! But why?"

"I'm not sure."

"You've only been in Dallas what, a couple of years now? I've never heard anyone speak an ill word about you or Mrs. Westcott, not a single ill word."

"That's very kind of you to say, Doctor."

The two men continued their walk in silence for half a block. The tobacco from Carter's calabash relaxed Sam, reminding him of various friends in New York and the hours spent with them relaxing while they puffed away.

"Sam, I've been thinking." Carter took a long draw and held the smoke for a moment. "Why don't you and your wife come stay with us for a while? We have an extra room, our son being off to college now."

"New Mexico A&M in Las Cruces, if I recall. How is he enjoying college?"

"Very well, thank you, a fine institution. He's studying chemistry and mechanics. I supposed that would make him a chemical engineer of sorts." Dr. Carter took another puff and then blew a stream of smoke out of the side of his mouth. "Please do consider it. We would enjoy the company. You have few possessions, you said so yourself. Your stay with us can be kept in confidence as well. Perhaps it would be safer than staying…"

"Safer?"

"I don't mean to sound alarmist, but assuming someone set your house on fire, won't they try to hurt you again? They didn't succeed in the first attempt."

"I said my conclusion, assuming the post mortem by the firemen was correct, was that it was purposeful. There may be many explanations of a purposeful act other than someone trying to do me harm. Perhaps they thought we were away and just intended property damage, maybe it was a case of mistaken identity, the wrong house, or it could have been a pyromaniac who just happened to pick my house."

"Perhaps." Carter seemed less than convinced.

"I do thank you for the offer, though. I'll mention it to Mary this evening."

"The offer is in earnest. Please consider it. And, if there is anything you need, let me know. Will I see you at the hospital tomorrow?"

"Thank you, yes. I have some additional work in the lab and then I hope to make the rounds later in the day."

"Excellent. Well, then I'll leave you here. I'll check with my wife on a convenient evening for you two to come dine with us."

"That would be lovely. We'd be delighted to accept such invitation."

The two men shook hands, and Sam continued toward the hotel, the aroma of the pipe merrily lingering in his nose. Passing an expansive newsstand he noted the headlines on the newspapers, "Europe Wants War," "Bosnian Crisis Ignites War Fuse," "Serbia is Angry, People Want War," and so forth. He stopped for a moment to take in some of the news, then continued on to the front door of the Oriental.

The hotel lobby was a lively place, with several guests milling about. He tried to avoid eye contact with any of them and made his way to the elevator.

"Good evening, sir. Floor, please?" asked the elevator operator.

"Third floor, please."

"Third floor. Thank you, sir."

Lost in thought, the ride up three floors seemed longer than he remembered. The elevator came to a sudden stop and the operator opened the door.

"Have a good evening, sir."

"You as well," he replied, planting a coin in the operator's outstretched hand.

He made his way down the corridor to his room. While placing the key in the door the knob turned and the door was abruptly opened from the inside.

"Sam, thank God you're back." Mary Cunningham gave him a strong hug as he reached back to close the door behind them.

"What's wrong, dear?"

Mary looked him in the eyes. He forgot for an instant the urgency in her voice and marveled at how lovely she truly was. Her ivory skin, her brown hair piled in a bun above her hazel eyes, her perfect mouth turning up slightly at the corners, her elegant neck—he was truly blessed.

"A man stopped by asking your whereabouts. How did he even know we were here? We checked in under my maiden name and specifically asked the front desk not to divulge our room to anyone. It scares me, Sam."

"What did he look like?"

"He had a long coat, a driver's cap, and a black beard that covered most of his face."

"Was he carrying a cane?"

"Yes, I believe he was. What's wrong? Do you know him?"

"A driver's cap over dark hair?"

58

"Yes, do you know him?"

"No, but I think I saw him on the street as I was leaving the hospital."

Sam took off his coat and set the cage on a coffee table. He sat down in the nearest arm chair and tried to clear his mind.

"Sam, it's simply not safe. We need to leave Dallas."

"And go where? I've sent a coded cable to Inspector Jenkins. It may take him a few days to arrange where we should go next. If we leave how will he reach us? I'm surprised I've not heard from him. I'm sure we will soon."

"We can contact him from wherever we go, maybe the ranch in New Mexico. At least we'd have men to protect us there."

"Mary, if someone is after me, might they be after Molly as well? We'd be leading them straight to her."

Mary sat down in an armchair and leaned across the coffee table toward him. "You think that's what this is about? Maybe we aren't the target. Maybe someone wants us to run to Molly."

Sam sighed. "I've wondered."

"That makes no sense. If someone wants Molly dead, it's because of black boxes. They'd want you dead too. But the black boxes are gone. Right?"

Sam shrugged and looked at his hands.

"No, Sam, it doesn't make sense. If this has to do with black boxes, shouldn't we get to the ranch and warn Molly? What is it, darling?"

"I've wondered, am I worth killing anymore?"

"What?"

"When I was in London, helping the inspector, he'd bring me black boxes, I'd look into them, and they would explode. Men tried to kill me for that."

"One almost did."

"Yes, and they'd surely kill Molly for it too. But what no one knew was…"

"Sam, tell me."

"It wasn't that simple. It got harder. Every time I looked into a box, it's hard to explain, but it became harder to come out again. The more I did it, the more difficult the task became. I began to wonder if I might one day look into a box and not come back again."

"What do you mean, not come back?"

Sam paused and took a deep breath. "When I look into the box I can see them, the creatures. They come toward me, snarling and snapping. I turn to a bright light. It's the way out. At first it was easy. I would turn to the light, and then it was over. The box was exploded. After a dozen or so it became harder. I had to push myself to the light. It was work and took longer, somehow. Then..."

Sam felt himself tremble. "Then another dozen or so boxes and they started catching me before I could get out, the creatures. I'd feel their claws latching on to my legs, pulling me away from the light. The more boxes, the longer we'd struggle before I got to the light. My faith began to waiver as to whether I could make it. I'm not sure I could make it if put to the test again.

"I mean, I would do it. If I saw another human being look into the box, I'd try to save them. It doesn't matter who they might be. I'd try to destroy the box in the hopes that I could bring them back, just like Molly brought me back. But to look into a black box just to destroy the box...I'm not sure I could do that. I'm afraid I might not come back. I...I don't know."

Mary put her hand on Sam's shoulder. "Oh, Sam."

"I wonder, if I can't destroy boxes, am I worth killing? Do they know I can't destroy boxes? Why would they hunt me down again?"

"Sam, look at me. All the black boxes are gone. But if they aren't, if that is how you feel, then I don't want you looking in any more black boxes. As long as Molly Bell is alive you don't have to do this by yourself."

Sam nodded and kissed her on the forehead. He said a silent prayer for Molly Bell. "God, please keep her alive."

"I saw Doctor Carter on the way here. He offered to let us stay at his house. He thought it would be 'safer' there. When I demurred, he asked that we have dinner sometime."

"Doctor Carter? God bless him. He's been very kind to us."

"He's a good man, about the only friend I really have at the hospital, at least the only one I trust fully. He seemed quite concerned. I told him we'd be delighted to dine with them when convenient."

"But of course. What's in the package?" Mary's focus shifted to the wrapped cage sitting on the coffee table between them.

"Oh, that." Sam stood up, broke the string, and proceeded to unwrap the cage.

"Two rats? Sam, why did you bring home two rats?"

"Good, they're both awake now. They seem to be getting along fine."

"Sam! Why are there two rats in a cage in our room?"

"Remember the sticky goo I took off the roses?"

Mary nodded but continued to look at the cage and the two rats.

"I've tried to analyze it to see what it is. It isn't a naturally occurring substance. That much I've been able to determine. I think it's possible that someone put it on our roses. If we had fallen into the rose bushes, the thorns would have acted like needles, injecting whatever it is into our blood. I know that sounds crazy, but I have a hunch it may be poisonous."

"Poisonous?" Mary's gaze stayed fixed on the cage as she sat in silence.

"It's only a hunch."

"What does that have to do with two rats in my room?"

"It's an experiment, off the books, so I couldn't leave them at the hospital. I've injected the one with the red markings with the residue I found on the roses. If it's poisonous, the reaction I

61

observe in the infected rat might give me clues about what it is. The other rat has not been infected, which gives me something to compare by way of behavior. They both seem to be acting identically at the moment."

"I don't understand. Why would you suspect that it's poisonous?"

"The night of the fire, I had a dream that the house was on fire. I jumped out a window into some rose bushes covered with a sticky substance."

"A dream? You dreamt our house was burning the very night it actually did?" Mary tilted her head and pursed her lips. "Isn't it possible the smoke induced such a dream? You smelled smoke and your brain deduced fire. The dream filled in the logical details."

Sam shook his head. "In the dream the rose bush thorns pierced my clothing. I felt a burning sensation and then I was—I don't know, exactly—I was affected some way. I was not myself. I was an animal, full of rage and anger.

"When I awoke from the dream the house was on fire. We were about to jump into the rose bushes on the side of the house until I saw something glistening on them, just like in the dream. Something triggered in me. I couldn't jump. I couldn't let you jump.

"Mary, we almost fell into those bushes. I need to know what was on those bushes."

Mary again went silent, staring at the rats.

"That's us here, Sam. We're rats in a cage."

She continued to watch the two rats rustling about the cage.

"Funny you should say that," Sam replied with a tremble in his voice.

"What, Sam? You have that look. Not another dream?"

The memory came rushing back. He tried to push it away, but the images pulsed forward. "Yes, they happen so often. I try to put them out of my head. But what you just said…"

Mary moved to his side and put her hand on his shoulder. "What, about rats in a cage?"

"I'm in a cage. Two angry red eyes spread far apart are looking in from the outside of the cage." He squeezed his eyes shut. Mary's arms were around his shoulders. "At first I think it must be some elephant-sized rat. Then the outside of the cage comes into focus. I'm in a cell of sorts in a basement. A stinky, smelly place. The two angry red eyes are not eyes at all, they are bright red moles on the back of a giant hand clenched outside the bars."

Sam looked down at his own clenched fist. "Then the hand turns around and opens. Inside the hand is a black box. The box floats from the hand toward my face, and then…" He put his hand to his eye and pinched the bridge of his nose, trying in vain to hold back a tear.

"Then, I'm back inside the box again." His body quivered.

"It's all right, Sam," Mary softly assured.

"The creatures are howling and shrieking. There are hundreds, maybe thousands of them. It's a bloodbath."

He squeezed his eyes shut again and gritted his teeth.

"First there's Inspector Jenkins. Molly is there, as is her mother…others, too. They're all fighting and screaming. The little monsters bite into them again and again, eating them alive in front of my eyes."

He stopped for a moment, taking a deep breath and forcing it back out through pursed lips.

"Then…then I saw you."

"Oh, Sam." She held him tight. "It's only a dream. Some dreams are just dreams. They don't have to come true."

Sam turned and held onto her waist, wiping his eyes on her shoulder. "I just wish they'd stop."

He clung to her. Only the sound of a ticking clock and the scurrying noises of the two rats broke the silence.

"I love you so, Mary. I'm sorry I've brought us such calamity. You deserve so much more."

Mary pulled back to hold his face with her hands.

"Listen to me, Doctor Sam Cunningham. There is no woman in the world more blessed than I. You have nothing to apologize for. This is my fight as much if not more than yours. One day at a time, Sam. We'll be fine. One day at a time."

He grasped Mary's hands in his, pulled them from his face, and kissed each one in turn.

"I thank God every day for you, my beautiful wife." He kissed her hands again as he looked up at Mary's sparkling eyes.

"I'll talk to Doctor Carter tomorrow at the hospital. I trust him implicitly. I'll explain that we need someplace new to lie low for a while and would like to take him up on his offer. We need to give the inspector a few more days to provide us with instructions. The Western Union office has standing orders to call me at the hospital with news of any cable. We should hear something any day."

"And what if the man with the cane comes back looking for you again?"

Sam turned away and glanced at the cage. The two rodents seemed quite at peace in their new surroundings, sniffing here and there and wandering about the cage.

"Sam, if someone is looking for you we don't have time to wait. We need to go somewhere now."

"I'll talk to the hotel manager. That someone could determine what room we are in is unacceptable. For two dollars a day I expect better."

"Move hotels?"

"We could, but it may be less conspicuous if we moved only rooms instead. There're six floors in this hotel. I'll get him to move us tonight and insist they move us to a new room on a different floor periodically for as long as we're here."

Sam moved to a coat stand and grabbed a jacket and hat.

"After that, I'll go out and get us some supper. We'll both feel better after a good meal."

"No, I'm not letting you out of my sight tonight. I'm going with you."

"Mary, you said something a minute ago, 'As long as Molly Bell is alive.' He wanted *her* dead first, the man with the black box. He picked Molly as a target. I merely stumbled into the mess. If I'm in danger, she's—"

"There's nothing to come from us worrying about Molly. That's the inspector's job. Right now we have to focus on you, Sam, on us."

Sam looked back at the rats. "I don't understand it. There's evil about. I feel it, but I don't understand it."

***

"What do you think?" President Roosevelt jutted his head toward his Secretary of State, Elihu Root.

"Interesting, tea and scotch, whatever led you to it?"

"Yes! Brilliant, I say. You take the two best things ever to come out of the British Isles and mix them in one cup. You like it, then?"

"I could certainly get used to it, but then I'd be cutting my daily allotment of scotch to make room for the tea."

Roosevelt slapped his knee. "Hah! Quite right, Elihu. Still, a fine combination, I must say." He took a sip out of his own cup before setting it down and folding his hands in his lap. "Now, where were we? First I digress to the ships and then tea."

"The report from our Austrian ambassador, Mr. Rives."

"Yes, we left off with the recent history of the Serbs...next they murder their king and his wife, brutally if I recall."

Root nodded. "Along with others, including the Prime Minister and the Minister of War. It was a complete change of government, from one friendly to the next-door Austrians to one decidedly not. Then two years ago the new Serbian government made its feelings abundantly clear when it awarded a substantial arms contract to a French firm instead of their traditional Austria-Hungary supplier. Austria-Hungary retaliated by closing its borders to Serbian agricultural exports."

"The 'Pig War,' I believe they call it." Roosevelt took another sip.

"Quite. A 'war' that is still being waged. According to Ambassador Rives, the new Serbian regime is not only anti-Austria-Hungarian. They are also very pro-Russian. And now the Russians see this little Slavic cousin as their charge. Russian protection in turn empowers the Serbs to greater ambitions, which they have in spades."

Root paused, gazing at nothing in particular with his sleepy almond eyes set above a strong nose and bushy mustache all arranged proportionally on a square face. Laconic, that's what Root was, Roosevelt concluded, laconic.

"A country should never bind itself to a weaker nation." The president interjected. "It's tempting to act provocatively when it's someone else's blood on the line."

"Indeed." Root took another sip of the fortified tea. "And this little Serbian nation, according to Rives, aspires to be a Serbian empire someday, cobbling together all the Serbian peoples of Albania, Rumania, Bulgaria, Montenegro and, important to the current problem, Bosnia. They even aspire to pull Dalmatia, Istria, Croatia, and Slavonia away from the Austro-Hungarians."

"But those places aren't all peopled by just Serbians. Why, in Bosnia-Herzegovina alone there's more Catholic Croats and Muslims than Serbs. Ridiculous."

Root shook his head. "That's a minor point to the Serbians. As far as they're concerned, they're all Serbs, some people just don't know it yet. As long as Bosnia and Herzegovina were under the nominal control of the Ottoman Empire, the Serbs were willing to bide their time. When they were suddenly annexed, well, the bee hive was kicked over."

Roosevelt held his cup short of his mouth and breathed in the peaty notes given off by the scotch. "And what does our man Rives propose we do at this point?"

Root leaned back in his chair and set down his cup. "He's a good man, thorough in his report."

"Yet?"

"Rather short on solutions, I'm afraid. He does note that the greatest proponent for peace in the region is the Grand Duke Franz Ferdinand. He's a moderating influence on the Austro Hungarian military. He preaches quiet caution whenever they rattle their sabers too loudly."

Theodore rubbed his chin. "Do what we can, Elihu. Perhaps a letter to the Austrian Emperor noting our appreciation for the keen insight the Grand Duke Ferdinand has shown during this crisis. We need to support that man. Ferdinand stomps on sparks, and there's lots of gunpowder lying around in the Balkans just waiting to ignite."

"Indeed, indeed. God forbid the Grand Duke joins the list of the assassinated. That list is too long already, and we need him."

Roosevelt shook his head. "God forbid, indeed."

"Theodore, you do realize you too are a target?"

"Now, Elihu, not a 'don't take unnecessary risks' lecture from you too. I've had two Secret Service men trailing me since McKinley was gunned down. I can't go to the privy without someone raising the alarm that I've gone missing."

"In light of the…"

Roosevelt waved him off with his right hand. "Did you hear that? I believe my stomach is growling. Will you join me for dinner? I'm told pheasant is on the menu this evening."

"I'd be delighted, Mr. President."

***

The boiling sulfurous water approached. Those in the front pushed back with all their might on the sea of naked bodies behind them. But their feet didn't hold as they were mindlessly pushed,

67

sliding forward toward the heat and the sulfurous stench. Suddenly the air filled with a shrieking noise that reverberated through their heads. Flesh burned for debts that could never be paid.

Molly sat upright. There was a rapping at her door. Images of writhing, pink bodies faded from her mind as she rubbed her eyes. The rapping came again, this time louder. She sprung from her bed and jumped at the door.

"Who is it?"

"It's me, Becky. You've got to get up. Hurry, open the door."

"Why? Why should I open the door?"

"There's no time. You trusted me to put you in this room, now you've got to trust me to get you out. They're here, Molly, the bounty hunters."

Molly opened the door and an icy hand grasped hers, pulling her from the room into the frosty night air.

"This way. No time to dress. I left you some clothes you can change into in your saddlebag."

Into the darkness she ran, the image of flowing red hair streaming in the night wind in front of her. They headed down a path through the pine trees, away from the buildings and stables. The chilly air bit through her nightgown, and the dry pine needles stung her feet. But she kept on running, following the flaming apparition down the hillside.

At the bottom of the hill the trail opened to a moonlit pasture. Pluck stood fully saddled, watering at a pond.

"I got him ready for you. There's food in the saddlebag along with the clothes. Dresses, though, that's all I had." She was pushing Molly toward her horse. "Ride hard on the road that starts on the other side of the pasture. It'll take you north toward Ruidoso and Hondo. Then head southeast toward the Lucas Triple X Ranch outside of Carlsbad."

Molly was trying to focus as she mounted the paint, now alert to the urgency, with head up and ears pointed skyward.

"Find Jay White. Tell him I sent you. Tell him Rebecca sent you and that you need his help. Got it?"

"Jay White, Triple X Ranch outside of Carlsbad. But why?"

"Now go!" She smacked the paint on the haunches. "Godspeed, Molly!"

Molly bent low to the horse's neck as it accelerated to a full gallop and entered the road.

***

The two rats made a bit more commotion than normal, interrupting Sam Cunningham's perusal of the morning paper. The unmarked rat, backed into a corner, eyed the other nervously as it drank from a water dish. Sam stole a quick glance at his wife sitting nearby having tea before returning to the news. She had not been herself since the fire, and this morning she wore worry on her face, apparent since the visit by the stranger two days before.

Sam returned to the paper. The news from Europe was still bleak. The British were sending a fleet to the Adriatic, and the Russian Black Sea fleet had mobilized. The Serbians were clearly the most agitated of the bunch. Austrian flags were being burned in the street, and the Serbian king threatened for not having declared open warfare yet over the annexation of Bosnia.

"Did you read about the motorcar?" he asked Mary between sips of tea. "Sixty-five miles an hour on average."

"The race on Long Island? I'm not much of a motorcar race enthusiast. All that speeding about, going nowhere as quickly as one can."

"It's simply amazing to think about, 235 miles in 219 minutes. Herbert Lytle…a new speed record. I doubt *that* one will fall soon. He'll be a household name fifty years from now. 'He's fast, but he's no Herbert Lytle.'" Sam paused, waiting a moment for a response.

"Besides, I'd rather think about fast motorcars than all the war talk. They seem like such children, the Bulgarians, Serbians,

Austrians. They'll drag the whole world into it if they're not careful."

Mary seemed disinterested as she put down and refilled her cup.

"Here's something truly funny, or maybe ironic is a better description."

She looked at him with a raised eyebrow.

"This article." Sam poked the paper. "About two cows."

"Two cows?"

"It strikes me that sometimes the answer comes from the strangest of places. Right here," He again poked at his copy of *The Dallas Morning News*. "Right here on the front page. On one side you have an entire column dedicated to the very childish behavior of the European powers, threats of war, fleets, armies, angry riots, and in a small article next to all that the story of two cows."

Sam could tell his wife was still not amused. He determinedly pressed on, even at the risk of overplaying the hand.

"Listen. 'Caldwel, Texas. Two cows were found in a pasture of T.W. Parkhill with their horns locked, and they had apparently been in this condition for at least ten days. They had been fighting, their horns got locked, and they could not get loose to fight any more and had to remain in that condition till discovered, at which time both animals seemed to be perfectly satisfied and in a hurry to get loose and go after water and something to eat. Their heads were so close together that the skin was rubbed off in several places, and the left eye of one cow had been gouged out by the horn of the other. Two men could not pull them apart. Two more men were sent for and the four tugged away as if for dear life, but could not get the cows pulled apart, and they got a saw and sawed the horns, after which the animals made a rush for water. Since they were given their liberty they have been best of friends, are in perfectly good humor, browse together, and apparently settled their difficulties for all time to come in that ten days' conflict.'" Sam poked the paper again. "There's a lesson there to be learned from these cows."

She shook head and frowned. "The truth of the matter is you men are like those cows, stubborn and aggressive until someone clips off your horns. This world will never be safe until women have an equal say in the matters of diplomacy."

"You mean the vote?"

"For starters, yes."

"For starters…I suppose it *is* inevitable. First the vote then the presidency. Perhaps you'll be the first. 'President Cunningham,' has a nice ring to it. What would that make me, 'First Gentleman'?"

Mary frowned. "My point is this, men are martial by birth. It's not a fault, it's the way God made you. Women are more maternal by birth. Men want to solve differences by action, sometimes aggressive action. Women want to resolve conflicts through conciliation and mediation.

"I see nations as being dangerous by degrees. The most dangerous is ruled by a single authoritative man, a king, for example. He makes decisions moderated only by his own moods and the persuasive nature of his advisors, all typically men. The next most dangerous is one ruled by a single authoritative woman, such as a queen. While she may be surrounded by male advisors, she, at least, still has the ingrained nature of a woman to moderate her behavior in the face of aggression."

"I see your point. The reigns of Queens Elizabeth and Victoria certainly support it."

"Presently, democracies ruled by men are the most resistant to war, but they are not immune to it. The more voices that have a say, the better. But, if half those voices were of the female persuasion, I doubt any democracy would ever clamor for war.

"It's not just the vote, Sam. The equality of woman and man may be essential to the preservation of mankind. Imagine if the world ever drifted in the other direction. The societies of the

Middle East, for example, where women are treated as cattle, covered head to toe to hide them from the world, under the absolute control of their husbands. Such dark and backward societies would doom mankind."

Mary stopped and glared at the two rats.

"Mary, I'm sorry we're in this mess. If I don't hear from the inspector today, I'll send him another urgent cable this afternoon."

"What if he can't answer you?"

"Can't answer?"

"What if he knows we are being followed and can't risk an answer, or what if he has been attacked himself?"

"If the former, I have no doubt he's sending someone to help us. If the latter, I assume someone in his office would pick up his mantle and carry on."

Mary sat silently.

Suddenly there was a commotion from the rat cage. Sam turned his attention to their wire prison. The cage rocked as the two rats slammed against the sides. One rat squealed in a high-pitched shriek.

"Sam, they're fighting!"

Sam leapt at a nearby pair of leather gloves, slid them on, and was quickly at the cage. The rats were a ball of bloody fury, one shrilly squealing and the other savagely attacking. He hesitated, contemplating the difficulty of grasping either rat as the battle bounced from side to side in the cage.

"Sam, he's killing the other. Make them stop." Mary came up alongside.

The brutal assault continued with the attacking rat ripping at the belly and neck of the other.

"I don't want to risk a bite or scratch. Whatever I injected him with might be transferable. I'm afraid we'll have to wait until we're clearly dealing with one rat."

They didn't have to wait for long. The victim stopped squealing and soon stopped moving altogether. The attacking rat continued ripping at the body of the other. Its face was covered in blood as it lunged again and again at the still corpse. The living rat's entire body quivered as it gorged on the body of its foe.

"Sam, it's the one you infected, the one with the red 'X'. He's gone mad."

Sam unlatched the cage and lifted the opening just wide enough to allow his gloved right hand into the cage.

"What are you doing?" Mary asked as she backed away.

"For starters I need to get the dead rat out. I don't think I'll get a better chance than now with the other so focused. Get me a bucket or something."

Sam thrust his right arm in the cage, pinning the attacking rat under his palm and closing his hand around its body. The rat jerked violently. Sam pushed down hard to keep the rat pinned to the bottom of the cage.

With his left hand he removed the dead rat and placed it in a trashcan Mary had set beside the cage. The live rat somehow began to wriggle free. Sam grasped hard with his right hand, jerked the struggling rat upward, and flung it at the far corner of the cage. Before he could pull his hand completely out, the rat bounced up and chomped on his gloved index finger.

"Ah, curses!" he exclaimed through clenched teeth. He fell back as that rat pulled the glove off his hand and into the cage. Sam latched the cage while the rat ripped into his now abandoned glove.

"Let me see. Sam, he bit right through the glove! You're bleeding!"

"It looks worse than it is. I'll need to wash it off and get a compress on it."

"But you said…"

"It's all right, Mary. The wound isn't deep. I'll get some alcohol on it to kill any infection."

He looked down at the cage. The rat was sitting on his glove staring back at him with a bloody face, the red 'X' on his back clearly visible.

"He certainly manifests aggressive behavior. I'll need to observe him and see what happens next."

"Observe him? Take him to the lab. I don't want a rat in our room anymore, especially not this one!"

"The lab is closed today. This is the critical time period. Someone needs to take observations at least every couple of hours. I've not told anyone else what I'm doing, in any event. I'm sorry. The cage needs to stay."

Mary turned away and walked toward the door. Her shoulders quivered.

"I need some fresh air," she whispered.

"That would do us both some good. Let me clean up this finger, and we'll go out for a walk."

He watched the cage as he moved to the bathroom. The rat glared back, following his every movement with two angry red eyes set above a bloody face.

CHAPTER 5
SETTING THE HOOK

Fred Miller kept trying to open his eyes, but the searing sunlight forced them shut with every attempt. His head ached. He felt suspended, rocking slowly back and forth, each rocking motion starting with a slight bump. A familiar Irish tune, whistled in rhythm with each bump, rose softly above the sound of sloshing water and the distant call of seagulls.

Where was he? He would have looked around to find out, but it was less painful to leave his eyes closed. An attempt to raise his head was met with splitting pain that caused his whole body to stiffen. He let out an involuntary whimper that added to the awful sensation of a sharp object being driven though his skull. He lay still, the gentle rocking providing his only comfort as his heartbeat pounded away in his head.

Staying as motionless as possible slowly brought relief. Sleep, blessed sleep was soon upon him again.

Fred blinked several times to moisten his dry eyes. Was it a dream? Where was he? Smoldering peat and coffee filled his nostrils as he took in a deep breath. Rotating his head toward the glow of a fire set off a stabbing pain in his brain. He reached up to feel a large knot on the back of his head. He re-closed his eyes and slowly, gradually sat up. With his eyes still closed he recalled the sensation of being carried and then placed in something—a cart? Then there was a soft bed, and a peat fire, and the smell of coffee and roasting meat. He must have fallen asleep again, but where was he?

He squeezed his eyelids tight before opening them, one at a time, to reveal the interior of a small, square room defined by short walls of fitted flat stones. The peat fireplace he'd been smelling was on one wall. The two walls perpendicular to that one each framed a single, grease and smoke-smeared window. The window on one wall was holding back a bright glow, while the window on the other wall, the wall next to him, sat in a shadowy dusk.

He twisted his body around to make out the fourth wall, the one opposite the fireplace. It held a rustic wooden door about five feet in height, the top being a bare foot or so from the low ceiling, a ceiling made of worn timber. He'd seen the likes of such a ceiling before, oak planks from a salvaged ship. Although rustic, it was all neat and symmetrical, the door opposite the fireplace and the two windows opposite each other, all in the center of their respective walls.

A wave of hunger tinged with nausea washed over him. He looked about for the source of the coffee smell and spied a kettle near the fireplace. Stomping came from outside, and then the door behind him opened. In walked a short, wiry man with stringy dark hair draped below his shoulders. The man closed the door, set a wooden staff in the corner, and removed a woolen over-garment and woolen cap, both of which he placed on a single peg near the door. He then retrieved the kettle and a tin cup, into which he poured the coffee that had enticed Fred from his slumber. The man handed the steaming cup to Fred and took a seat on a low wooden stool by the fireplace.

He sat erect while calmly observing Fred sip coffee. In the glow of the fire, his face was bronze and weather-beaten. He stared at Fred with small piercing eyes perched narrowly over a proud aquiline nose. While he looked to be the backside of fifty, his gait displayed no age or infirmity.

"Hello," murmured Fred softly, not knowing what else to say.

The man sat silently for a moment, and then reached for another tin cup, into which he poured coffee for himself.

Fred took a swallow of the hot, bitter brew. Strong stuff. He felt his body warm and the throbbing in his head began to subside. He gulped down more.

His new companion moved to a small table in a corner near the door. He picked up a knife and cut off a chunk of bread from a flat, round loaf. Handing the chunk to Fred, he retook his seat on the stool.

Fred gingerly bit into the hard, dense bread. He chewed and swallowed, washing the first piece down with the last swallows from his cup. The man dutifully retrieved the cup from Fred, refilled and returned it. Fred gave a slight nod in gratitude and smiled, as the man again returned to his stool perch.

"Thank you."

Fred took another bite, chasing it again with a mouthful of coffee.

"You're most kind, for the coffee and bread. Fred, Fred Miller. May I ask where I am?"

The man took a sip from his cup, but made no response.

Fred looked around the room again for clues to the many questions that raced through his head. It was simply furnished. He was sitting on the only bed, which was as wide as his shoulders and not much longer than his five feet ten inches.

Across the room hung a canvas hammock with both ends stowed on a hook between one of the windows and the corner of the wall in which the fireplace resided. There was a matching, empty hook on the opposite wall. The few other bits of furniture were modest, but the place was neat, if not exactly spotless. The wood staff that his companion had propped near the door caught Fred's attention. It was longer than the height of the ceiling and sharpened to a point at the upright end, more like a spear than a staff.

"Habla Español?" his host finally uttered.

Fred swung his head back toward the stranger, which was a mistake he wouldn't soon repeat, as he was reminded that sudden movement had consequences. He steadied himself and waited a few seconds for the throbbing to subside.

"No, I'm sorry. I don't know Spanish. I don't suppose you speak English then? English?"

His companion shrugged his shoulders and took another sip of coffee.

"Well, then we'll find very little to disagree about. To your health," Fred raised his cup in toast and took another sip. "I don't suppose you have anything with which we could give a proper toast?"

***

"I agree with your analysis, Charles. I simply don't arrive at your conclusion."

Hardinge clenched his jaw and breathed in deeply. "May I try a different tack, then?"

"By all means." Sir Edward unfolded his arms enough to flutter his right hand in Hardinge's direction.

"Turning to the Russians, can we agree that it is not too late to change our response to their ambassador?"

"Change? In what regard?"

Hardinge leaned forward in his chair, lowering his voice. "When the ambassador spoke with you yesterday…"

"He asked me point blank what we would do if Russia went to war with Austria-Hungary. My response as Foreign Secretary would be considered the official position of His Majesty's Government."

"Thus, you gave him no substantive response at all."

"Exactly." Grey unfolded his crossed legs and shifted in his seat.

"Yet ten minutes ago you agreed that it would be very difficult for us to stay out of such a conflict."

"True as well."

"Isn't it better that our allies know something of our support for them? Otherwise they operate in the dark with no context to discern the consequences of their action."

"I need a drink." Grey rose abruptly and moved toward a nearby cabinet from which he retrieved a bottle. "Scotch, or would you prefer sherry?"

"Scotch, thank you."

"You drive me to it, you know…you, the Russians, the Germans, the Serbians, the whole lot. Instead of fishing in Scotland I'm stuck in London drinking their liquid solace." Grey handed a glass to Hardinge and smiled.

Sir Charles seized the opportunity and raised his glass. "To Scotland, then, for the trout and the solace."

"To Scotland."

"Excellent stuff, Highland?"

Grey nodded while staring out the window. "I despise this town. There is an aggressive…" Grey paused and looked down at his glass. "Stiffness to the buildings, a brutal hardness in the pavement. In summer the smell of the streets festering in the sun, the glare of the light all day striking upon hard substances and the stuffiness of the heat from which there is no relief at night…for no coolness comes with the evening air and the bedroom windows seem to open on to ovens. Now, as winter approaches, the buildings block the sun and turn the day grey and bleak, receding into the icy night. Add to these hardships what is worse than all…" He glanced up at Hardinge with a wrinkle on his brow. "The sense of being deprived of the country and shut off from it."

Grey took a sip from his glass and nodded approvingly. "It does bring solace. Enough of the black mood. More to your point, and since you mention trout…" Sir Edward took another sip. "I recall fondly the beginning of my keenness for angling. I believe the ardent anglers are born and not made, that the passion is latent in them from the beginning and is revealed sooner or later according to opportunity. In some cases it may be that the passion perishes unsuspected and unrevealed, because there is no opportunity of indulging or discovering it, till too late in life. The longer we live the deeper becomes the groove or the rut in which our life moves"—Grey moved a forefinger around in a circle pointed at the floor—"and the more difficult it becomes to go outside it.

"Fortunately, for me the opportunity for fishing, and the lessons therein learned, came early. The passion for it awoke suddenly. I remember very well being seized with the desire to fish."

Grey stood before the window with a wistful gaze at the street below. "I was about seven and riding a Shetland pony by the side of a very small burn. A mill was working higher up the stream, and the water was full of life and agitation, caused by the opening of the sluice of the mill pond above. I had seen small trout caught in the burn before." He looked at the floor with his eyes darting about at imaginary shadows. "But now, for the first time and suddenly, came an overpowering desire to fish, which gave no rest till some very primitive tackle was given me. With this and some worms, many afternoons were spent in vain."

Grey raised his hand with palm out toward Hardinge while savoring another sip before continuing.

"The impulse to *see* the trout destroyed all chances of success. It did not suit me to believe that it was fatal to look into the water before dropping a worm over the bank, or that I could not see the trout first and catch them afterwards, and I preferred to learn by experience and disappointment rather than by the short, but unconvincing, method of believing what I was told.

"For some years this burn fishing was all that I knew." Grey took another drink and sat back down. "It was very fascinating, though the trout were so small." He held out his left hand with forefinger extended and thumb in the air. "One of four ounces was considered a good one, whilst the very largest ran to six ounces.

"These larger trout taught me a second lesson: self-restraint. The first lesson was, as I said, to refrain from looking into the water before I fished it. All the trout of every size combined to teach this. The second difficulty was to restrain the excitement when I had a bite. Setting the hook takes a patient approach. The natural impulse was to strike so hard..." Grey jerked his arm back. "As to hurl the fish into the air overhead. This answered very well with trout of two or three ounces, though once a small one came unfastened in the air, and flew off at a tangent into the hay behind, never to be found. But with a six-ounce trout this violent method did not answer so well. Neither the angler, nor the rod, nor the tackle, was strong enough to deal with them so summarily. Catastrophes occurred, and by slow degrees and painful losses I learnt the necessity of getting keenness under control."

Grey ended his lecture with a sniff of his glass followed by a long, relaxed draw.

Hardinge sensed a response was required. "Don't look into the water and keep my keenness under control. Do you think I'd do better in these respects if I started fishing this late in life, or is my groove too deep?"

"I think you'd be less inclined to urge hasty commitments to allies with such skills better honed."

Hardinge let out an audible sigh. "When the weather turns, then, I'll endeavor to take up the sport."

"Excellent." Grey slapped his knee. "Since we are in one accord, there is another matter I wish to thrash out. I've had ample time to review the file on Special Department B. Now that I am in the loop, I wish to discuss certain conditions."

"Conditions?"

"B is a joint effort between this office and Scotland Yard. I may not agree with the initial decision to keep the workings of this operation from my attention, but now that I have been briefed, it is imperative that I become involved."

"With conditions?"

"Inspector Jenkins must report to me."

"Edward, I may have given the wrong impression. Since the establishment of Special Department B, Jenkins has not reported to me or anyone else in the Foreign Office. He runs the effort, and I assist as best I can while he keeps me informed. Given that the operation has come under assault, it became important to share knowledge of the operation with a larger base of authority."

"What is the purpose of informing me if I have no say in the direction of future events?"

"Jenkins may need additional resources beyond those of the Yard and Department B. Requests for assistance may need to flow more officially through this office."

"Then I'm to be a rubber stamp, informed of the need, responsible for the outcome, but with no ability to shape it."

"Special Department B was formed with autonomy expressly in mind. There are cracks in our government that have been exploited in the past and are being exploited again."

"Autonomy? To whom does Jenkins report?"

"Edward, you are now one of the few of His Majesty's Government to know about the effort at all. The goal is still autonomy, but B needs greater assets at its disposal. It needs your support."

"To whom does Jenkins report?"

"I don't know."

"Unacceptable." Sir Edwards lowered his voice to a barky hush. "Unacceptable. I shall bring this up with the Prime Minister."

"Edward, what you're sensing is a very large fish nibbling at your line."

Grey lowered his head and rubbed the bridge of his beaklike nose.

"My apologies, Charles. It's been a rather tiring day. First there was a meeting with the Home Secretary to discuss violent labor strikes. Gladstone seems to think a foreign influence is at work, or perhaps anarchists. As I left that meeting a militant suffragette threw her umbrella at me whilst I was boarding my motorcar. It's as if civil society is falling apart.

"Then I met with His Majesty, who again expounded endlessly about my never having traveled outside the British Isles, insinuating that extensive travel is a minimum qualification for a

British Foreign Secretary. I'm rather tired of that chorus. Hmm, my glass is empty."

Hardinge repressed the thought that he too was a member of the choir singing that tune. "No apology needed, but accepted nonetheless." Hardinge tipped the remainder of the contents of his glass into his mouth. "My glass as well. May I join you for another?"

Grey smiled broadly. "Point well taken. If we can't have the fish, we should at least enjoy the solace."

***

Fred Miller finished his breakfast and emerged from the hut to a grey misty morning. Sheep bleated in the distance. There was no sign of his companion, a repeat of the day before. The little man was up and gone, with breakfast cooked and his share eaten, before Fred had opened his eyes.

He rubbed the receding knot on his head and looked back at the hut, the lone structure on the island. It sat like an organized pile of rocks with a roof plopped on top. The hut was sheltered from the prevailing wind by a low ridge.

Fred glanced up at the ridge, picking out the only other evidence of man on the island, a sloping door built into the side of the ridge. Some sort of cellar? What might be behind door, or even if the door had anything behind it but the rocky ridge, he couldn't tell. The door was solidly secured by an iron padlock and he'd yet to spy a key about.

"Well," he announced to the hut, "the least I can do is offer my service." Despite knowing nothing about tending sheep, off he went to find their shepherd.

The island, rock and grass, with not a single tree to break the monotony, did not immediately reveal his companion. The bleating of sheep echoed from every direction, giving him no clue as to which way to proceed, so he just went.

Occasionally he stumbled upon a few casually grazing bleaters in a defile. There were lots of defiles where the grass generally grew. No doubt these defiles also provided refuge for the sheep when the wind swept across the island, like it had the night before. The wind blew so hard that the windows rattled and the roof whistled, a sinister sounding symphony that kept him up half the night. The old shepherd slept soundly through it all, adding his rhythmic snoring to the score.

What was a patent agent from Manchester doing wandering aimlessly about this barren landscape? Perhaps this is hell? Fred chuckled to himself.

"Well, maybe purgatory," he commented to a passing sheep. "I say, old chap, can you direct me to the nearest pub?" When the sheep made no reply, Fred continued his quest.

"Old man! Hello, good fellow! Where are you?"

***

It was time to end this tomfoolery. The same two gentlemen followed Inspector Jenkins, again. They were easy to spot, one in a long coat concealing a lumpy object underneath and the other with a peculiarly shaped cane with a shaft that branched out into an upside down "U" shape at the ground end.

If they wanted a target, he'd give it to them, but on his terms and where they couldn't escape. He *was* dressed for the occasion, after all.

Jenkins ducked into the entrance of the Underground Electric Railways Company of London's Holland Park station. As he descended the stairs in the sharp electric glare of the bulbs hanging overhead, he heard the two sets of footsteps following. He turned for the eastbound platform.

A few customers milled about waiting on the next train. It always confounded him that the underground railways were so lightly used, particularly since they had all been converted from steam to electric. They were so efficient. Maybe they were too new for the general population to trust? Old habits die hard. So people would go on riding carriages, hansoms, and the above-ground trollies. The new motorized buses seemed to be quite popular. They'd probably replace hansom cabs someday.

Hansom cabs—where was Jim Talbot? Was he alive? Mick had yet to turn up a single clue about the young hansom cab driver's whereabouts. No corpse had drifted up from the Thames. He had to be alive. He must be alive.

Jenkins pushed the image of young Talbot out of his head and returned to the puzzle of the sparsely frequented underground railway. Perhaps it was the subterranean aspect that kept Londoners out of the tube—too much like a rat's existence. In any event, the venue served his purposes nicely, for his assumption that the midmorning crowd would be light had proven correct.

Jenkins moved to the center of the platform. The two stalking men hovered nearby. The train pulled into the station with a handful of passengers trickling off. The conductor in the last car appeared bored, standing stoop-shouldered behind the iron entry gate and looking at his feet. His must be an empty car.

As Jenkins approached the conductor snapped to attention and swung the gate open.

"Tuppence if you please, sir. Thank you."

Jenkins nodded, stepped up to the conductor's landing, and entered the car. Upholstered benches lined each side with a row of rectangular windows above them. He took a seat on one side and checked his scarf. It still covered his entire neck, concealing what he wore beneath it—his insurance. He leaned back, stuck an unlit cigar in his mouth, and closed his eyes. He placed his right hand over his right trouser pocket, the faux pocket that led to the pistol he always carried. He thrust his left hand into the other trouser pocket and gripped the handle of the knife that was sheathed therein.

He focused on the sound of two additional customers entering the car. The rise and fall of the cushion meant that one of them was sitting to his right. If his hunch was correct, the other, the one with the peculiar cane, must be across from him on the opposite bench.

What Jenkins concealed under his scarf should buy him time to deal with the man off his right shoulder.

"All clear," came a cry from outside the car. "Next stop Notting Hill Gate, gents," came the voice of the conductor from the direction of the single door into the car. That door snapped shut, leaving Jenkins and the two strangers alone.

The train lurched forward and accelerated. The clattering of the rails picked up tempo until it reached a steady rhythm. Jenkins rolled the cigar around on his tongue. If they were going to act it would be immediately before the next station. He felt a jiggle in the seat cushion. Too early, he thought to himself, leaving his eyes closed and continuing to roll the cigar from side to side in his mouth. The car swayed through a bend in the track and then swayed back again in the other direction. He sensed a body nearby and smelled the ripe tinge of nervous sweat. After another swaying motion the clattering rhythm began to slow as the car decelerated.

There was a jostling in the car, and his seat cushion flexed downward and then sprang upward. He thrust his right hand to his gun and pulled his left hand up with the knife. He opened his eyes to the sight of the peculiar cane being thrust toward him, knocking the cigar out of his mouth. The man on his right held down his right arm, but Jenkins pulled his left one quickly enough for it to be free. The other assailant pushed the "U" shaped end of the cane around Jenkins' neck, pinning his head against the side of the car. There was a click followed by a smack against the steel collar he wore under his scarf. He still breathed. He *had* dressed for the occasion.

Jenkins swung his left arm across his body toward the man next to him, jabbing the assailant under his ribcage. The man with the cane hesitated, looking surprised and momentarily stunned. As the seated man crumpled from the knife piercing his heart, Jenkins gripped the shaft of the cane with his right hand and pushed the other assailant back, knocking him into the seat on the opposite side of the car. The attacker to his right would die, but the one with the cane must not get away.

Jenkins leapt at him just as he dropped the cane. The man struggled toward the opposite seat. Jenkins glanced to his right while grasping at the man's waist. A black box rested on the seat next to the dying assailant. Jenkins tugged at the struggling attacker, but he grabbed the box and pulled it toward his face.

"Redeem me!" he shouted. He went limp, dropped the box, and slumped to the floor.

CHAPTER 6
DISCRETION

Molly Bell peered down at the sleepy town of Hondo, New Mexico, a smattering of small adobe houses scattered about the Rio Hondo. The whitewashed exteriors poked through the thin grove of trees that followed the riverbed. She heard two dogs barking in the distance, not urgent barks, but the bark dogs make when bored. They're just talking to each other, she thought, wondering what they were saying. A slight breeze blew up behind her, and she hunched down in the saddle to stay warm.

Her hunger was getting the better of her. It must be about dinner time. She looked longingly at the small hamlet and imagined all the meals being prepared and what they might taste like—warm beans, moist chicken, soft tortillas. She was famished. She'd do almost anything for a warm meal. Not stealing, though, it wasn't Christian. But she needed to eat, and she knew no one in the little town. In fact, she'd never been to Hondo.

She made a quick survey of each of the little white buildings. Something told her to look harder at one on the edge of town. Smoke wafted from a chimney at one end of the squat structure. The breeze shifted, and the smell of bacon settled in her nose, making her feel suddenly weak.

"God, what should I do? Are you listening? I don't know what to do." Molly wiped away a single tear. In doing so she had loosened the reins, and her paint started toward the house she had been watching. She started to rein him in, but upon reflection, decided to let the horse judge the best course. She'd once heard a cowboy say, "If your horse don't want to go there, then neither should you." Was the opposite true? Maybe the horse knew something she didn't.

On they went, the paint steadily picking its way down the hill. As they got closer to the house a blond dog wandered out from a grassy clump under an apple tree and eyed Molly and her horse.

89

The dog neither growled nor wagged its tail, but stood its ground, watching intently.

Closer on they went. When Molly and her horse entered the roughly defined yard of the house, the blond dog stretched a back leg and slowly approached them. Through a greying muzzle the dog sniffed at Molly's foot in the stirrup, but remained neutral toward the intruders.

Molly stood in the saddle and examined the single rustic door. Wooden shutters hung closed over windows on either side of the door to keep out the chilly breeze. She strained to hear anything from inside, but the gurgle of the nearby river masked whatever noise might come from the house.

"Well, boys, here goes nothing."

Molly cautiously dismounted and put out a hand to the big dog. The dog sniffed, and, either satisfied or maybe just not interested anymore, limped off to the grassy bed whence he came. Molly tied off Pluck to a bush in the yard and turned to the house.

She stopped at the door and listened again. Still nothing, but the distinct smell of bacon caused a sharp, hard knot in her stomach. She reached up and rapped softly on the door.

A rustling noise came from inside. The door opened to reveal a Mexican man standing in front of her, not much taller than she, with straight black hair peppered with strands of grey, cut bowl-shaped around his head. Several days of white stubble framed his round and jowly face. He wore a loose-fitting white shirt, but there was nothing coming from the left sleeve. His left hand was missing. Molly checked herself from staring at the empty sleeve and, instead, looked into the man's brown eyes.

"I'm sorry, I mean, perdóname, Señor. Habla usted Ingles?"

"Yes, I speak English," came a soft response in the singsong accent of the locals.

Molly felt relieved, having already used a large chunk of her Spanish vocabulary. "I'm so sorry to bother you. I'm traveling and, well, I'm very hungry. I have money. Do you have enough to share? It smells so good. I mean, I can pay you if you let me have some food."

The man stepped aside and ushered her in with the open palm of his right hand. "Please, come in."

Molly walked inside as the man closed and locked the door behind her, an action she noticed but elected to ignore given her hunger. It took a moment for her eyes to adjust, but soon a small, tidy room came into focus. A bed stood in one corner made up with a colorful red blanket with a zigzag of blue cutting across the middle, like a fat, blue bolt of lightning splitting the sunset sky. A similar blanket, but smaller, draped lazily across a chair on the other side of the room, and a floor rug in the middle of the room repeated the pattern. In the corner opposite the bed a softly glowing kiva oven warmed a skillet with fried slabs of bacon mixed with chunks of onion. The wonderful smell was overwhelming, and her stomach gripped harder.

"Please, sit." The man pointed at the chair with the blanket draped on it. Molly dutifully obliged, all the while keeping her eyes on the skillet and its enticing contents.

The man produced a cup of water and handed it to Molly. She drank while watching with amazement as the man used but one hand to simultaneously hold a plate and fill it with bacon and onions from the skillet. Without missing a beat he secured a fork in the same hand while still holding the full plate, and then handed both to Molly.

She tried to eat slowly and politely, but she failed in the task as she shoveled mouthful after mouthful of the delicious food into her mouth.

"I'll tend your horse. No, please, don't get up. Eat. Then rest." The man pointed at the bed. "Mi casa es tu casa."

"Thank you. I'll pay you. Thank you, but I can't stay long."

"Eat, then rest." The man disappeared outside, leaving Molly to the food and the warm fire emitting from the little, round fireplace. An occasional pop came from the burning wood.

She wondered what time it must be, surely close to dusk. Her host seemed harmless. Could she trust him? Could she trust anyone? She trusted Mick. Where was he? He was always there when she needed him. Why hadn't he come?

She found herself gazing at the little bed. She ate until the plate was empty. Perhaps she could rest a moment. The thought alone seemed to add weight to her eyelids. She blinked a few times, set down the plate, and trudged to the bed. She could rest a minute without actually going to sleep, and then...

"Wake up."

Molly felt someone urgently shaking her shoulders.

"Wake up, mija. You must leave before the sun comes up."

The sun? Molly sat up and blinked. "Did you say the sun? Oh no, I fell asleep!"

"Hurry. Your horse is saddled. Venga. Follow me."

Molly sprung to her feet. The man was pulling now, urgently, to the door and then outside. Sure enough, in the darkness she could see Pluck, fully saddled, pawing the ground with wet legs, seemingly sensing the urgency of the situation. Molly jumped into the saddle.

The man grabbed the reins and started the horse toward the sound of the river.

"Wait, I need to pay you."

A strong "shush" came from the man as he continued to lead Pluck to the water.

As they approached the riverbank the glint of the coming dawn peaked over a distant rise. The man walked her paint right into the river and turned it downstream.

They trudged in the babbling water, her horse occasionally slipping and stumbling on the slick river rocks, for what seemed like twenty minutes, until they were well beyond the little village. Oddly, not a sound came from the village the whole while, not even a dog bark. Finally, the man stepped out of the river onto a shelf of solid rock forming one bank. The rock shelf extended about fifty feet right up to the edge of a thick pine grove.

"I walked your horse upstream first, to buy you some time. Go, and don't look back."

"But—"

"Go!" The man slapped her horse on the rump. Pluck snorted and bolted across the rock shelf toward the pine grove.

Molly rode the paint hard until they were out of the little valley that cradled Hondo village. She followed a deer trail as it wound its way up to higher ground. Soon the sun was up, casting a long shadow across the valley.

She came to a point on the trail where she could peek over a slight rise back down toward the village. She searched for the white house with the apple tree on the edge of town. Despite having gained a fair amount of altitude on Hondo, it didn't seem that far away. There was the blond dog, now lounging in a spot of sunshine in the yard.

From her vantage point she had a good view of the front yard to the Mexican's home, but she was fairly sure no one could see her head peaking above the ridge, unless they spotted the steam snorted by bursts from her exhausted horse. The rest of her and the paint were concealed by the terrain, and the sun coming up behind her would blind anyone looking in her direction.

It looked so serene and peaceful below. She lingered for a moment to take it all in and to let the horse rest.

Suddenly the blond dog rose and started to bark. A moment later the Mexican opened the door and walked into the yard, putting his one hand on the scruff of the dog's neck, which silenced the barking. Other dogs in the village took up the call, though. A chorus of howls, yips, and woofs rang across the valley, barks with a purpose.

The reason for the commotion soon became clear. Four horsemen rode into the yard and stopped in front of the Mexican and his dog. They were trailing a fifth unsaddled horse. One of the men was smaller than the rest. By the angular way he gripped the waist of his horse with his legs she guessed he must be an Apache. The largest of the four horsemen sported a black hat and headed straight for the Mexican, who stood holding the blond dog.

The man in the black hat pointed at the Mexican, who worked harder to hold on to the big dog with his one hand. The rider pulled out a long pistol. She saw the flash first and then heard the bang echoing through the pines. Everything went silent, even the Hondo dogs stopped barking briefly before picking up the chorus again, louder and more furious now.

The blond dog was lying on the ground with her kind host standing over it glaring back at the riders. The man with the black hat dismounted and smacked the Mexican across the face with his long pistol, sending him sprawling onto the ground. Molly watched in horror as the assailant then began to kick the Mexican while he rolled on the ground. Others dismounted. The Apache collected the reins while three men surrounded the poor Mexican, who was curled up in a ball on the dirt.

The man with the black hat grabbed the Mexican by the hair and starting pulling him toward the house. The other two men joined in the effort by grabbing him on either side. Together the three dragged the poor man across the yard, into his house, and shut the door behind them.

Molly suppressed the urge to charge down to rescue him. It was her fault. Anger welled up inside her as tears filled her eyes. There was nothing she could do. She gritted her teeth and wiped her cheeks. "Discretion," she whispered, shakily at first, then more resolutely. "Discretion." She silently prayed for mercy on her host and courage for herself as she took a deep breath, turned the paint around, and rode away.

***

President Roosevelt set down his pen, leaned back from his writing desk and rubbed the back of his neck. The soft glow of the electric lamp to his right gave the papers strewn before him a warm yellow hue.

It was a delicate situation, one he'd struggled with the better part of the day, an urgent plea for help from London, a secret request. What could he do without exposing his involvement and endangering those he sought to help? Applying the power of the United States military to such a domestic issue was out of the question, but what power short of that could possibly rescue the situation?

He was about to pick up his pen when a noise came from the doorway. Looking back he spied the form of his youngest child, Quentin, tiptoeing toward him. The president grinned and turned to meet his unexpected companion.

"My boy, what are you doing up and about? It's past midnight."

The ten-year-old, clad in nothing but a long nightgown, smiled at his father with the impish glint that never failed to bring a larger smile in response. He pulled a chair over to his father's desk and plopped himself at the president's left shoulder.

"I see. Joining me for work, are we? Well then, let's put you to good use."

"Are you angry at me, Father?"

"About?" Teddy rocked back in feigned surprise.

"For playing with the Secret Service men. Mother was very cross. She said you would talk to me about it."

"Ah, that." He sighed and put his arm around his son. "Well, first, it *was* an unfair advantage. Why, you were on the roof and those poor men were on the ground. Where on earth did you get the snowballs?"

"Charlie and I made them when it snowed last and put them in the basement icebox. You're not cross, are you?"

"Your mother also tells me that you and young Charlie Taft have been riding on top of the elevator again."

"Do you think it would hold a pony?"

"A pony? In the elevator?"

"Charlie doesn't think so, but I've measured it."

"Quentin, you must stop riding on the top of the elevator, and, henceforth, you may only engage the forces of the United States Secret Service on equal footing. No more surprise attacks from the roof. They're on our side, you know."

"Yes, Father." Quentin leaned his head into his father's breast and stared thoughtfully at the papers on his desk. "Why are you up late?"

"Various matters of state. This letter is to the British Prime Minister explaining our neutrality on this Bosnian mess, but offering a few suggestions. This one involves a discrepancy in the accounts of the Post Master. What a den of thieves that is. And this, ah that devilish Senate, I have to constantly cajole and prod them into action. They're quite a stubborn bunch of mules."

"Why don't you just order them what to do? You're the president!"

"Shh, not so loud, son. You'll wake your mother."

Quentin sighed and snuggled his head against his father's breast.

"Excellent question, lad. You share my instincts completely, but not the discretion learned from experience. Have I ever told you the legend of the mountain Indian tribe?"

Quentin sat up, looked attentively at his father, and wagged his head in the negative.

"Long ago there was a mountain Indian tribe, proud and strong. Like many tribes out west, each brave could take as many wives as he was able to feed and care for, but the older braves got first pick. A chief, why he might have as many as a dozen. The youngest braves had none, since they picked last.

"To give the younger braves a fighting chance at a wife of their own, the tribe held a contest every year right after the snow melt. Those men without a bride would assemble at the base of their most mystical and holy of mountains. A like number of older

96

braves would also assemble there, each with one of their wives. The older braves and their wives with them were then given a head start on a race up the mountain to the summit. After a time, the younger braves were cut loose to chase after them.

"The contest worked like this, if a younger brave caught up to an older brave and his wife before they reached the summit, then the younger brave could claim that squaw as his wife, and the older brave must surrender her forever. If the older brave and his wife reached the summit before any younger brave caught them, then he retained his wife.

"The chief of the tribe, being a good chief, always entered the contest. For many years he reached the summit with his wife ahead of the younger braves. But as time went on he began to slow, and the young braves began to come closer and closer to catching him.

"The older braves, chief included, got to pick which of their wives each would take with him up the mountain. It was a matter of pride to pick a valuable wife to risk in the contest."

"Like Mother?"

"There are none as valuable as your mother, but, yes, you get the point. One year the aging chief's wives begged him to take the youngest and strongest with him into the contest so that she could help get him up the mountain ahead of the young braves. He wouldn't hear of such a cowardly plan. Instead, he picked his favorite wife, even though she too was beginning to slow and may need *his* help up the mountain."

Quentin leaned back but remained transfixed on his father.

"Now, the rules of the contest required that everyone stay on a single trail up the mountain, so that the younger braves would know where to find any couple they caught on the way up. This trail was difficult with no creeks or streams nearby to quench your thirst. Carrying water up the mountain would slow you down, and the braves knew better than to burden themselves with such weight.

"The morning of the contest was unusually hot. The chief and his favorite wife got off to a good start, but they soon began to tire, especially his wife. The old chief urged his wife along, pulling her at first and then carrying her short distances while she rested. He too began to lose his strength and energy, and his thirst was high. Before they were halfway to the top, they both were exhausted.

"The chief could hear the sounds of the young braves whooping and hollering as they gained on the couple. He couldn't lose his favorite wife. She had born him fine children and been a good and loyal companion. He knew of a shortcut, though, a secret trail with ample water and an easier route up. He picked up his wife and headed off the prescribed trail toward the quicker and watered route.

"His wife implored him to stay on the proper trail. She cried aloud and promised she would work harder at climbing with him on the proper trail, even if it killed her. The old chief couldn't bear the thought of losing her and ignored her pleas. He carried her to the secret trail.

"When they got to a clearing near a stream, he set her down on a boulder. She was crying and wouldn't look at her husband as he went to fetch them both some water.

"When he came back into the clearing from the stream, instead of finding his wife, he found a large grizzly bear sitting on the very boulder where he left her. Fearing that the bear was stalking his wife, who was perhaps hiding nearby, the chief charged at the bear with his knife drawn." The president paused, raising his right arm clenched around a pen. "A single man with a knife is no match for a grizzly bear."

Quentin audibly gasped. "Not even you, Father?"

The president chuckled softly, ignoring the question.

"The next day, the tribe sent out a party to search for the missing chief and his wife, as neither ever made the summit or returned to the camp. Eventually they tracked the couple to the secret trail and the clearing near the stream. In the clearing standing guard over the mauled and partially eaten body of the old chief was a large she-bear. When the braves in the search party looked into the eyes of the bear, they saw the eyes of the chief's favorite wife looking back at them. Frightened by this apparition, they all fled, and neither the chief nor his wife were ever seen again.

"Now, what moral do we draw from this story, son?"

"Don't trust women."

The president sputtered as he tried to suppress another chuckle.

"No, although, exempting one's mother and one's wife, that might be a good rule in general. No, you asked why I can't just order people around. You see, in the United States we have a saying, a saying that I believe that legend represents. 'No man is above the law,' not even a chief, not even a president. These senators follow the law in being stubborn mules, and I must follow the law as well."

"Or you'll get eaten by a bear?"

"That's right, or I'll be eaten by a bear." The president beamed at his son and then turned to see his wife enter the room.

"Or by his wife, who also eats little boys who stay up too late. Oh, Teddy, that's such an awful story. Why do you fill his mind with such a tale, and right before he goes off to bed? Besides, you'd take the secret trail just so you could fight the bear."

The president's smile widened as he rose to greet her.

"Now Edith, it has a good message in the end. Every boy should learn to listen to and respect the women of the species." He laughed aloud and kissed her on the cheek. "Quentin, off to bed. Your mother looks hungry tonight. Let's not put her to the test."

"But, Father, aren't you still a colonel in the Rough Riders?"

"Ceremonially, that's true. But that was a volunteer cavalry disbanded after the war in '98. They've all scattered to the winds, back to their ranches and mines in Arizona, Texas, and New Mexico. Now what does that have to do with our bear problem?"

"Can't a colonel order his men to do his bidding?"

"He can, but the best ask the men to take the hill and lead the way. I've seen soldiers do amazing things when they want to do it, when they feel compelled by loyalty, by love of each other, to do the deed."

"I know the Rough Riders would do anything you asked them, Father." With that, the boy scampered out of the room.

The couple watched the boy depart and then looked at each other. Teddy reached out and playfully pinched his wife at the waist.

"Teddy, you're incorrigible. That boy gets it from you, you know."

He kissed her on the bridge of her nose. "I won't be long."

Edith Roosevelt sighed, smiled and left the room.

Turning back to his desk, a wave of happiness washed over him. A thought expressed as a fully formed phrase popped into his head, and he endeavored to write it down quickly before it faded away. "There is no form of happiness on the Earth, no form of success of any kind, that in any way approaches the happiness of the husband and the wife who are married lovers, and the father and mother of plenty of healthy children."

He sat back and read the words he had written, quite satisfied at the expression. Then, something else popped into his head. It was something Quentin had said. "I know the Rough Riders would do anything you asked them."

"I believe he's right," he muttered out loud. Quickly reaching for a fresh piece of stationery, he started a new letter.

***

"Sam, what's wrong?" Gripping her husband's trembling hand, Mary Cunningham turned him toward her and pulled him out of the foot traffic to the side of the street.

"Sam, why are you trembling?"

He gave her a bewildered stare. His lips quivered. He closed his eyes, took a deep breath, and his body stilled.

"Sam, are you all right?"

"Yes…strange."

"What is it?"

"I felt, I felt cold. Then…I'm not sure. One moment we're walking along the sidewalk, and then I'm…" He paused and looked about. "Here."

"Do you need to see someone at the hospital?"

Sam breathed deep and looked down at his hands, turning them over from front to back several times. He pulled a watch from his vest and grasped the wrist of that hand with his free hand. He focused on the watch in silence.

"Pulse is fine. I feel fine. Perhaps it was just a heart palpitation. No, that's not right. I mean, I'll be fine."

"We should go back to the hotel, then."

"No, the walk will do me good. It was more of a feeling, like rage welling up inside me. It wasn't painful. Let's continue on for bit." Sam offered his arm.

They strolled silently on, Mary holding him secure. He seemed steady enough.

"What is it, Mary? I can tell when you need to speak your mind."

"Sam, we need help. No, listen to me this time. You've heard nothing from the inspector. We live like gypsies moving from room to room, with that infernal rat watching us like he can't wait to get to us and have another bite. If we went to the ranch at least we'd be safe."

"And possibly endanger Molly."

"So you've said, but we'd reduce the liability we create by staying here in Dallas, so helpless. If in fact someone is trying to hurt us…"

"No, *me*, Mary, someone is trying to hurt *me*. I'm endangering us both. It has something to do with black boxes, I'm sure of it. I see them in my dreams. I'm the one they want."

"It doesn't matter. My point is…"

"Mary, I've thought on this considerably. Please, now hear me out. The logical course would be for you to go to the ranch. I'm the one who'll be followed. At least you'd be safe. I'll wait here until the inspector makes contact. Then he'll make sure I'm safe. When this blows over, we'll be back together.

"I won't hear of it. Sam I...why are you pulling on me?"

"Please, walk quickly," Sam whispered urgently. "Don't turn around."

"What's wrong?"

"The day I brought the rats home, when I bumped into Doctor Carter, there was a man with a strange cane. I thought he might be following me, but he disappeared when I turned around."

The couple walked on, weaving between the oncoming pedestrians.

"I just saw him cross the street. I believe he is following us now."

"Where are we going?"

"I have an idea."

The electric "Wonderland" sign marking the entrance to the Wonderland movie theater came into view. Sam motioned to the sign with his head.

"Remember the tour we took of this theater when we arrived in Dallas?"

"The rear exit behind the screen?"

"Precisely." Sam stopped in front of the caged ticket booth. "Two please."

"Ten cents," the ticket agent responded. "You'll need to hurry. It may have already started. Great show, *Doctor Jekyll and Mr. Hyde*. Here you go. Head straight in, sir, ma'am."

"Thank you." Sam took the two tickets, surrendering them to an usher at the door.

They entered the theater from the center, but turned left toward a side aisle. They worked their way forward and were taking their seats when the lights dimmed. A piano played an ominous chord. In the moment of blackness before the film started, they were up and soon behind the screen.

The glow from the projector gave them enough light to locate the back door. Once they were in the alley, they ran. Mary clutched Sam's hand and glanced over her shoulder. The alley was empty.

***

President Roosevelt looked up from the book he was reading and into Edith's eyes.

"What troubles you, my dear?"

"Troubles me? I was just watching you read."

Teddy smiled, put his book down, and shook his head.

"Edith, after all these blissful years of marriage, I may be a self-centered, stubborn bull moose like that reporter fellow said yesterday, but I think I can tell when my wife is troubled."

Edith Roosevelt sighed and looked away.

"Is it Quentin again? Has he put another pony in the elevator?"

"I do wish you would be more careful."

"Me, careful? Why, I avoid elevators with ponies at all cost!"

Despite his broad smile, Edith did not appear amused.

"Teddy, after your press briefing yesterday you took a two-hour walk, by yourself, without a secret service agent. They were looking all over the city for you!"

He smiled again. "Yes, I had to sneak out a side door just to get some time to breathe. That press meeting was quite taxing. 'Bosnia this' and 'Europe war that.' I found myself wishing I was back on a ranch somewhere."

Edith set her jaw and glared at him.

"Now what's all this about? I only took a little walk."

"Without the secret service men!"

"Edith, if I came back unscathed from the Spanish War, charging up all those hills with bullets zinging here and there, what can be so dangerous about a walk in the park?"

"What can be so dangerous? For starters you wouldn't even *be* president but for the assassination of President McKinley by an

103

anarchist! But let's go in order, shall we?" Edith straightened her back and began counting off on her fingers.

"How about Alexander II of Russia—blown up with a bomb. President Carnot of France—stabbed to death by an anarchist. Prime Minister of Spain Canovas del Castillo—shot to death by an anarchist. Empress Elisabeth of Austria—stabbed to death by an anarchist. Umberto I of Italy shot four times with a revolver by an anarchist. Then…" Edith stopped momentarily holding her pinky before moving to the next hand. "We have our President McKinley."

"Next there was Alexander I of Serbia—he *and* his wife shot and mutilated." She extended two fingers on that account. "Followed by Greece's Prime Minister Dilgiannis—stabbed to death. Grand Duke Alexandrovich—blown to bits by a bomb tossed into his lap."

Edith held up her hands. "Look. I've run out of fingers, but the toll continues. Bulgarian Prime Minister Petkov—murdered by an anarchist. And most recently Carlos I of Portugal was shot by assassins!

"That's what's so dangerous…dead, every one of them by assassins' hands! And the number could have been much higher but for providence. I've not even mentioned all the attempted assassinations against Prince Edward, King Leopold of Belgium, French President Loubet. Anarchists have tried twice to blow up King Alfonso of Spain!"

The President waited a moment to make sure he wouldn't step on a further point. "Quite a list. Poor King Carlos, he was such gentle man. He loved the sea. I think he would have been perfectly happy being an ensign in the Portuguese navy. But your order was off slightly, dear. I believe the Grand Duke of Russia was killed in February 1905, while Prime Minister Diligiannis was murdered in June of that year."

"It's not funny!" Edith's chin quivered as her eyes both steeled and watered.

"Oh, my dear Edith," he replied. "I've gone on walks before. What is it about this one that troubles you so?"

"The whole world, it seems so unsettled. Anarchists, nihilists, nationalists…all these bombings, explosions, assassinations, riots, heads of state, disappearing, dying before our eyes. Where is it all headed?

"Oh, Edith, come now…"

"Don't patronize me, Teddy. Tell me. Where is it all headed? You're the president of the United States. Where is it all headed?"

She clenched her fists and flashed back a fierce look.

"I don't know," he replied softly. "I suppose at some point the whole thing may explode. I'm doing my best to make sure that doesn't happen."

Edith relaxed her hands and bent her head. She shivered slightly before reaching for a handkerchief.

The president rose and embraced her.

"Edith…now, now my dear Edith."

"I have visions. You're speaking to a crowd. It's outdoors, and you're on a platform. A man steps forward. He pulls a pistol, aims, and shoots you in the heart."

He held her firmly in his arms. Then he pulled a handkerchief from his vest and lightly blotted her face.

"Look at me, dear. I promise. I promise I'll keep myself guarded…no more walks alone. And…" He held her face in his hands and her eyes in his gaze. "I promise that no assassin is *ever* going to kill your husband."

***

"It is true that all these issues are important. But none can be addressed until society recognizes the right of women to elect their leaders." The speaker at the podium continued as Mary Cunningham's thoughts drifted back again to her husband and the uncharacteristic exchange just hours before. Checking herself, she sat up in the folding chair and tried to focus on the present. A dozen or so women's hats nodded in approval around her.

"I find it encouraging that two other former British colonies, New Zealand and Australia, have granted the basic human right to vote to their female citizens. Just last year Finland joined these enlightened countries. I once hoped that our daughters might benefit from our efforts. I say the time has come, now. Yes, not just for them and their daughters, but for us, for me, for you, for all our sisters in this great nation."

The hats bobbed back and forth again accompanied to the sound of clapping and "hear, hear."

Mary glanced at the clock in the corner. Sam was not himself. He hadn't been himself since the night they escaped from the man with the cane by going through the movie theater. But today, he'd never been *that* bad. That had not been Sam talking this morning. She could still see him standing over the cage in their hotel room.

"Most perplexing—it seems to come and go," he said. She remembered clearly every word thereafter.

"One minute it's calm, normal, the next the fur goes up and fury breaks out."

"How much longer, Sam?"

"How much longer, what?"

"The rat, it's in our room night and day, calm one minute, ripping at the cage trying to get at us the next. How much longer do you have to observe it?"

"And what do you want me to do, kill it?"

"Yes, kill it. You've observed its behavior for two weeks. Why can't you do an autopsy now?"

"And now you're the doctor, is that it?"

"What? You know I don't mean anything like that. I only..."

"I'm tired of you questioning everything I do. I explain myself until I'm out of breath, but you stay after me."

"What are you talking about?"

"Rational facts seem to have no effect. You don't have..."

"Sam, please, slow down. I don't understand what you mean."

"Do *not* interrupt me! You're always interrupting me! Do I interrupt you?" Sam's body quivered. He strode toward her, his fists clenched, his arms shaking.

"And don't look at me like that! I'm your husband. I deserve your respect, not this constant questioning and interruption."

"Sam, you're scaring me!"

"Shut up, I say! Can't you be quiet for one minute? Must I shake some sense into you?"

"Sam, let me go! Stop!" she yelled as he threw her to the floor.

She shivered now at the image of him standing over her with a look of animal rage. His eyes had darted around the room as if looking for something to attack. She had started to cry. Slowly, then, the look on his face changed. He put his hands over his face and backed away with tears leaking through his fingers.

He apologized profusely. She held him in her arms, and they cried together. An hour later he was napping on the sofa. She tidied the room and left for the suffragette meeting, as he had urged her to do before drifting off into slumber.

He could use the rest, she'd concluded. He'd been sleeping so poorly of late. The stress was clearly taking a toll on him. Or was it something else? Did the bite from the rat…? No, it must be stress. The bouts of anger, coming on suddenly with that wild look, that wasn't Sam, though.

The hats around her suddenly rose and applause filled the room. The last speaker left the podium, and the meeting was adjourned.

On the way back to the hotel she played the scene over and over again in her head. There was some truth to what he said. She had questioned many things lately. Why were they still in Dallas? Why not retreat to the known safety of the ranch in New Mexico? Why keep that infernal rat alive in their room? Why was he shaking?

She found Sam's answers unconvincing. But he was her husband, and he did deserve the respect of being listened to. His inability to explain didn't necessarily mean he was wrong. But he was wrong.

The hotel lobby was the usual busy place, with guests lounging, packages and luggage arriving, customers at the front desk. The ride up the elevator seemed too short as she pondered what to say to Sam. Perhaps he'd still be resting on the couch, and she wouldn't need to say anything.

She rounded the corner and reached the door to their room. She fished a key from her purse, turned the lock and quietly opened the door.

"Sam? No! Sam, where are you?"

The room was a wreck—furniture overturned, clothing flung about, curtains torn from the windows. Frantically she searched, pushing pictures and chairs aside.

"Sam? Where are you, please? Sam!"

She came across the wire cage, empty on the floor with the small door ajar.

"Sam! Please God, no! Where did they take him?"

There was no answer. She was alone.

***

Mary Cunningham stepped off the train and onto the platform. The ride to Fort Worth from Dallas had been a short one, and the early morning departure meant that there were few passengers in the day cars. She watched as a handful of others got off the train followed by another handful who boarded.

"Help you with your luggage, ma'am?"

Mary looked down at a boy, perhaps eight or ten years old. "Thank you, no. I'm traveling light as you can see. Can you direct me to the nearest Western Union office?"

"Yes, ma'am. There's one here at the station." The boy pointed to a sign further down the platform.

"Yes, I see it. Thank you."

At that the boy trotted off to find another customer. Mary looked around as the platform began to clear. Somewhat satisfied that she hadn't been followed, discreet at every turn, she made her way down the platform toward the sign the boy had pointed out.

The Western Union office was a simple structure, one door, two windows, one on either side of the door, and a waiting area inside with wooden chairs along the walls. Two clerks stood behind a counter that faced the door. One looked up from a stack of paper.

"May I help you?"

"Yes, I'd like to send a cable to London."

"Price is on the wall." The clerk pointed behind him with a pencil he held in his hand. "I'll need to get some information from you."

"Certainly. Here are the delivery details, and here is the text." Mary handed the clerk two sheets of paper.

The clerk studied the two sheets and began to write something in a ledger on the desk.

"May I read the message back to you to make sure I get it right?"

"I thought my handwriting was quite legible, but if you must."

The clerk looked up and smiled. "Just procedure, ma'am, anytime we get a handwritten note."

Mary nodded. The clerk looked back down at the two sheets.

"I see this is to the attention of a Mr. Wainright at an office located in Victoria Station, London."

"Yes."

"Message as follows: 'Can begin on Sunday. Schedule tomorrow morning is most quiet. Monday was worst morning. Reassured knowing your skill will solve this deplorable rot. MS.'"

"You've read it perfectly, thank you."

The clerk scratched at a pad with his pencil, tore off a sheet, and slid it across the table. "This is your receipt. I'll need payment in advance."

Mary took the receipt, glanced back at the door, and handed the clerk the amount due.

"Will you be expecting an answer?" The clerk looked up as he stuck the pencil behind his ear.

"Yes."

"And where can we find you when it's received?"

Mary looked about the room eyeing the benches. "I'll be right here."

The clerk frowned. "Ma'am, it's well past noon in London now. Chances are the earliest answer will come tomorrow."

"Isn't this office open twenty-four hours?"

"Monday through Saturday, yes, but..."

"I'll wait for the answer here, thank you."

***

Inspector Jenkins sat at his desk reading the latest dispatches. Another Foreign Office agent had been found dead and another missing now for a week. He absentmindedly reached for his teacup and lifted it to his lips before realizing it was empty. Setting it down, he plucked a short, unlit stub of a cigar from his desk and stuck one end in his mouth. He hated being hunkered down in his office day after day, but discretion demanded it.

Clearly everyone associated with Special Department B was being hunted. The report two days ago that Mick had narrowly fended off an attack was unsettling. Talbot was still missing, and there was no news from America. Why hadn't Dr. Cunningham responded to his telegrams? Where was Molly Bell?

"Excuse me, Inspector."

Jenkins looked up to see a dispatch clerk at his doorway. It wasn't just any dispatch clerk, though. Sensitive messages were entrusted only to particular dispatch clerks, who were more trusted messengers than ordinary clerks. Knowing where this man was assigned, Jenkins immediately knew the message was important.

"Sorry to interrupt, sir. I have a message delivered to our drop at Victoria Station. It's addressed to Mr. Wainright."

Jenkins sat forward in his chair and took the offered envelope. Wainright was Mary Cunningham's address identifier. He checked

110

the unbroken Western Union seal on the envelope and opened it, producing a folded sheet of paper with typed text on one side.

"Please be a good chap and fetch the cryptologist from the office around the corner and five doors down on your left. Tell him I'd like to see him immediately. Then please wait in the foyer in the event we need a message returned."

"Yes, Inspector."

Jenkins bit down on the cigar stub and set the paper on his desk. He recalled the coding convention specific to Mary Cunningham despite not having used it in years: the number of letters in the first word indicates the number of letters in the first coded word; the location of the first vowel in the second word indicates the location of the key letter in the word clues specific to the first coded word; the number of letters in the third word indicates how many letters to count up from in the alphabet from the key letter found in the word clues; the next word would begin the sequence of word clues; decode one key letter from each word clue until the first coded word is revealed; then repeat the process.

Jenkins smoothed the paper flat on his desk and retrieved a pencil. He placed the number "3" above the word "Can." There were three letters in the first word. He circled the vowel "e" from the next word "begin" and wrote "2nd" above it. He would look to the second letter of each word clue. Next he wrote the number "2" above the third word "on." He would count up two letters in the alphabet from each of the second letters found in each word clue.

He made a quick review of the first sequence to check himself. The first coded word had three letters, the key letter would be found at the second letter position in each word clue, and he needed to count up in the alphabet two letters from each key letter to determine the coded letters making up the coded word.

The next word, "Sunday," was the first word clue. He circled the second letter, "u," and counted back two letters in the alphabet to the letter "S," which he wrote above the word clue, "Sunday." Next he circled the letter "c" from the word "Schedule." He counted back two from "c" to arrive at "A," which he wrote above that word. In the third word "tomorrow" he circled the "o," counted back to "M," and wrote the "M" above that word clue. He had his first coded word, "SAM."

"Excuse me, Inspector Jenkins." The cryptologist had arrived. "I was told you had an urgent need of my services."

"Please, I won't be but a minute." Jenkins removed the cigar from his mouth and pointed it at a seat in front of his desk. He returned the wet, brown stub to one side of his mouth. "I'll need you to check my work and draft a response," he instructed through clenched teeth.

The next word was "morning," above which he wrote the number "7." He circled the vowel "i" from the word "is" and placed a "1st" above it. Above the next word, "most," he wrote the number "4" and then tackled the next phrase.

The clue words "quiet Monday was worst morning reassured knowing" revealed the coded word "MISSING." Repeating the process again he revealed the last coded word "HELP" from "solve this deplorable rot."

He spit out the cigar, which landed with a "plop" on his desk, and looked up at the cryptologist.

"The convention is first word designates the number of letters in coded word, the first vowel position in the next word designates the key letter position, and the number of letters in the third word sets the number of letters from the key letter to count up in the alphabet. Repeat the sequence after every coded word. Understood?"

The man seated across his desk nodded.

Jenkins held up the paper showing his notations. "'SAM MISSING HELP.' Check my work. If it is correct, I need you to encode the following in return and have it wired out within the hour. 'Go to ranch immediately.' Understood?"

The cryptologist took the paper and smiled. "Immediately? You don't want to make it easy on me, do you? I don't suppose 'now' would be an adequate substitute?"

"No, 'immediately.' I don't want there to be any ambiguity."

"It will be out within the hour, sir."

CHAPTER 7
IT MUST BE DONE

Fred Miller scanned the shoreline and then looked wistfully at the sea. It wasn't a big island. He'd by now seen it all many times over, following after the strange little man with his long staff as he tended to his various chores, most of which involved checking on the numerous sheep that were the only other inhabitants of their rocky plot of terra firma. Despite watching his companion daily, Fred was still perplexed about how the shepherd did his job. Fred had nothing better to do, though, so he dutifully tagged along. Perhaps eventually he'd figure it all out. In the meantime he was well fed, well recovered, and perpetually thirsty for something other than water and coffee.

What a beautiful and clear day, one of the rare days when the faint outline of a low shoreline in the distance off the east side of the island revealed itself. It appeared around five to ten miles away, depending on how high the terrain might be on the other side.

The wind blew lightly on his back. The sound of the rhythmic splashing of waves, seagulls overhead, and the nearby bleating of sheep blended seamlessly together, the island's song played over and over, as if it had always been so.

He sat down on a rock and scanned the seascape for any sign of life. Over the past weeks he spotted an occasional ship in the distance, but ships never came close to the island, and they never passed between the island and the mainland. The prevailing wind and current must cause ships to give that stretch of the mainland a wide berth. Was the opposing coastline rocky and dangerous? He reached out his hand toward the far shore.

Suddenly appeared the little man, the only other inmate on this rocky prison, sitting next to him.

"I've been thinking, old man," Fred announced. He had long since determined that the man understood not a word out of his mouth, but he was the only person he could speak to, and so he did. "Why am I here?"

Fred's companion gazed out to sea.

"I guess I've been asking that for going on two years now, regardless of where I am. I don't understand it. I can't die, even when I want to. And sometimes, maybe now many times, I think I..."

Fred breathed deeply of the chilly sea air and rubbed the crown of his head, which still sported a tender lump, though much reduced in size.

"Yes, for two years I've been asking that question, ever since I met him, the man with the black box, that is."

Fred paused and looked again at his companion for any reaction, but the old man continued to gaze toward the sea and the coastline beyond.

"I'll never forget what he said. He doused himself with lantern fluid, and right before he lit himself on fire, he told me, '*You, Mr. Miller, you will witness my departure. You will live to witness what follows, with sadness, frustration, and horror all to my honor. Just imagine, Mr. Miller, an entire world aflame! Millions upon millions trudging to their deaths, like dimwitted slaves directed by the hand of an uncaring and stupid master. The end of mankind comes, and no one will have the sense or the will to stop it.*'

"I stood there frozen. I couldn't move, I couldn't speak. He told me I'd live to see it all, the death, the destruction, the horror, that I'd be his chronicler, his 'Mark.' Then, he said we'd meet again. After that he lit himself on fire. I watched him burn. All the while he laughed."

The old man turned and faced Fred with a look of puzzlement.

"I don't want it. I never wanted it. I don't want to be his chronicler. I don't want to be his witness. I don't want to see death, destruction, horror. I don't want to see him again. I want to be left alone. 'Why me,' I ask. Why am I here?"

Still no response from his companion…only the music of the sea, the gulls, and the sheep.

"Eventually it became evident that I can't escape. I can't die, even if I want to, I can't. Something always intervenes. If I tried to drown myself in that ocean…" Fred paused and pointed at the water. "You'd pull me out, or someone else who I don't even know is here. It happens every time."

Fred waited for a reaction that again didn't come. The little man turned back to the sea. Fred dropped his arm and shrugged.

"At first it all seemed coincidental. One day I was walking to my office in Manchester. I'm a patent agent by trade. Well, that's not relevant to what happened, is it? 'Stick to the point, Mr. Miller.' That's what my boss, Mr. White, would say. Former boss, that is. He let me go five, no, six months past.

"In any event…" Fred waved his hand in the air as if rubbing clean a chalkboard. "I was walking to work when a motorcar came careening around the corner. It was going too fast to stay in the roadway and was headed straight for me. Someone, I don't know who, grabbed my arm and pulled me to safety.

"A few weeks later, I was at a train station in London walking along the platform when I slipped on something. I fell into a man in front of me. As he righted himself he knocked me toward the rails. A train was pulling into the station, and but for someone, I don't know who, a stinky grubby man, grabbing ahold of my leg, I would have fallen in front of the train.

"I became careless. It made me sad, in a way, that I hadn't been killed. I don't know that I actively wanted to die, yet." He stopped and swallowed. "But I just didn't care. Every time, I was jerked back from the precipice by someone. Sometimes I thought there couldn't be anyone near enough to help, but there always was.

"I started to drink. Well, I've always had a nip now and then, but I mean *really* drink. Hard at it I was. Without my mate, James Aston, around, there was no one to check me. I think I even tried to kill myself a couple of times. I don't know. I don't remember. In the back of my mind I knew it wouldn't work, and it never did. So I kept drinking. Can you imagine, a life you can't exit from even if you tried? Where's the free will in that? Drinking was my only escape. It wasn't really up to me. That's all that was left, the glass and the mug.

"And so I lost my position, the only chemist in the firm. Can't blame them. What good is a patent agent who's never sober? But I just kept drinking. The money ran out, so I drank on credit. Then the credit ran out."

The old man turned away. Fred felt a sharp pain rising in his chest.

"It's all my fault, really. I've let my friends down. I've let Mr. White down. I've let, well…

"And now I'm here, on a rock, on an island, with an old shepherd, hundreds of sheep, and not a drop of ethanol in any form to be had!"

Fred shouted out the last pronouncement and made a broad sweeping gesture with his arm. The old man hardly noticed, and continued sitting silently, facing the sea.

"Ethanol, you know, alcohol?" Fred stretched out the last word and then pretended to take a drink making a glugging noise as if downing a mug of beer.

"Oh, what's the use?"

Fred stared back out at the sea. "James Aston, I mentioned him a moment ago. He was my closest friend. He's been missing all these years. He left behind a wife and child. Some think he ran away with another woman. I don't believe it, not the James I know."

Fred wiped his nose on his sleeve and blinked to clear his eyes.

"Thank God my mother's not alive to see me now. Faith— that's what she would urge, faith. I don't know. I think faith left me long ago."

Fred dropped his head, letting his chin rest on his chest. The word "faith" reverberated in his head, but he pushed it away.

"And then, there's Inspector Jenkins. I shouldn't even mention him, but for the fact you haven't a clue what I'm saying. Jenkins must know I'm a drunkard. You can't keep anything from that man. No, I've seen him in action. Believe me, he knows. I've let him down, too."

Still no reaction from the old man, he just sat, holding his staff. The ocean splashed. The seagulls called. The sheep bleated. The breeze blew.

The staff *was* peculiar. Fred thought upon it frequently. The little man was never without it. He might not know a thing about sheep, but he couldn't imagine the functional purpose to a shepherd of a long staff with a sharp pointed end, on an island inhabited by nothing but sheep and the shepherd. All the shepherd's staffs he'd ever seen had a blunt end used for whacking the occasional stubborn ram on the head or a crook for pulling a lost ewe out of a ravine by the neck.

He tapped on the old man's shoulder. Having his attention, Fred pointed at the end of the staff. Then he brought his hands together at the fingertips but sloping away from each other at the wrists, thus forming a point. Fred looked at the old man and shrugged, trying hard to show confusion on his face.

"Why?" Fred looked down at his hands and then at the tip of the shaft. He got up from the rock, took the end of the shaft in his hands, and pointed to the sharp tip.

"Why?" Again he shrugged his shoulders and tried to appear confused.

"El lobo," the old man said reverently. "El lobo blanco."

"'El lobo'? What does that mean?"

The old man stared blankly at Fred and then shrugged his shoulders in apparent imitation.

"Here," Fred tugged on the shaft, which the old man let him have with little resistance. "Here," Fred pointed the sharp end of the stick at the ground and moved the tip back and forth right above the surface. "Draw what you mean. 'Lobo,' draw it for me, 'lobo.'"

The old man got up from the rock and looked about. He found a palm-sized stone with a jagged end and got down on his hands and knees. He cleared away a section of the hard ground and started scratching on it with the rock.

A form began to appear on the ground. It had four long legs and a body that sloped from front to back with a long tail. Some sort of dog? There was a large head and alert ears. Then the old man added large sharp teeth to a powerful muzzle. The picture became unmistakable.

"A wolf? Are you crazy?"

The old man pointed at the drawing scratched in the ground. "Lobo! El lobo blanco!" he exclaimed emphatically.

Fred laughed. "You are crazy, old man. There's nothing on this island but you, me, and more sheep than I care to count."

The old man indignantly pulled his staff away from Fred, pointed the sharp end at the drawing, and thrust it at the wolf's head.

"Lobo, muy malo...hijo del diablo. Todos lobos son hijos del diablo."

Fred sat back on the rock and tried to contain his laughter.

"Oh, what a pair, you and I, old man. I carry the ghost of evil in my head, and you imagine wolves on an island full of sheep."

The shepherd stood silently holding his staff and looking back out to sea.

Fred sighed and shook his head. "I could sorely use a drink right now."

***

Father Philip Cornish sat in quiet contemplation. The late afternoon sun glowed through the three stained glass windows above the altar of St. George's church in Bloomsbury, London. There were a few other worshippers, mostly silent as well, scattered about the pews of the square sanctuary. Occasional murmuring came from somewhere in the front of the church, probably a parishioner praying aloud, carrying on a conversation with his savior.

He rubbed his right knee and contemplated the boxy organ pipes crammed into a corner to the right of the altar, standing close-packed together, sentinels at attention waiting to blow their horns. His stomach growled, reminding him of the late hour. He braced his forearm against his right leg and pushed himself up, noting a gentleman sitting behind him. Curious, he hadn't noticed the gentleman before or sensed him sitting down. Father Cornish didn't recognize him as someone from the congregation.

The stranger smiled, rose, and followed Father Cornish down the aisle. When the pair reached the vestibule, the gentleman cleared his throat followed by a tap on Father Cornish's shoulder.

Cornish turned in response to face a tall, slim man, about his height, with wavy blond hair, a button nose, and a boyish face which, being slightly creased from the march of time, clearly didn't belong to a young man—more like mid-thirties, he guessed.

"Father Cornish?" the stranger whispered.

Cornish nodded.

"May I have a word?" he asked, pointing at the door exiting to the street.

Cornish nodded again and gestured for the stranger to proceed. He followed the man outside, all the while studying him for any clue as to what the stranger wanted. Once in the street the gentleman donned a top hat and turned back to face him.

"Father Cornish, please forgive the abrupt introduction. I was given your name by a dear mutual friend, Father Tate of Saint Martin's in Leicester."

The gentleman paused, as if waiting for a reaction. But Cornish just smiled, content to give no reaction.

"Father Tate, before he died, was of great assistance to me. He mentioned you often, as he felt we had much in common. I miss his counsel tremendously."

Cornish allowed a second or two to pass before answering. "I'm sorry to hear that." Cornish paused again. "I'm sorry, sir, I think I missed your name."

"Oh, sorry, my fault entirely…James, for now." He extended his right hand to Cornish.

The priest looked at the hand, pale with two red moles forming eyes to the nose of the middle knuckle. He took the offered hand and returned a firm shake. "For now?"

"Yes, I'm in a bit of a pickle and need to remain somewhat anonymous for now. It will all make sense. Do you have a moment?" James smiled and looked on expectantly.

"I'm afraid I have an engagement this evening, but if you'd like to walk with me, I'd be delighted to listen on the way." His engagement had to do with his growling stomach reminding him that it was well past the dinner hour.

"You're so kind. Please, lead the way."

The two proceeded in rank down the sidewalk with Cornish on the left and James on the right.

When James didn't begin, Cornish offered, "You say you were acquainted with Father Tate?"

"Ah, so you do remember him. Yes, he took my confessions at first. As you know he subscribed to the Oxford movement in that regard. We became fast friends and occasionally dined together. As I said, he spoke frequently of you. It's strange to think of now, but he once told me that if anything happened to him, I was to seek you out."

"He died two years ago, as I recall," offered Cornish.

"Indeed, quite unexpectedly. The obituary said heart troubles, but I never knew him to be anything but fit. I assume you were at the funeral as well?"

"Two years, and now you've decided to 'seek me out'?"

"It has taken me that long to think all this through."

"Well, you've found me."

"That wasn't the difficult part. You're easy to find. What took me two years was convincing myself that I should do it."

Cornish made a hard left turn at an intersection and, given the quick pace he had set and the fact that James was following off his right shoulder, he fully expected that the gentlemen would fall back slightly and be forced to catch up. Instead, James opened his gait and remained abreast of Cornish throughout the entire turn. Clearly he couldn't outwalk this man, not that the thought fully preoccupied his mind. Hunger was a more immediate concern. The question was how long this interloper would talk until he could settle in at some nice pub for dinner. They'd already passed his favorite. He could always double back.

"Father, I believe you and I have a similar background and, shall we say, similar difficulties."

"How might that be?"

"This is not an easy conversation on a public street, but..."

"Then, might I suggest, sir, that we meet again at the church tomorrow morning. I can obtain a private office where we can speak in earnest and at our leisure."

Cornish was taken aback when the man put his hand on Cornish's shoulder and pulled him to a stop on the sidewalk.

"Father Tate told me he had a suspicion about you. He thought you might be in search of someone, the man with the black box. If so, I can help."

Cornish flinched from a jolt running up his spine. He'd not heard mention of the man with the black box in two years. He focused on appearing as calm as possible and looked hard at the man's face. Was he sincere? There was no hint of fear or cruelty. His brow was raised in what appeared earnest anticipation of an answer. James stood with one thumb latched to his trouser pockets, thus spreading open his jacket and exposing a dark blue waistcoat.

"Tate was a good friend of mine. If he recommended you to me, my appointment can wait this evening. Have you had supper?"

James smiled and rocked back slightly on his heels. "I thought you'd never ask. Only if you'll let me treat."

"Only if you'll come to the point." Cornish replied as he returned the smile. "I can hardly be of any assistance if I have no idea what you're talking about."

"Quite right, Father, I can be a little chatty. Will this do?"

James pointed to the pub at the next corner, whereupon Cornish nodded and the two set off together.

The pub was not crowded, with most of the patrons huddled along a short bar. A haze of pipe smoke hung in the air at about eye level. James led them to a table in a corner, furthest away from the group and lacking any direct lighting.

"Please." James pointed to the bench built into the wall on one side of the table as he took the chair opposite.

No sooner had Cornish's eyes adjusted to the dim corner than a young girl appeared tableside. "Do you sup with us, or just a beer?"

"Both, I think." James looked at Cornish who confirmed with a nod. "Two ales, and what might we have for supper?"

"Cold is yesterday's roast with bubble and squeak, hot is Yorkshire pudding with beef and gravy."

"Father?" James motioned toward him with his right hand.

"I think the pudding for me, child, thank you."

"Yes, the pudding as well," James quickly interjected as he set his right hand on the table palm down. Cornish again noted the two red moles staring at him from the top of his hand. "No, on second thought, the roast if you please."

"Thank you, sirs." The young girl half curtsied and scampered off.

"How did you know Tate?" Cornish inquired.

"I think he was looking for me. He found me."

"Looking for you? Why?"

"Excellent question, Father. I'm not sure I can say." James tilted his head and scratched his temple. "A mutual friend, I think. I suspect she commended me to him. Regardless, find me he did. And, I might add, he was of great comfort and assistance to me. I'm glad he found me."

James paused and looked around the room, seemingly taking stock of the patrons, like a man who didn't want to be found at the moment.

"As I noted, he was my confessor. But more than that, he helped guide me during a very difficult time." He lowered his head toward Cornish and continued in a soft voice. "I've been absent from society for some time. I need assistance reentering. If Tate were alive, he would help me, but he's not. The day before he died, he told me that if something ever happened to him that he knew a likeminded priest whom I could trust."

The conversation was interrupted by the return of the small waitress who plunked two mugs on the table, half curtsied, and scurried off again.

"In fact, he told me, this priest may be particularly understanding of my plight. This priest," James picked up his mug and thrust it toward Cornish, "is you. Cheers!"

"Cheers." Cornish returned the toast. He downed a healthy draught of the warm, nutty ale and returned the mug to the table.

"And so, here we are." James set down his mug as well and looked expectantly at his tablemate.

"Despite your repetition of the recommendation of our mutual acquaintance, I'm afraid I'm still a bit lost. What possible assistance could I, a school chaplain, give you? And who is the man with a black box?"

"Oh, him. Never mind about that. He's dead."

"Then why did you say you'd help me find him?"

"The man with the black box was but an intermediary to something much bigger, much more important. *That's* what I can help you find." James grinned as he picked up his mug and took a swig, the entire time keeping his sparkling eyes focused on Cornish. The two red moles on the back of his hand were redder now, two angry little eyes that focused on Cornish as well. "Interested?"

"I'm still confused, I'm afraid. You said that I might have a particular understanding of your predicament."

"Predicament! Yes, that's what it is. That's not what I said, but I believe you're right. I do have a predicament. You see, part of the society from which I have been absent includes a wife and son, a wife who surely doesn't approve of the reason for my absence. I confess to bedding with another."

Cornish pushed his mug away and stood up. He glared coldly down at his new acquaintance.

"If you're going to tell me that you think I will help you because of what you've heard about the Lady Brompston affair, I'm afraid you've wasted your efforts and my time."

"Father, please, sit down. I would never presume such a thing. Please, don't force me to play my high suit just to convince you to join me for supper."

"If you have a trump card, perhaps you should play it. Otherwise, if you'll excuse me, I have other matters to attend to."

"I do, sir, I do! And I think you'll be of quite a different attitude when I play it. Just five minutes, allow me to explain." James pointed at the bench, his countenance having quickly changed to reflect a deadly earnest.

The priest sat slowly, nursing the right knee he had set off by the preceding sudden rise.

"Anyway, why would I inquire into the Lady Brompston affair? That would be a futile line of questioning, would it not?" James took another drink from his mug.

"I could say 'to this day the true identity of the lady's lover has never been confirmed. Poor Lady Brompston, wasting away in an asylum, she'll never tell.' At which point you might say 'why do you speak of this matter? Years have passed.' I would dodge your question and reply 'her lover was rumored to be a priest, much below the station of her deceased husband, the late Sir Reginald Brompston. In fact, some newspaper accounts floated your name, Father Philip Cornish, as a prime suspect and father to the child she was carrying.' To which you would respond 'if I were an adulterous priest, why am I still wearing the collar?' You would then expect me to counter with the stories about your divorce from your wife and her sudden departure for America, far away from the hounding London press. That is what you would expect, no?"

James smiled and took another drink.

Cornish gritted his teeth and forced himself to breath slowly. He must remain calm.

"You'd be surprised, however, when I described how you visit the asylum once a year, incognito. But then the entire exercise would get us nowhere. The mystery is much deeper than all that, isn't it?"

Father Cornish's blood was up. He'd heard it all before, with the exception of his annual visits to the asylum, a fact never reported in the newspapers. His face felt warm and the sound of his heart throbbed in his head.

"If that was your trump card, sir, I'm afraid you have indeed wasted my time." Cornish braced his leg with his right arm and started to rise.

"Sit, Father, for I'm *about* to play my trump card," James commanded. He kept his gaze on the priest as Cornish slowly rose to standing.

"I play the king of hearts. What a story he tells! He desperately needs to slough off a card, quite a troublesome card, but he can't be seen doing it. He's nearly been caught before, sloughing off, that is. Ah, but what if there were two 'identical' cards, one interchangeable for the other?" James held up the back of his right hand and raised two fingers above the fiercely crimson moles. "But then, it would be quite dangerous to talk about the women, sisters, identical twins after all. Please, have a seat, Father.

Every deck has a joker. They're indispensable, especially to the king of hearts, especially when the joker is a priest."

Cornish sank back down, trying hard not to show any emotion.

James smiled broadly, exposing perfect white teeth. "Excellent, then, we'll talk no more of cards or affairs. You can count me a friend in that regard. Look, our meal comes!"

The young girl reappeared with a towel of sorts on the top of her head, upon which she skillfully balanced a large bowl. In her hands she carried a plate piled with the roast and a healthy portion of the accompanying vegetables. She placed the plate in front of Cornish and removed the pot from her head, making sure to use the towel between her hands and the vessel. She placed the bowl before James.

"Please be careful, Father. It's quite hot." She produced assorted cutlery from her apron, half curtsied, and again vanished.

"A blessing, Father?"

"The Lord be with you."

"And also with thy spirit."

"Bless us O Lord, for these gifts we are about to receive from your bounty, and steel us for the journey that awaits us."

"Amen! 'Steel us,' indeed, Father. You and I have quite a journey before us."

***

Fred Miller rolled away from the wall, barely catching himself before falling off the narrow bed. He blinked at the morning sun streaking through a window in the stone hut. Something was different, no smell of coffee, no smell of breakfast. He glanced at the hammock, tied off on one side of the wall. Springing to his feet, he looked left and right about the small room. He was alone.

He threw on his clothes and bolted outside.

"Hello, where are you?" His voice seemed swallowed by the island. He listened while searching the distance. The gulls called. The sheep bleated. The steady swishing of the waves sounded the muffled rhythm to the normal island symphony. He turned round slowly, scanning the horizon in every direction. Nothing—just gray rocks, patches of green grass, and the occasional dot of a sheep or two.

He returned to the hut and scrounged some hard bread. As he chewed he noticed the staff with the pointed end leaning in a corner. Strange, he'd never seen the little man without the staff or the staff without the little man. A sense of anxiety washed over him. Finishing off his bread with a sudden sense of urgency, he added a jacket to his attire and retrieved the staff, hard, cool and solid in his hand.

He spent the better part of the morning scouring the island for the staff's owner to no avail. Occasionally he called out. "Hello, old man. Where are you, good fellow?" He listened intently for the whistle response. The sheep were all there, but no shepherd.

The sheep seemed a bit out of sorts, too. They watched him nervously as he passed them by—little black faces that stopped chewing, brown eyes that followed him until he was out of sight. What did they know that he didn't?

After several hours hunger compelled him to return to the hut. As he passed the sloping door built into the side of the ridge near the hut, something caught his eye. The lock was missing. Was the shepherd inside? The door appeared latched, though.

Setting the staff aside, he pulled back the iron bolt. It took considerable effort to swing the door away from its position leaning against the slope of the ridge. When it passed the halfway point, he allowed the door to fall away toward the rocky surface, revealing a cave.

"Hello. Anyone in there?"

Hearing no answer, Fred retrieved the staff and entered, stooping to avoid a low rock ceiling.

The smell of damp wood and mold hung in the air. He blinked several times and waited for his eyes to adjust. Objects in the back of the cave appeared, perhaps ten paces on. He approached slowly, holding the staff with the pointed end toward them.

"Well bless my soul, could it really be?"

He blinked again and smiled. They were large, eight of them altogether, piled two high in a confined space at the back of the cave, round along the sides and flat in front. He eagerly tapped on each with the wooden staff, and his grin grew with each responding bass thud.

"Well bless my soul, eight full barrels."

He knelt at one and gripped a wooden plug near the bottom of the barrel face with his right hand while cupping his left hand underneath. He gave it a twist and then a gradual pull until liquid flowed into his cupped hand. He pushed the plug back and raised his wet, now-trembling hand to his mouth. The familiar scent of whiskey filled his nostrils. He licked his palm.

"Yes!"

He leapt to his feet, causing a sharp collision with the low ceiling. He crumpled back to the dirt floor, giggling and rubbing his head.

"Just when I got rid of the last knot! Nothing that a little Irish whiskey can't cure."

He wobbled back on his feet again, more cautiously this time. He let his hands drag across the cave ceiling as he staggered back outside. Once in the daylight he raced to the hut for a cup, laughing and rubbing his head there and back.

Once filled he raised the cup to his lips.

"Hah! How rude of me. First, a toast."

Fred's voice boomed in the cool, confined space. He raised the tin cup toward the glow coming from the cave entrance.

"To you, strange little man, wherever you may be. I fear you've left me alone on this island with all these sheep, but at least you unlocked the treasure before you left."

Fred took a satisfying gulp.

Alone with all these sheep...the thought snapped his mind to attention. He made a stooped dash to the outside and frantically scanned the surrounding rocks and pastures, but still no little man.

"I'm not a shepherd! Why did you leave me here?"

There was no answer, only the gulls and the sheep and the sea.

"You can't leave me here," he muttered. He looked down at the tin cup half filled with whiskey. He felt cold. He stared at the cup in silence.

"I'm not a shepherd. Why did you leave me here?" he whispered despondently at the cup.

A gust of wind whistled across the wooden door lying against the rocks. The cave let out a hollow hum as the wind whipped by the opening. He retreated into the stillness inside and sat cross-legged on the dirt floor, propping his back against one of the big oak casks.

It all seemed sadly fitting, alone in a dark hole in the ground.

"No need for a casket, good shepherd. You need only close the door when you find me. I'll take care of the embalming from the inside out. *That*, I can do."

Fred took a long drink from the cup and licked his lips. The hunger pains that had brought him back to the hut subsided as the warm liquid flowed into him. His head stopped throbbing from the collision with the ceiling.

Fred's sense of time decreased with every fresh pour. He was trying to work out in his head the number of cups he'd downed when he lost sight of the cup held firmly in his hand. In fact, he couldn't see much of anything in the cave. He held his free hand up to his face—just a shadow where the hand should be. The cave entrance was hardly perceptible. Had he drunk himself blind?

"But of course, you sot, you've lost your daylight."

Fred dropped the cup and crawled outside on all fours. Using the sloping rock face beside the cave entrance, he haltingly pulled himself to his feet while leaning into the rock.

The wind had died down. Thousands of stars twinkled down at him from a clear sky.

"Why did you leave me here alone?" he pleaded to the stars. He gazed forlornly at the tiny lights dancing above him.

"Well then, it must be done." He thought of his mother. He wanted to cry, but his heart seemed long past it. He felt empty, hollow. He looked away from the sky in shame. "No, it's time. It must be done."

He spied the shepherd's long staff with the pointed end leaning nearby. Using it as a crutch he started on his journey, stumbling along but always in the same general direction toward the high cliff.

The moon, low on the horizon, cast long shadows across the landscape. It appeared positioned perfectly, acting as a beacon toward his destination. On he trudged, past the occasional clump of sheep huddled together sleeping. They ignored him as he tripped and tromped his way to the cliff. The moon seemed to move around, but he always adjusted his course to keep heading up the slope and toward the glowing spot in the sky.

As he ascended the last few steps the wind rose over the top of the cliff and pressed on his face. The waves splashed below. He approached the edge and looked down. The rocks at the bottom were shrouded in darkness, but the sea stretched out far into the distance in the beckoning moonlight. He turned back toward the island, a grey landscape of long shadows.

"Who?! Who will save me this time?!"

He waited for an answer to his shouted demand. The waves crashed below and the wind whispered past his face.

He turned to face the ledge and, planting his feet, threw the shepherd's staff over the edge. A stretch of silence was followed by a distant crack and then a barely perceptible splash. It must have bounced off the rocks into the sea. Just as well, perhaps it will wash up for someone, somewhere. It was a well-made staff, and a shame to waste it just to confirm the drop.

He looked back over his shoulder one last time. Something moved. He blinked and rubbed his eyes. Nothing, but then, there it was it again, a form floating across the landscape. It disappeared, and reappeared. There it was again. Was it his savior? Someone coming to pull him off the ledge yet again?

He turned toward the vision, mesmerized, as it moved from shadow to shadow, up the rise toward the cliff. It shimmered in the moonlight, but stayed low to the ground.

Fred rubbed his eyes again. He must be seeing things. But the form kept floating closer, moving rapidly toward him.

If he focused, perhaps it would go away, merely a product of his well-lubricated imagination. He could barely walk. Perhaps he could barely see straight as well.

On came the apparition, darting from one shadow to the next, inexorably up the slope toward the ledge, toward Fred. He blinked again and again, but the image kept dashing toward him.

As it got closer it began to trot. There was no darting about now, just a steady jog straight at him. It was an animal, a big animal. It moved confidently but silently, slowing to a walk. Then, but yards away, it stopped and growled, a low, raspy growl.

Fred rubbed his eyes once more in disbelief. He refocused, but it was still there, a snarling beast, ears erect, head bent low, and white fur waving in the breeze.

Fred instinctively picked up a stone and cocked his arm. He heaved it at the wolf. The monster backed away, the stone clanking off the spot that the wolf had vacated. He picked up another and threw it. Again, the animal retreated to avoid the stone as it harmlessly bounced down the slope.

He furiously threw stone after stone. His effort kept the beast at bay, but he soon ran out of projectiles. He started his way downslope along the ridge, gathering stones and throwing them as he went. If he could only make the water, he could stand at a depth that would cause the beast to swim. Then he'd have a chance.

Time slowed in the descent. He mustn't turn and run. He kept his face to the wolf as has worked backwards toward the beach. When he slipped the wolf lunged to close the gap between them, but as Fred recovered he sprayed the oncoming beast with a fusillade of smaller stones, and the wolf retreated.

The ground began to flatten, and he heard the sound of the surf behind him. Then everything began to fade. He looked to the sky to see a cloud drifting over the low moon, extinguishing what little light there was. When he looked ahead he couldn't make out the wolf. He turned and ran to the sound of the sea.

He tripped when his feet caught the surf, sending him sprawling head first into the foam. Up quickly, he raised his legs and splashed ahead. Something was running along the beach. Fred kept pressing deeper into the water until the waves came nearly to his shoulders. He turned and faced the shore. A form waited at the edge of the surf. It hesitated a bit longer, and then charged into the water.

Fred felt frantically around the surf. He had nothing to defend himself, no stone, no…and them something brushed up against his arm. Looking down at the water revealed a long object—the staff? His mind saw the sharp weapon in his hands, thrusting and stabbing at the beast. Now he had a weapon. Now the odds had turned. He felt an urge for revenge. He wanted blood.

He reached out for the black object floating near him. With excited anticipation he raised it from the sea.

"No!" he screamed staring at the object, a soggy and limp tree branch. "No, no, no!" he shouted at the dark sky. Fury mounted in his breast. He screamed a primal scream and charged the shore.

On, he splashed, screaming and wielding the soggy branch like knight's lance. His charge picked up speed as he came closer to the water's edge. Soon he was moving faster than the surf that broke behind him.

The beach suddenly glowed as the moon broke through the passing cloud. On he ran, screaming, his soggy lance held out before him.

Several yards into the beach he stopped. He spun around swinging the branch in a circle until he faced the island again—

nothing. Then he spun around in the other direction—still nothing. Salt from his hand stung his eyes as he wiped his face—still nothing. He heard a single bleat in the distance, then another. The sound of a gull came from overhead. The waves splashed behind him. But he saw nothing, just the island before him. He collapsed to his knees and wept.

CHAPTER 8
A MAN'S SOUL

"Come in. Please, Inspector, take a seat." Sir Charles Hardinge directed Inspector Jenkins to an overstuffed chair next to a small round table. The inspector always looked out of place in formal surroundings. His scarred face, square shoulders, and compact fists gave him the look of a street brawler dressing up as a gentleman. "I understand you have some news. May I get you something to drink?"

"Yes, thank you. Tea with a splash of scotch."

"Of course, your usual." Sir Charles nodded at a young man who had accompanied the inspector to his office along with a wooden trunk that he held in front of him like a platter.

"Tea with a splash of scotch," repeated the young man. "And where shall I deposit this, sir?"

"Anywhere near the inspector." Hardinge waved in the inspector's direction as he walked to a liquor cabinet on the other side of the room.

Jenkins motioned at a position near his chair.

"Thank you, sir," acknowledged the young man to the inspector as he set down the trunk and left the room.

"What in heaven's name have you brought in that?" asked Sir Charles, pointing with the bottom end of a retrieved bottle. "You've put scotch in my mind. I believe I'll skip the tea dilution, though."

"Many of the foreign office agents found dead over the past few months had something in common."

Hardinge paused for a moment holding the bottle above a shot glass. "Do you mean the knife in the throat or the calling card from 'Charlie'? Quite a mystery."

"I believe I've solved the mystery, at least partially. May I?" Jenkins pointed at the box.

"By all means." Hardinge filled the glass and dropped into another overstuffed chair on the other side of the round table.

Jenkins retrieved a key from his jacket and unlocked the trunk. He peered inside and removed a knife.

"You may recall that all of the knives found in necks of various 'Charlie' victims, whether they entered from the front or back, traveled through the entire length of the neck with the blade buried to the hilt, thus severing the spinal cord of each victim." Jenkins demonstrated by placing the knife next to his neck with the handle facing forward and the blade pointed behind him. His was no elegant neck, but rather burly, and the knife tip did not protrude beyond the back of it.

"Yes, ghastly." Hardinge absentmindedly took a drink. "Sorry, quite rude of me. Do you mind?"

"By all means," responded Jenkins to the glass held high by Sir Charles.

"To your health and long life."

"Thank you. Further, in every case bruising was noted on the neck underneath the hilt, with the structure of the neck crushed, flattened if you will. This evidence indicates that the knife was still traveling at a high velocity through the throat when slowed by the hilt contacting the neck."

Hardinge rubbed his neck and took another drink.

"This fact created quite a puzzle. The autopsy coroners at the Yard all concluded that it would take enormous force to consistently achieve such results, force that a human might be able to muster only if the victim were lying on the ground and the assailant shoved the knife through the throat by stomping on the top of the handle. It's hard to imagine such an attack, unless the victims were incapacitated or held down. Yet evidence of many of these murders suggests that the victims were standing upright when the knife was embedded into their throats and that they thereafter fell to the ground.

"Upon inspecting the knives, we noted that many had a peculiar mark on the top of the handle." Jenkins pointed the handle at Hardinge, revealing a small X-shaped mark embedded in a metal surface. "I believe we now understand the source of this mark and the purpose behind the savagery of the attacks."

Jenkins reached in the trunk as the young man who brought it in appeared at the door to Hardinge's office.

"Your tea, Inspector."

"Thank you," Sir Charles answered and motioned to the small round table.

The tea service was placed on the table, and the young man again left the two gentlemen alone in the room.

Jenkins waited for the door to close and then produced a metal cane from the trunk and handed it to Hardinge.

"This is our answer to part of the riddle."

"What is it?" Sir Charles set down his glass and began inspecting the cane, turning it around in both hands.

"It's a specially built walking cane. You'll note the inverted U-shaped base connected to this shaft. In the shaft is a spring, presently uncoiled. A knife, such as this one, is inserted in the hole you see going through the base of the U-shape into the hollow shaft. The knife is then forced further into the shaft with the top of the handle pressing against an X-shaped metal tip at the end of spring. We suspect some smaller diameter hollow tube is used to force the knife all the way into the shaft and compress the coil. Given the strength of the coil, there must be a further device that provides significant leverage to push the knife back against it."

Hardinge continued to roll the cane around in his hands, fascinated by the device.

"Once the knife is fully inserted in the cane, meaning the coil is fully compressed against the top of the knife handle, the knife is locked in place by a lever connected to the button you'll find at the top of the handle."

"My God! It's a loaded weapon! The button is the trigger that releases the spring. It works like a crossbow, but the dart is the knife."

"Exactly, Sir Charles. And this…may I?" Jenkins reached for the cane, which Hardinge readily surrendered.

"This upside down U at the end acts as an aiming device, like this." Jenkins placed his neck in the U shape with the shaft now pointed straight at the center of his throat.

"Dastardly!"

"As you can see, if an assailant can place this end of the cane around a victim's neck, whether from the front or the rear, then pushing the button on the handle releases the trigger mechanism—"

"And," interrupted Sir Charles, "thereby releasing the spring that drives the knife straight through the neck of the victim."

Hardinge picked up his glass and downed the contents.

Jenkins set the cane down, picked up his cup, and raised it toward Hardinge. "To *your* health and long life."

Hardinge responded by quickly pouring another glass of scotch.

"The force of the spring on the top of the handle of the knife leaves the telltale X embedded in it from the metal tip attached to the end of the spring," Jenkins added before taking another sip.

Hardinge sat still in his chair, staring at the cane with his now full glass suspended before him.

"What on earth is the purpose of this bizarre method of execution? Why not just stab your victim in the heart or some other conventional method."

"Excellent question. The purpose is to paralyze. A victim subjected to such attack becomes immediately paralyzed from the neck down, but remains alive and aware for a short period of time. Think of the severed head from the guillotine, still cognizant of the earthly world for a few seconds after removal from the body. These knife victims are conscious for a few seconds after the attack, just long enough for someone to force one of these onto their faces."

Jenkins reached back into the trunk and produced a black box. "Just long enough to look into a black box."

Sir Charles remained still and silent with his untouched second drink still held high in his hand.

"Where did you get that?"

"Two assassins attempted to use one of these cane devices on me. Fortunately, they did not succeed. Unfortunately, I killed one and the other killed himself. He did so by looking into this box."

"I thought they were all gone," Sir Charles muttered to himself.

"From this anecdotal event, I surmise that Foreign Office agents and agents working with Special Department B of the Yard have been impaled by knives and then quickly forced to look into black boxes. The cane enables assassins to easily target, stab, and immobilize the victim and allows a few seconds to force a black box to the victim's still perceptive eyes before he loses consciousness."

"Incredible. Then you've solved the mystery of the knife."

"Not entirely. You see, only some of the knives exhibit the telltale X associated with this cane weapon. There are others, all found in Britain, that have no markings on the handles of any kind. Yet, they were used with the same force and effect as the others."

"How do you explain it?"

"I can't, yet, other than to conclude that there are at least two methods of knife attacks, only one of which we have discovered. The undiscovered method is used by an assassin who doesn't need the cane. But I can't yet explain how that is possible."

Hardinge rolled the problems around in his head. "Is it conceivable that someone might be strong enough to thrust the knife into a victim's neck to the same effect? What if the assailant were a brute of a man?"

"He'd have to be stronger than any man *I* know. We've experimented on cadavers. Even my strongest man taking a full swing didn't produce the kind of crushing and bruising we see in the victims."

A chilling thought crossed Hardinge's mind. "Your box busters, Molly Bell, Jim Talbot, and Doctor Cunningham, are they…"

"Alive? If they were dead, we would know. My presumption is that they are all still alive. If so, I'll find them."

Hardinge prayed he was right. Jenkins certainly seemed confident. "And the cards. 'Charlie.' Why the calling cards?"

"A statement, clearly. We're being taunted."

"Taunted? What does the statement mean?"

"That we can't stop them. It's…" Jenkins paused appearing to choose his word carefully. "Bravado."

"To demoralize? Cause us to chuck up the sponge?"

"Perhaps, not sure, exactly." Jenkins took another sip of tea.

"Then this really isn't about knives, it's the black box again."

"So it appears."

"But why?"

"I've thought on that point considerably. The best I can come up with is that it must not be enough to dispatch. Collection seems to be a necessary component."

"Collection?"

Jenkins took another sip, set down his cup, and looked Sir Charles square in the eye. "Do you believe man has a soul?"

* * *

"Do you believe man has a soul, Father?"

The word "Father" seemed almost in jest. Cornish took a moment to finish chewing, set his bag of chips on the park bench, and swallowed.

"James," he replied in the same mocking tone. "Do you believe man does not?"

142

James laughed before shoving a chip into his mouth. He chewed for a moment and swallowed.

"A man's soul. In the end, isn't that's what it's all about, Father?" He shoved another chip into his mouth and continued between swallows. "Beautiful day. I love Regents Park. I love this lake, so serene and peaceful."

Cornish reached for the chips wrapped in a newspaper, flinging one of the greasy strips of fried potatoes at a gaggle of passing geese. A duck scurried up from the bank, instead, to retrieve it.

"Speaking of souls, isn't this the disaster end of the lake?"

The priest flung another chip at the geese, but the duck again rushed in for the prize. "The disaster end?"

"January 1867. You've not heard of it?"

Cornish thought on the date, but nothing immediately came to mind.

"The ice skating incident. Surely you..."

"But of course, now I recall. Hundreds of Londoners came out for a skate on an unusually warm winter day. Yes, I believe it was this southwest corner. Men, women, and children, but mostly women and children, all crowding onto the ice. It gave way. Heavily laden with winter clothing, many perished. I believe more than forty in all. A sad day for London."

"That's it." James smiled. "You remember correctly."

"Why do you bring that up on such a lovely day?"

"To illustrate a point. After that accident, the city reduced the depth of the lake a few feet. Several years ago a similar incident occurred, hundreds skating on the ice when it gave way. No one died. They all waded out of the cold water, quite embarrassed but no worse for the affair. Why the difference?"

"Obviously, because someone had the foresight to order the depth decreased."

"Exactly my point." James popped a chip into his mouth. "And what would have happened the second time had such foresight not be exercised by someone? More lost souls!"

Cornish sighed. "Yes, we've rather established that." If James was trying to make some further point, Cornish wished he would get on with it. "You certainly enjoy talking in riddles."

"The foresight of one man saved many. But what if that one man had never lived?"

"Perhaps another would have come to the same conclusion."

"Perhaps, and perhaps not. When insightful men act, lives of others are affected, sometimes saved. If there are no insightful men to act, then what?"

"More riddles, as far as I can tell."

"Think on it, Father." This time the "Father" seemed in earnest. "Most men are sheep. They skate on the ice, oblivious to the danger. Shepherds keep them safe, but they are few. Imagine a world without shepherds. Imagine a world of only sheep, lost and oblivious to the danger."

"What do you want of me?"

"You've been a great comfort to me over these past days since I made your acquaintance. You do remind me of Father Tate in many ways."

"I'll take that as a compliment."

"As intended." James stuck two more chips in his mouth and slowly chewed while staring out at the lake. After swallowing he resumed the conversation while still gazing at the still water.

"Aston."

"I beg your pardon?"

"You've been wondering, no doubt, what is my name. It's Aston, James Aston."

Cornish ate another chip and chewed in silence, purposely showing no reaction. The geese were moving out to the middle of the lake now. He tossed another chip to the industrious duck.

"Is my name familiar to you?"

"Yes, I'm remembering now. I believe Father Tate mentioned you once or twice as a man who could be trusted."

"The world is changing." Aston continued staring out to the lake. "You and I will sit on this bench ten years hence having witnessed cataclysmic changes. We need to prepare. Power will shift dramatically, and the world will require men like you and me.

"Do I believe men have souls? Most certainly, Father. They're there for the taking."

***

The gulls woke him. Fred Miller blinked and wiped sand from his brow. The sun bore down, flickering red to brilliant white with every blink. The surf splashed nearby.

What time was it? How long had he been on the beach? The image of a white wolf pushed the questions out of his head. He sat up and blinked again. He cupped his hand to his forehead, shielding his face from the sun, and scanned the shoreline. Nothing, he was alone…almost alone. A group of five or six sheep stared placidly at him as they lay sunning near a clump of rocks. One bleated in his direction, as if to say "about time you got up."

"Yes, quite right you are," Fred responded meekly.

He gained his feet and again surveyed the scene. Was it a dream? It had to be. There were no wolves on this island. He had never encountered any evidence of them, despite what the old shepherd wanted him to believe. Fred had just been a little drunk last night. His head ached. All right, maybe very drunk.

He glanced back at the rolling surf. Something washed toward the beach, something long and skinny. He splashed in after it, and soon had the familiar shepherd's staff in his hand, the one he'd thrown from the cliff. The point was blunted, but otherwise it appeared in good shape. The chatty sheep bleated at him again.

Fred gripped the staff, feeling its strength and weight. Then he gazed at the distant mainland. The sea sparkled between it in the sun. He stood transfixed. His mind sharpened onto a single, powerful thought. Again came a bleat.

"I agree. Enough…it must be done." With that Fred trotted out of the surf and turned toward the cave. Whether an apparition or imagination, the wolf had made his point. Life was worth fighting for. "It must be done."

When he arrived at the cave entrance his heart raced. Stepping inside he took a moment to adjust to the shadows. The scent of whiskey mixed with the damp, earthy mold. Still eight barrels, just as he remembered.

He approached one of the lower barrels. Setting down the staff, he gripped the plug near the bottom of the cask, gave it a hard twist, and pulled it out with an accompanying plop. The brew chugged out the opening and onto the floor of the cave. He moved to the next barrel and repeated the exercise: grab the plug, twist, and pull. Then he opened the next, and the next. Soon all of the barrels were chugging their contents onto the floor of the cave, a sloshy symphony that echoed in the small space. The cool liquor flowed past his feet.

The floor of the cave sloped downward slightly in the direction of the entrance. From there the land sloped to the beach. Fred picked up the staff, sloshed his way to the entrance, and stepped outside to observe the whisky creek he had created rushing down the hill. Satisfied with his work, hunger moved his attention to the little hut.

There was much more work to do, but he'd eat first. After that, he'd scrounge for the materials he needed to lash the eight empty barrels together. It made sense to roll them down to the beach first, he thought. The staff would do nicely for part of the sail. It must be done. Yes, but first, food.

He followed his new creek as it swirled past the hut. Just before entering the door, a single sheep trotted toward the creek, sniffed at the amber liquid, and bleated at Fred.

"Don't get started on that stuff. That's all I have to offer, my woolen friend. I'm not a shepherd, much less the good one. I'm not even the hired hand. I don't know the first thing about sheep. I only know I have to get off this island and make things right."

Again the sheep bleated.

"Look here, I promise to send someone. You can make it on your own for a few days. I'm sorry. I've let everyone down, and now I'm letting you down too. But, you see, I can't help here."

The solitary sheep stood silently, staring at him. Fred's stomach growled. He opened the door.

"I'm sorry, but I want my soul back."

CHAPTER 9
LOTS OF HEARTACHE

Clayton Spake stood high in the stirrups, one hand on the saddle horn and the other reining in the stout, blue roan to keep it as still as possible. His head, topped with a worn straw hat, peered above the scrub cover on the tip of the rise in front of him. He squinted hard to focus, making out the horses hobbled in the clearing. He took his time to make sure he counted all of them. Five. They were all there, the same five he had followed for the past two days, getting closer by the hour and then waiting for the opportunity that lay before him.

They were easy to follow, four riders on five horses. They weren't concerned about being followed. If his hunch was correct, they were hunting and not expecting to be hunted. They'd moved fast, aided by the extra horse, but were stopped for a midafternoon break from the searing New Mexico sun. They would eat, nap, and rest their horses before riding on through the night. Now was the perfect time to confirm his hunch and, if confirmed, deal with them.

Spake sat back in the saddle and thought about his approach. He dismounted and posted the roan to a nearby creosote bush. Snapping his fingers brought his dog out from the meager shade of a squat cactus. Spake grabbed his nearly empty canteen, removed the cap, and poured straight into his mouth, holding the warm liquid there so as not to swallow the precious stuff. He produced a tin cup from his saddlebag into which he poured the rest of the water. He screwed the lid back on and secured the canteen to the saddle. He held the cup near the ground and let the muscular dog lick it dry before returning it to the saddlebag.

The dog looked up quizzically. Spake thrust a finger toward the dog and then pointed to the sky. The dog understood; he'd be quiet. Off they went toward a clump of trees where the four men were resting, Spake striding silently across the desert sand, the dog close on his heels.

They approached from the opposite side of the trees from where the five horses were hobbled. No need to alert the men sooner than necessary. As they got closer he heard them talking, a low muttering with an occasional chuckle. He slowed his pace and swallowed what was left of the water he'd been carrying in his mouth. He turned to the dog and signaled stop with an open hand. Then he pointed to the ground. The dog dutifully obeyed, squatting to a prone position with his hind legs cocked and ready.

He was a formidable beast, larger and more solid than your average cattle dog, probably close on ninety pounds, with a compact muzzle built for a crushing bite. Spake needed him to keep the odds close.

As he came upon the camp, Spake purposefully stepped on a stick. The crack brought the four men to their feet, each one pulling a revolver and pointing it toward the approaching stranger. Spake paused and held out his hands, palms open.

"What do you want?" shouted one of the men.

"Same thing you do, and I can help you get it."

The four men stared at him in silence.

"Can I come in? Let's talk."

"Who are you?"

"A man lookin' to make some quick money, just like you."

The four men went silent again. These were hard men. Three sets of glaring eyes set in dirty, bearded faces watched him intently for any sudden move. One man was different, shorter than the rest with no facial hair. His high cheekbones set upon a broad face and flat forehead framed by coarse black hair set him apart as an Apache, probably Mescalero. The Indian no longer looked at Spake, but instead scanned the area around the camp. He must be the tracker. Spake hadn't counted on an Apache. His odds just got longer.

Spake eyed the other three men. The tallest of the four, a broad-shouldered man with a speckled beard shaded by an enormous black hat, held a long Navy Colt. That long pistol would take a while to un-holster once he returned it to his side.

A shorter, stocky man with sandy hair slowly chewed something as he stared at Spake. The stocky man held his revolver at hip level, slowly turning the barrel in a tight circle pointed in Spake's direction.

The last man looked the youngest, and more than a little anxious. A skinny cowboy with blond hair and smooth hands, the left one jiggling at his side, he held his revolver high with his right arm extended. He canted his head to the right, squinting his left eye as he looked down the barrel with the other eye at Spake's chest. He'd be quick to fight without thinking much first.

The fellow with the black hat stepped forward. After eyeing Spake up and down, the man stuck the big Colt into his belt, keeping one hand on the gun and rubbing his chin with the other.

"Come on in to me, stranger. Let me take look at ya."

Spake cautiously approached the man with black hat while still holding his hands out in front of him. A breeze wafted the smell of the men Spake's way, a mixture of sweat, horse, and dust. He stopped a few paces from the man and returned his stare. The man glared down at Spake from under the dusty black felt hat with a brim wide enough to cover his shoulders.

"Do I know you?" asked the man with the black hat.

"I doubt it."

"Where's the rest of your party?"

"I don't need no party. Just me."

The man with the black hat smiled. "You shouldn't walk up on a camp like that unannounced. You could get yourself kilt."

"I stepped on a twig."

"I appreciate that. You look part Indian to me. You one of them half-breeds?"

"Not half."

"Part, huh? The sneaky part, I reckon." He tilted his head and squinted at Spake. "What was that you said about helpin' us?"

"I can help you find her."

"Find who?"

"Molly Bell."

The name seemed to slice through the group, causing all but the Indian to flinch.

"We already got a tracker."

"You found her yet?" Spake looked toward the Apache. "You'd think he'd know I was followin' you, goin' on two days now."

The Indian ignored him and continued to scan the surroundings.

"Come on in. Let's talk. But first, you'd make me feel a fair sight better if you'd unbuckle that gun belt and hand it over."

Spake complied with slow deliberate motions, handing the man with the black hat his gun belt. The man smiled again and nodded his head toward the center of the camp. Spake headed that way with the man following him. The other three, having holstered their guns upon Spake surrendering his, positioned themselves to form a loose circle around Spake as he approached. Once he was surrounded, Spake turned to face the man with the black hat.

"What's your name?"

"Clayton. What's yours?"

"Boss. You can call me 'Boss.'"

"All right, Boss. How long you gonna meander looking for this girl?"

"Meander? I suppose you know where she is?"

"That depends."

"On what?"

"Do you want her?"

"A big pile of dollars split four ways says so."

"Zero split four ways ain't as good as a big pile of dollars split five ways."

Boss laughed and put his hands on his hips.

"That bulge in your shirt pocket"—he pointed at Spake's chest—"I don't suppose that's tobacky?"

Spake nodded.

"Well, hand me some, Clayton."

Keeping his eyes on the man, Spake pulled a brown wad out of his shirt pocket. He reached toward Boss with the wad protruding half out of his fist.

Boss unsheathed a knife. Cupping Spake's fist with his free hand, Boss scraped his knife across the top, cutting the protruding portion of the wad and slicing a sliver of skin off Spake's thumb in the process. The man then let go of Spake's hand and cut a smaller piece off the plug. He placed the smaller piece in his mouth, stashed the rest of the plug in his own shirt pocket and sheathed the knife. He chewed a bit, swallowed, and grinned.

"Not bad tobacky. You a tracker?"

Spake made no notice of the blood coming from the back of his thumb and placed the tobacco back in his pocket. "The best."

"Can you handle a gun?"

"Yes."

"How about a knife?"

"Better than a gun."

"That's big talk, Clayton." Boss rubbed his chin again and took another swallow. He looked away from Clayton at the stocky man with the sandy hair, who in response stopped his own chewing and moved his jaw slightly to the left while pushing out his left cheek with his tongue. Boss pursed his lips and nodded before turning back to Spake.

"See, here's the deal, Clayton. This Indian feller, we call him Jo 'cause we can't say his name. Jo's a damn good tracker and mighty handy with a knife. I don't know why I'd split money with two trackers. So here's my offer. You and Jo can figure it out. I'll give you a knife, and Jo's got one already. Whoever's left standin', why that man can have the tracker job."

"And what if I don't want to fight Jo?"

"Then we'll have Jo here cut your throat, and we'll have six horses instead of five. No hard feelin's. It's just business." Boss swallowed and looked toward Jo. "What do you say, Jo, don't that sound fair to you?"

Spake glanced over at Jo. His face was tense and his eyes, narrowed to almost nothing, focused on his adversary. He slowly nodded his head without breaking his stare at Spake.

"Deal, Boss," snarled Spake as he turned to face Jo.

The other three men backed away as Jo pulled a knife from his belt with his right hand and advanced on Spake.

"Shucks, Clayton, I forgot to mention, we don't need no tracker. I just like Jo. And I hope you have a knife handy, cause I ain't got one to spare right now."

Spake had two, in fact, one in each boot. But Jo was close on him and would make him pay if he reached for either. Instead, Spake removed his straw hat and used it as a cover for his right hand. As Jo made his first test lunge toward him, Spake feinted a grab at the knife blade with his hat-covered right hand. He now had Jo's attention on his right hand. Jo was evidently right-handed; Spake was not.

The two men circled each other, Jo making the occasional thrust, but always pulling the knife back before Spake could grab the blade with his hat. Then the Indian committed. He thrust again toward Spake with the knife in his right hand. As Spake countered with his hat, Jo grabbed at the hat with his left hand. Spake let him take it, but grabbed the blade of Jo's knife with his bare left hand. The blade bit into his skin, but Jo pressed his attack instead of retreating and pulling the knife away.

With his now-empty right hand Spake reached for his right boot. With quickness that he had purposefully concealed, Spake pulled his knife from his boot. Thrusting downward on Jo's knife with his left hand, he threw Jo off balance and exposed Jo's left side. With one continuous movement Spake completed the dance with a thrust of his knife deep into Jo's left side below his armpit. Jo crumpled and let go of his knife. Now the odds were shorter.

Clayton let loose a sharp whistle. The sound of his dog thundering from the brush toward the camp turned the attention of the three men. As expected the young one was already on his gun, yanking it up quickly with his right hand and trying to get a bead on the dog. Spake threw Jo's knife into the young man's right shoulder and finished the throwing motion by retrieving his other knife from his left boot. That knife was soon lodged in the throat of the stocky man with the sandy hair.

The dog was on the man with the black hat and long revolver. The animal had Boss's right hand firmly in his jaws as the man howled, flailing at his holster with his left hand.

Clayton moved on to the young man who, despite the knife in his shoulder, was valiantly raising his right arm with his left, trying to get a shot off at the dog, the focus of his attention since he first drew the gun. Clayton punched the young man hard on the chin, sending him reeling to the ground. He then rushed Boss, knocking him down.

The dog let loose of the man's hand and went for his throat. Boss used both hands to keep the dog at bay, allowing Clayton to pull the long Navy gun from its holster. One shot to the head quickly stilled the man.

Turning around, Clayton saw the stout man with the sandy hair writhing in pain on the ground, grasping at the knife lodged in his throat. Another shot to the head quieted the stout man too.

Jo had managed to remove the knife from his side, but the growing puddle of blood next to where he lay made it clear that the heart was pierced. The Indian was out of the fight, permanently.

The young man was coming back to his senses, though. The dog started a charge toward him, but Clayton brought him to heel with another loud whistle. The dog looked up at Clayton and reluctantly obeyed his signal to lie down.

The young man sat up, Jo's knife lodged in his shoulder, and stared at Clayton with glassy eyes, still gripping his revolver in his right hand. Clayton discharged the big Colt into the young man's lower stomach. The young man dropped his gun and began screaming in pain, a high-pitched gurgling scream.

"Sorry about that. But I need to talk with you in a minute."

Clayton ignored the screaming man and retrieved his knife from Jo's side. Jo was dead. Just as well. Clayton preferred the Indian not know what was to come. It was best Jo died with honor.

Clayton pulled the Indian's head up by his hair making it easier for him to take his scalp. He then did the same to Boss and the stout man.

Turning his attention to the screamer, Spake squatted down beside him, holding the three scalps in front of him to see. The sight of them made the cowboy moan. Spake set the scalps on the ground and pulled the tobacco from his shirt pocket. He wiped off his knife on his pants and cut a piece of the brown wad.

"You know why Apaches scalp a man?"

The cowboy stared at the scalps. Clayton put the plug of tobacco in his mouth and returned the rest to his pocket.

"It's the man's soul they want. You take his scalp, you take his soul. The more souls you take, the more powerful you are."

Clayton spat, the brown stream landing in a puddle near the scalps.

"It's like you consume the man. You take all his power from head to toe."

He spat another brown stream at the same spot.

"I reckon the devil operates the same way. A man can't get to heaven if his soul's down here on earth." He pointed the knife around the camp. "These poor fellers ain't gonna get there any time soon."

Clayton stopped to ponder his statement and shook his head. "Hard business all around, I know. Lots of heartache in these parts lately cause of fellas like you. Way I figure it, you got to fight evil with evil. Sinners like you don't cotton to sweet talkin'."

He spat again, enlarging the small brown pool on the ground.

"Now, here's *my* deal." Spake spoke slowly and deliberately. "You got a knife in your shoulder, your jaw is broken, and I put a good size hole in your stomach. You're a dead man, but it's gonna hurt for a spell first. It's gonna hurt even more when I take your scalp."

His moaning stopped as the man continued to stare at the scalps with wide eyes. "Don't scalp me, just kill me, mister, please." The cowboy spoke in a half whisper out one side of his mouth. "I don't want no part of this. Just kill me. Please, don't scalp me."

"That all depends. You need to get real honest with me real fast." Again he spat at the brown puddle. "You answer a few questions, and I'll make it quick and painless. Otherwise, I'm takin' your scalp and leavin' you here for the wolves to eat. Hmm, I wonder where a soul goes if it can't get to heaven."

"I'll answer you, just promise you'll bury me. Don't leave me to be eaten by wolves."

"I can't promise that. I'm kind of in a hurry. But I won't scalp you, and I'll make it quick."

The man let out another moan.

"You trackin' Molly Bell?"

The man nodded.

"You lost her trail two days back outside of Hondo. That's why you circled back today a bit."

The man nodded.

"And you intend to kill her when you find her."

"No scalping, please."

"No scalping, if you answer me that question."

"We wanted the money. It's $100,000 dead."

Clayton put him out of his misery and left his scalp alone. Leaving a scalp behind would cost him, but he gave his word to a dead man. He put the three he had in his saddlebag with the others.

He picked up his straw hat, noticing for the first time how bloody his left hand was. He made a fist, then opened it and looked at the gash across his palm. He took the tobacco wad out of his mouth and squeezed the juice onto the wound. He stripped some greasy leaves from a creosote bush and matted them together. He then used a long yucca leaf to tie the creosote clump over the gash on his hand.

His hat had a few cuts too from Jo's knife. He sauntered over to Boss and retrieved the big black hat from the ground near his head. He dusted it off and, after a short inspection for evidence of lice, tried it on. It was a good fit.

***

Jay White pushed down on the stirrups and stretched his back. He took off his Stetson and ran his fingers through his hair. The late afternoon breeze chilled the damp ring of sweat where his hatband had been. He looked to the west at the setting sun. He'd best get back to the ranch. He reckoned he was about two hours' ride away. He'd have to make the last hour in the dark.

He hadn't intended to stay out this long, but his search for strays was frustrated by a pack of wolves that had followed him since noon. Every time he turned to chase them they scattered, only to reassemble a while later, always staying just outside of rifle range.

The last time he turned he was determined to close on one and get off a shot. Across the desert he charged, picking out one of the elusive grey figures zigzagging between clumps of brush. He never got off his shot. To make matters worse, he had charged away from the ranch and lost track of time. Now he rode a tired horse, two hours away from the ranch, with one hour of daylight left.

He let out two clicks from the side of his mouth and shifted his weight forward in the saddle. The horse reluctantly plodded toward the setting sun.

The horse knew the way, so Jay let his mind drift. His thoughts floated to where they normally went when he was tired, to Rebecca. She haunted him when awake and asleep. The image of her flowing red hair and teasing smile made his heart ache. A purple dress with black trim, what was that about? The white heart-shaped brooch was familiar enough. He'd given it to her. But why did she always appear in a purple dress with black trim? He couldn't recall ever seeing such a dress before. She wore it well in his mind's eye. He'd give a lot to see her in it now.

He tried to think of something else. The ranch boss would be irritated with him getting back so late and nothing to show for it. Chasing wolves wasn't much of an excuse.

A motion in the distance caught his attention. He put his hand over his eyes to shield out the sun and squinted. A horse and rider were headed his way.

"That's about the way I was goin' anyway. Might as well see what he wants," he muttered.

Jay made another clicking noise with his mouth and applied a slight lateral pressure to the reins. His weary horse turned and trudged toward the approaching stranger.

As they got closer, details of the other rider came into focus. It wasn't anyone he recognized. The rider was not big. Maybe a boy? He didn't recognize the horse, either, a paint.

The distance closed rapidly. He was mistaken. It wasn't a boy at all, but a girl. What was a girl doing riding out in the desert near dusk by herself? Was she lost?

When they were within speaking distance she abruptly pulled her paint to a stop. Jay obliged and halted his mount with a slight backward pull on the reins. The girl stared at Jay, sitting as straight in the saddle as any cowboy he'd ever seen. There was a wire cage tied to her saddle horn with what looked like a horned toad sitting on top of some straw inside. There was something familiar about her. Her dress, he'd seen it before.

"Are you Jay White?"

"Who's askin'?"

"They told me at the ranch I'd find you looking for strays out this direction. I wasn't sure I'd find you before the sun went down, but I had to try."

"A good thing you did. There's a pack of wolves about. Now, who found me?"

The girl sat perfectly still, eyeing him suspiciously.

"Please, tell me for certain, are you Jay White?"

"Miss, you got a lot of nerve comin' upon me near dark and demanding to know who I am."

The girl trembled, the bravado dropping momentarily. Her eyes showed fear. Her paint pawed the ground and snorted.

"Yes, I'm Jay White."

"I'm Molly Bell."

The name sent a jolt down his spine. He instinctively patted his rifle to make sure it was hanging in its place near his left leg and scanned the horizon for evidence of any other riders. Every scoundrel and lowlife from New Mexico, Oklahoma, and Texas was looking for this girl. Men were killing each other to get within a day's ride of her scalp and there she stood, right in front of him. How did she get this far east?

Jay's mind raced. "Miss, I don't want no part of this. You need to keep on ridin'. I'm just one little cowboy, and it ain't gonna do you any good to leave one more set of hoof prints to follow. I'll give you my water if you want and I promise not to tell a soul, but I can't help you. You need an army, not one cowboy."

He'd let her ride on and then gather some brush to sweep the ground in case someone was following her. Maybe that would buy her some time and erase any evidence of their encounter.

"I'm sorry, miss, I don't want no part."

"Rebecca sent me."

The name fell on Jay like a blow. He grabbed the saddle horn and steadied himself.

"What did you say?"

"Rebecca from Cloudcroft sent me. She said you would help and that I should mention her name."

"What color was her hair, this Rebecca?"

"Red and worn long."

"Wh-what sort of game are you playin' with me?"

"I'm not playing a game. She was kind and warned me when men were closing in. I've been riding to find you ever since."

"What was she wearing?" He wasn't sure why he asked the question, but he did.

The girl hesitated a moment, looking puzzled. "A purple dress with black trim. She wore a white brooch shaped like a heart."

Jay felt dizzy. He gripped the saddle horn even harder.

"She said you would help me. Mr. White, I'm sorry, but I need help. I can't keep running like this. I'm tired, I'm hungry, and I'm scared."

The sound of a sniffle brought him back to his senses. The girl sat as erect as ever, but he could see water welling in her bloodshot eyes.

"Aw, dang it," he muttered under his breath. He searched the horizon again and rubbed his chin with a quivering hand. He looked back at the girl who still maintained her brave appearance, even if her eyes gave away the fear she felt, a fear he was beginning to share.

"I-I kn-know a place. No one will e-ever find you." He shouldn't have said it, but he had.

She let out a long breath and relaxed her shoulders. "How will you keep someone from tracking us there?

"You leave that to me."

Jay's mind worked faster. He was committed now. Was he a dead man? Probably, but maybe he could save the girl. He scanned the horizon one more time and then looked for a landmark off his left shoulder.

"See that rise with the bump in the middle over yonder?"

"Yes."

"Get off that paint and start walkin'. Head just to the left of that bump. When you get there, stop until you can see me comin' up on the other side. I'll take your horse and meet you around the back of that rise."

"Why?"

"It's easier for me to cover your walking tracks. If someone's on your trail they'll see that we met and then rode off together over that direction. There's a road over there that heads to Carlsbad. It's full of tracks and about a mile down the road passes a rock ledge. I'll get off the road at the rock ledge and head to the back side of that ridge where you'll be waiting. Then we'll go where no one will ever find you."

"How do I know you won't ride off with my horse?"

The poor girl had no one to trust. Jay didn't know what to say. He pointed at the rifle slung from her saddle. "You know how to use that?"

"Yes."

"Take it with you, but don't you shoot it unless those wolves are bearin' right down on you. Yell at 'em and throw rocks, but you just keep on walkin' until you see me on the other side."

"But how do I know I can trust you?"

"Didn't Rebecca say so?"

"Yes, but..."

"Well, that's all you've got to go on, and were runnin' out of time and options. Now, are you gonna get off that horse or not?"

***

"Get! Get, you!" Molly yelled as she hurled another stone from her rock pile at the snarling shadow that flashed from behind a creosote bush. She looked down at her dwindling supply of rocks. The wolves kept their distance while she was moving, but now that she had stopped where Jay White told her to wait, they were circling in, tightening their circle with alarming intensity.

How many were out there? The way they'd dart at her from different direction, there must be at least four. Her rifle was cocked and ready to fire for when they left her no choice.

"Get, you!" she screamed at a charging blur, turning around in time to lob another rock at a shadow coming from behind her. "Get! You too!"

A voice rang out from the darkness. "Molly Bell!"

Turning toward the sound of the voice she soon made out the outlines of a rider and two horses. She hesitated.

"It's me, Jay White."

"I'm over here."

She waived her rifle above her head and then reached down to pick up her last two rocks. Turning round in circles she didn't see any more darting shadows.

A sudden wave of exhaustion came over her as the two horses entered the clearing where she had piled her rocks an hour earlier. It was cold, and she started to shiver.

"You all right, miss? Don't cry. Here, you got to be cold."

White pulled a blanket off his horse and wrapped it around her. Feeling his strong arms against her shoulder she leaned into him and sobbed.

"It's OK, miss. Once we get to some lower ground we'll light a fire and have some food. The wolves won't have any interest with the two of us together. They're damn cowards when you come right down to it. We'll get some rest and then start off in the mornin'."

Jay walked her to her paint and helped her into the saddle. She wiped her eyes with one end of the blanket and checked another sob.

Soon they were headed down a gentle slope toward lower ground. She listened close for a sign of the wolves, but all she heard was the crunching of horse hooves on the sandy desert floor and the occasional snort from one of the two mounts.

"Thank you for helping me. Where are we going in the morning?"

"Miss Bell..."

"Please, call me Molly."

"Molly, God dropped you in my lap somehow. It may not be the smartest thing I've ever done, but when I was out there makin' us disappear off the trail, I promised Him I'd put you somewhere safe."

"Where is that?"

"A cavern, a cavern like you've never seen in your life or even read about in a book. I'm the only one who knows how to get in it, and it's so big it would take a hundred men months to find you in there even if they could find the entrance."

***

President Roosevelt rubbed the back of his neck and surveyed the stacks of papers on his desk. "Is there any good news in here?" he muttered to himself. He knew the answer.

Riots in Serbia, protest marches in London, ridiculous threats of war in the French and German press...had they all gone mad? He was afraid he knew that answer, too.

He wouldn't miss the papers, always stacks upon stacks. Reports from ambassadors, generals, and admirals pressing for more of something, politicians complaining about this or that...no, he wouldn't miss the papers. He strummed his finger on the hard wood that framed the leather writing surface. Taft would deal with it all. He'll make a fine President. No need to worry. The papers, no he'd not miss these stacks.

He sighed and murmured to himself. "A promise is a promise. No third term."

He looked toward a wall at the picture of the deck of the battleship *Connecticut*, the crew's football team proudly arrayed around one of the gun turrets of the flagship of the Great White

Fleet, which now steamed toward the gateway to the Mediterranean, the Suez Canal. A ragtag group of confident men in dark knit sweaters bearing a "C" across the chest stared back at him. Some had leather shoulder pads built into their uniforms. A few wore leather helmets. All projected bravado and grit. Their faces ran the gamut from English, to Irish, to Polish, to Russian, to German—American mutts through and through. Tough dogs...they gave him comfort.

"We may need you boys sooner than you think, only this won't be a game."

Connecticut, a good state name for a battleship...and what of New Mexico? He had no news from that front at all. New Mexico...

"You, sir!" he shouted at a shadow passing outside his office door.

"Yes, Mr. President?" A servant poking his head into the room.

"Do we have any of those peaches left from Carlsbad, New Mexico? You know, the big ones? They must be a pound each."

"I'm sorry, Mr. President, I believe your son ate the last few we had?"

"Few? There were a dozen or more yesterday."

"Yes, Mr. President. Is there something else I can get for you?"

"Humph. How about a torch so we can burn all these confounding papers off my desk?"

"I'm sorry, Mr. President, a torch?"

"All right, just bring me a cigar, one of the Havanas."

"You gonna burn your desk with a cigar, Mr. President?"

"No, not today, just recalling the spoils. War produces few benefits, you know...lots of heartache, but not much on the positive side."

"I'm sorry, Mr. President. I don't know."

He looked up and smiled. "A Havana, if you please."

The servant disappeared, leaving him to his papers.

"Lots of heartache." He looked back at the football players. "It won't be a game this time, lads."

***

Molly jerked her head up and opened her eyes. Jay was still there, riding ahead of her. She shifted in the saddle, finding a more comfortable spot. Her horse plodded on without noticing. She must try harder to stay awake. Surely they'd be there soon. Jay said if they left early they'd be there before nightfall.

The going was slow all day. Jay insisted on frequent direction changes and kept stopping to cover their tracks. They even doubled back a few times.

She started to doze again. Her head filled with images. There was a pretty Mexican girl she'd never seen before. The girl cleared tables at a cantina as men caked with dust leered at her. She saw an older priest sitting in a small office with a rat. The rat stared at the priest with two beady red eyes. Next she saw a sack of some kind in a hand cart. Why was Inspector Jenkins cutting at it with a knife? Then the image of a saddlebag pushed out all the others. The saddlebag smelled bad and had black flies as big as bumblebees around it. She opened the saddlebag and peered inside.

"You all right, Molly?"

"What? I'm sorry. I must have fallen asleep."

"Hmm." Jay looked back at her with a frown. "Must have been a bad dream."

Molly put her head down, resting her chin on her chest. "Must have been." She let her body rock with the steady motion of the horse. The fading sunlight warmed the back of her neck.

Jay nipped the next nap in the bud. "There's somethin' I been meanin' to ask you. Why do you carry a horny toad around in a cage?"

"He's my friend, Joshua. I talk to him."

"I suppose if I can talk to a horse, you can talk to a horny toad. I got somethin' else I been meanin' to ask you."

"Yes?"

"What makes you so valuable?"

"I beg your pardon."

"You know, that big bounty on your head. A man would never have to work another day in his life if he cashed in on it. He'd live high on the hog the rest of his days."

Molly pondered the question, wondering how to answer. "I'm not certain."

"What's your best guess, then?"

Molly thought on the question further. Jay was risking his life to help her. "I suppose it has to do with the black boxes."

"Black boxes?"

"It's kind of complicated. When I was a little girl I lived in New York City. One day I was playing in the park, and a man asked if I wanted to look into his black box. I don't know exactly what happened after that, but Mother said I went into a coma. To me, I was somewhere else. It was a terrible place. My doctor, a good man, he saved me from that place. Ever since then, well..."

"You don't want to talk about it. That's all right. I was just curious."

"Not the bad stuff, no."

"A black box, you say?"

As she struggled with how to explain she looked out at a familiar sight.

"We're here!"

Jay stopped his horse and turned around in the saddle. "What did you say?"

"I said, we're here. The cavern, it's just over that rise."

"How...how..." Jay stammered and stared at her with eyes open wide.

"I had a dream last night. We rode to this spot. Just over that rise, at the bottom of a gorge was a gaping hole in the ground, like God had stuck his finger in the earth."

"You had a dream?"

Before she could answer something else caught her eye. At first it looked like black smoke rising from the ground. It seemed alive, though, arching toward the sky. The wave continued up, followed by another wave and then another, first up and then streaming away. She sat mesmerized as the horizon filled with wave after swirling black wave.

She pointed even though Jay was now looking at the same thing. "What is it?"

"Bats."

"Bats?"

"Yep, that's how I found the cavern in the first place. You've got this rise here and then the next behind it. There's no reason to climb the first rise. Common sense says you ride around both. But if you do that, you don't see the cavern entrance in a gorge between the two rises. Unless you happen upon the bats leavin' just before dusk, you'd never find the thing. And you have to be close when it happens even then or you can't figure out where they come from. This here cavern's been hid forever, until I found it. Come on."

Jay led the way up the first rise, and then down a steep incline. At the bottom of the incline the cavern suddenly made itself known just as the last wave of bats circled up from the earth. Cool air wafted toward Molly from the gaping cavern entrance located on the side of the gorge between the two rises.

"It's just like I saw it. It's beautiful. How deep does it go?"

"Miles, as far as I can tell."

"Miles?"

"I haven't seen it all yet. I come and explore when I can. Someday this here cavern is gonna make me a rich man, cause of those bats."

"You're going to sell the bats?"

Jay let out a chuckle. "No. See, them bats eat bugs at night. In the mornin' they hang upside down in a part of the cavern near the entrance. Their droppings, guano, builds up below them in big piles. They been doin' it for hundreds of years. Only God knows how much guano is in that cave."

"You sell the guano? Who would buy it?"

"Fertilizer! That's the ticket. It's like mining for gold, only easier. Once I save up enough money, I'm gonna open up a guano mine. That's why I keep this place a secret. If anyone with the means finds out about it, they'll swoop in here and get to that guano before I can."

"A guano mine." Molly tried to imagine what one would look like.

"You'll see. I'm gonna be a rich man someday. They'll call this place White's Cavern. I'll build a city nearby to support the mine. I'll call it White's City. I'm gonna be big someday."

"I hope so, Jay. That would be wonderful."

"Yep." Jay sat and gazed at the cavern entrance. "Someday. But for now we're gonna stow you away in there, in a big room about a mile inside."

"A mile underground?"

"Oh, it ain't anywhere near the end. Like I said, I ain't figured the whole place out yet. I been learnin' all about caves, though. This one's full of big icicle rocks hangin' off the ceiling, called stalactites. Underneath each stalactite is an upside down icicle called a stalagmite. Some of those stalagmites are taller than three men standin' on top of each other."

"I can't wait to see it."

"We'll camp here tonight. In the morning I'll take you down inside."

"I'm glad you're going to be rich someday. That must be important to you."

"Yep. I tell you, no more heartache for me. Pretty soon I'll be on easy street. This cavern's my ticket."

"Why don't you turn me in? You'd be on easy street tomorrow." She wasn't sure why she said it, but knew she had to.

"What? Turn you in?"

Molly stared silently at him, trying to show no expression.

Jay turned his horse around to face hers. "Molly, the reward is for you dead."

Molly shivered but kept staring at him.

Jay squared his jaw and leaned forward in the saddle. "Thou shalt not kill. I don't care how much money they want for you. I can't abide killing. I told you last night, I promised God I'd put you somewhere safe. That cavern is the safest place on earth. A mile underground will put you thousands of miles from all those bad hombres out there lookin' for you.

"Molly Bell, you're gonna have to trust me on this. I may be the only friend you've got right now."

CHAPTER 10
THE DEAL

Jay White couldn't help it. She was a Spanish beauty if he'd ever seen one, and completely out of place, at least in his eyes. He couldn't stop staring at her from his seat at the bar.

The cantina was a small, dingy affair in a low, flat-roofed adobe. One little, shuttered window let just enough of the late afternoon light sneak in to save the proprietor the trouble of lighting a lamp. Keeping it shuttered also hid the worn-out nature of the place, although fresh air might do a lot to relieve the stale smell. Jay preferred bat guano, now that he thought about it.

The low light also meant that anyone opening the front door during the day would need a minute or two for their eyes to adjust before seeing what and who was inside. Jay liked that just fine, with all the hired guns spilling into the territory, some probably stopping at this very bar before heading out of Texas into the deserts of southeastern New Mexico. They'd never find Molly, though. Only he knew where she was, and his mouth was sealed shut. A hundred men couldn't pry it out of him.

He gazed again at the señorita. Her clean, white blouse gave her an angelic look in the low light as she busied herself with various chores, collecting the used glasses from the night before, wiping off tables, sweeping the dirt floor, and other tasks that needed to be done before the nighttime crowd arrived.

He took another sip of the bitter drink he'd been served. "Strong stuff," he muttered as he stared down into the nearly empty glass before clunking it on the grimy wood bar.

"You say somethin'?" the man behind bar barked.

"Naw, just pour me another." Jay looked back across the room, but the little señorita had slipped away again through the low doorway in the back of the bar. He started to get up to follow, but checked himself. "Say, what's that gal's name?"

"What gal?"

Dumb question, he thought. There were only four people in the whole dang room. There was him, the man behind the bar, an old man with his head down on one of the four wooden tables, either asleep or too drunk to keep his head up, or both, and the pretty girl who kept disappearing right when Jay was getting up the courage to say something to her.

"The little Mexican gal who keeps poppin' in and out."

"Ask her yourself," replied the bartender as she appeared again bustling through the little doorway and headed toward the bar.

"Maybe I will."

Jay straightened up on his stool and turned to face the doorway just as the lovely creature slipped onto the only other stool in the place, which, to his good fortune, or so he thought, was right next to his stool.

There she sat, within touching distance and looking right at him. She didn't say a word, but the look on her face jerked his heart clean out of himself. He almost pinched himself to see if he was still there, but he couldn't seem to bring himself to do anything but stare back, frozen in place.

She was even more beautiful up close. She had coal-black hair pulled by a red ribbon on one side and dangling down loose to her left shoulder on the other side. Her face was round and prominently displayed the most enticing mouth he'd ever laid eyes on. It was broad, rising slowly along its length, and then turned down slightly at the corners. She had a square chin that matched the square shoulders peeking above her white blouse. Below her brown, bare shoulders, just concealed by the blouse, were ample breasts riding high on her chest. She peered at him through dark brown eyes with a look that said she knew exactly what effect she had on him and was amused; a satisfied cat contemplating a trapped mouse.

He thought about turning back to the bar for another drink, but that seemed dumber than just sitting there in stunned silence. He hadn't thought of another girl since Rebecca. In fact, that's all he had thought about for more than a year now. Maybe this new gal was his salvation? Yes, for the first time in a while he did think of something else, the girl sitting in front of him, staring at him as he stared at her.

"Name's Jay," was all he could muster.

The corners of her mouth turned up slightly and she leaned in toward him, squinting, as if trying to get a better look. Both actions made him feel dizzy. He turned away and grabbed his glass.

"Dang, where's my manners, miss? Can I buy you a drink?"

She still just sat there, pulling him back in with her dark eyes.

He momentarily forgot to breathe, but fixed the error with an audible sigh that he quickly regretted.

"Habla Ingles?" he asked, not knowing what else to say.

"Thank you, I don't drink alcohol."

Her English was perfect with hardly an accent at all. Of course she wouldn't drink alcohol! Angels don't drink alcohol!

"It's OK if you want to, though. Everyone drinks in here, except for me."

Now it was Jay's turn to sit there silently. He was content just to look at her, branding her image into his mind, knowing he'd surely want to recall its details for a long time.

"Catalina."

"Sorry?"

"My name. Catalina."

Jay rolled the name around in his head. It sounded like a verse in a song. "Catalina, that's beautiful. I mean, I'm pleased to meet you."

She let out the prettiest laugh, tilting her head back, and then smiled at him. Her voice was low and soft. Her laugh relaxed him like a shot of good whisky.

"Why are you watching me, cowboy? Haven't you ever seen a girl cleaning up a bar before?"

"Well, don't know if I have, but darn sure never saw one as pretty as you."

Her broadening smile caused his heart to race. What should he say next? He suddenly felt very small even though he surely had six or seven inches on the gal. Her square shoulders made her look taller, though.

"You poor cowboys. You don't see anything but cows for weeks, and then you fall in love with the first woman you see."

"No, that ain't true. I mean, not the first woman thing. I mean..." Darn it, what did he mean? He took a sip from his glass to steady himself. "I mean, I'm pleased to meet you, and would like to see you again sometime."

"Are you hungry?"

"Beg pardon?"

She paused and frowned at him. "Are you hungry? I'm getting ready to have dinner."

"Oh, thank you kindly. I believe I am."

"Follow me."

Jay found himself pulled in her wake through the little doorway and into a small back room. She motioned to a wooden table hardly big enough for the two chairs that surrounded it. He parked himself in one that allowed him to watch the girl as she dipped some stew from a kettle into two bowls.

She was beautiful from every direction. From the back, the white blouse tapered down along her waist and disappeared into a red skirt that had white lattice trimming at the hem. She wore a white apron over the front of the dress tied with a perfect bow in the back that rested above her hips, like a store-bought gift box.

She turned around, placed the bowls and two spoons on the table and sat opposite him. She leaned her head sidewise and gave him a quizzical look. His heart fluttered.

"Will you say grace?"

"Oh, grace, yes." Jay cleared his throat. "Heavenly Father, please bless this meal we are about to eat." Was that the best he could do? A sense of shame washed over him. He surely wasn't making a good impression.

"Amen."

She picked up the spoon and scooped up a bite. Jay watched transfixed as she placed the spoon in her mouth. The downturned corners of her mouth moved slightly with every chew.

"You're not very hungry?"

"Oh, no, I mean, I'm sorry." Jay stuck a spoon in his bowl and took a bite. He felt foolish. Why was he flustered? She was just a girl in a bar. He looked down at his bowl and took another bite. But she wasn't just a girl, she was the prettiest thing he'd ever seen.

"Where are you from, cowboy?"

"A ranch up near Carlsbad."

"Carlsbad, New Mexico? That's two days' hard ride from here. What brings you to Toyah, Texas?"

"Provisions…they gave me a list. I already got what I need and head back in the mornin'."

"You're staying at the boarding house down the street?"

"Yes, ma'am. I took a bath and come right over here."

"To see me." She smiled.

"Well, I didn't know you were here, but I'm darned glad, I mean, I'm pleased to meet you." He looked back down at his bowl and shoveled in another bite.

"What's your full name, cowboy?"

"Well, it really ain't Jay at all. Truth be told, my name's James Larkin White, but my friends call me Jay. I guess cause James starts with a J…I don't know."

"James Larkin White," she parroted back slowly.

He liked the sound of his name in her mouth. She said it like she owned it, and that didn't bother him one bit.

"I like James. Reminds me of a friend of mine. He's named James too. Can I call you James and still be your friend?"

He wanted to say "You can call me anything you like," but thought better of it. "That would be just fine, Miss... What's the rest of your name?"

The sound of the door opening in the dining room intruded into their conversation.

"Catalina! Véngate!" shouted the bartender.

She stood up and wiped her mouth with her apron. "I have to go, James. You finish and then let yourself out the back." She pointed at a wooden door that led outside the cantina. "There's a big elm tree behind the boarding house."

She bent down and kissed him softly on the cheek, the corner of her mouth touching the corner of his.

"Meet me there at ten tonight. It gets too rowdy in here for me after that, and you can take me for a walk, James."

Whatever wind she hadn't knocked out of him with the kiss was certainly gone with the utterance of his name. He sat stunned as he watched her head for the dining room and disappear from view.

"Catalina," he said to himself as he touched the corner of his mouth and then abruptly gasped for air.

***

"Now, that's different."

The stocky mare champed on the bit and shook her head in seeming response.

"We're almost there," Mary Cunningham softly replied to her mount, patting it on the neck.

It *was* different. Even at this distance the silhouette of the sprawling ranch compound outside of Alamogordo was clearly different than she remembered. For starters there was the new tower at the center of the compound. The exterior fence was taller and more substantial. There was no activity in sight, no familiar smoke from the various cooking stoves that seemed to burn non-stop when she and the Bells had sought refuge here years before.

"Well, I've come this far. Let's go see." She nudged the mare with her boots, and it plodded on toward the ranch.

As they got nearer Mary thought she saw movement in the tower. Closer on she noted a lone figure peering over the fence near the entry gate, a man in a straw hat that curled up tightly along the sides of his head. Then appeared the barrel of a gun pointed in her direction. She held her left hand out to her side with her palm out and fingers spread.

She forced herself to look straight on and not at that barrel as it got larger and more distinct with every clomping step her horse took toward the gate. A few whiffs of smoke came from the main building. Another man emerged from the building and walked toward the gate. A rifle poked through an opening in the tower.

She and the mare arrived at the gate at the same time as the man from the main building. He had a broad chest and bald head, with beads of sweat built up on his brow. The man with the rolled straw hat leveled his barrel squarely at her heart.

"What's your business, ma'am?" barked the bald man.

"I'm Mary Cunningham. I've come to see the Bells, Molly and her mother."

"Are you trying to be funny?"

"I lived with them for a while, here, a couple of years ago. Is the foreman about, by chance?"

"I'm the foreman, and I asked you a question."

A commotion from the doorway of the main building caught Mary's eye.

"Mary!" shouted a woman running toward them. "Mary Cunningham! God be praised! You're safe! Open the gate!"

"You heard what Mrs. Bell said, Billy," the bald man shouted at the man with the rolled hat. "Open the gate."

"God be praised, Mary! Have you any news about Molly? Where is Doctor Cunningham?"

***

Stalactites jiggled and swayed above the cavern from the flicker of the diminutive fire. Smoke curled up and out of view toward the invisible ceiling far above. Molly Bell warmed her hands and turned the stick spit skewered with her meal, the last of the rattlesnake meat that Jay White had left for her during his previous supply drop.

The wood was gone. This was her last fire until the next drop.

"Maybe he'll come early," she said wistfully to Job, the fat stalagmite squatting across the fire from her. She no longer had Pluck or Joshua to talk to. Jay took her paint to a remote homestead of a trusted friend, and she let Joshua loose at the mouth of the cave when she first arrived. Jay was right. A horned toad would never survive in this chilly damp cavern. She looked for Joshua every time she emerged from the cave entrance for the supplies Jay would drop on occasion, but he never appeared. All she had was Job, silent, patient, Job.

She grabbed the spit and gingerly poked at the meat with her finger. Satisfied, she rested the spit on a nearby rock to give the meat a moment to cool.

Yes, this was the last fire until his next visit.

"Jay left plenty to keep us going. Look here, Job, candles, matches, oil for the lantern, and food. This bread will last a while now that the meat is gone. That rattlesnake was six feet long or more." She pointed at meat on the spit.

"It's longer than the last one he left. There must be a lot of them slithering around up there." She looked wistfully toward the cave ceiling, far too high to be seen with the light from her fire. The stalactites appeared to float above her, unanchored as they receded into the blackness of their thickening bases.

"I like them, though. It's good meat." She poked it again. "I think it's ready now." She pulled a chunk off the spit, blew on it, and took a bite.

"I wish he'd bring more firewood. It's never enough to last until his next drop. I know, Job." She held her hand up to shush him. "He can't fit much in the bundle he leaves in that hole near the cave entrance. I'll check it again tonight. Maybe I won't be disappointed this time."

Most nights she was disappointed. Job knew that. At least he'd heard enough about it that he should. But maybe this time she'd feel the cloth bundle deep in the hole and pull it out to find a bounty left for her.

"I'd offer you some snake, Job, but I know you're never hungry." She pondered that fact for a moment. What was it like to never be hungry? "I bet the cook at the ranch would make something special with snake."

She felt a pain of longing in her chest and clenched her jaw.

"How long, Job? Mother has to be worried to death. Papa's probably back at the ranch by now. I wonder who else is at the ranch. They'll all be looking for me. No, don't get all gloomy on me, Job. My cowboys are out looking for me. So're Mick and Papa." She sniffled and brushed back a tear.

"I miss them something awful."

She pulled off another piece of meat and chewed slowly, not feeling particularly interested in swallowing.

"I have this feeling, Job. I don't know how to explain it, but they all need my help. All of them, Mother, Papa, Mick, even Inspector Jenkins, even people I don't know, they all need me."

She peered at the blackness in every direction. "But I can't help anyone in here!" Her shout echoed about, reverberating back and forth until dying with a last soft "here."

She let out a sigh and pulled the last piece of meat off the spit.

"It's like I'm back in the box, this time with food, but all alone. Heck of a deal." She wondered which was worse, having food with no friends, or friends with no food. She decided not to dwell on the question.

At least Jay White knew where she was.

"I told you already, Job. Jay will keep his mouth shut until things calm down. Then he heads to the ranch when no one is watching and lets my folks know where I am. He can't go now. He'd be intercepted when he got near to the ranch and found out. He says men, bad men, would kill him to find out where I am. Remember, Job, I told you that yesterday and the day before and the day…"

Perhaps she should stop trying to convince Job—thick headed piece of rock. It did help to talk about it, though.

Jay won't tell. Thank God for Jay. He always left little encouraging notes, passages from the Psalms.

I called upon the Lord in distress; the Lord answered me, and set me in a larger place. The Lord is on my side; I will not fear: what can man do unto me?

If I say, Surely the darkness shall cover me, even the night shall be light about me.

Cast thy burden upon the Lord, and He shall sustain thee; He shall never suffer the righteous to be moved.

She had lots to be thankful for. The water was plentiful from pools so clear that it was hard to tell there was anything wet there. The deep cellar temperature was tolerable with the blankets Jay had left her. The food was sufficient. It was the darkness…

Molly shivered at the sight of her small fire dying. The darkness—the relentless, silent, total darkness—it was unnerving. Once the fire died or the lantern or candle extinguished, the darkness took the stage, so absolute that she couldn't see her own hand held inches from her nose. It was complete and total nothingness.

Could God see through such enveloping gloom? Did he know where she was once light gave way to impenetrable black? She was a mile underground. How deep was hell? Could God see her? He must. Surely he could.

Is this what hell is like? Nothing? Separated from everyone you loved? Separated from God?

"No, He can see me! I know it!" she shouted at Job.

"Yea, the darkness hideth not from thee, but the night shineth as the day; the darkness and the light are both alike to thee."

Job shrugged from a final flicker of her exhausted fire.

***

Jay White pulled out his pocket watch and tilted the glass face toward the moonlight. Seventeen minutes after ten, only two minutes later than the last time he checked. He held the watch to his ear and listened to the steady, metallic clicking. After standing under the elm for forty minutes, all he'd encountered was one of the town's dogs, who wandered out of the darkness, sniffed his leg, and then wandered back into the darkness.

"I guess she ain't comin'," he mumbled.

He took off his Stetson for one last look toward the side of the boarding house nearest the saloon. He shrugged and put his hat back on.

"Hello, cowboy."

He half-jumped and spun around in the direction of the voice. Only the fact that it was a woman's voice kept his pistol in its holster.

"Dang, Catalina, you shouldn't be sneakin' up on me like that."

"Maybe you shouldn't be so easy to sneak up on." She took his hand and tugged him toward her. "Come on, James, let's walk."

He dutifully obeyed, feeling like a lassoed puppy.

"Did you miss me?"

"I reckon I did. How long were you standin' behind me?"

"I said I'd meet you at ten."

"You weren't here at ten!"

Her laughter came down like cool rain. He felt foolish, but the warmth of her hand in his suddenly made nothing else matter. The night sky twinkled down on them. It seemed infinitely big. Jay took in a deep breath of the sweet air and gave her hand a slight squeeze.

"That sky's awful pretty tonight," he offered.

She squeezed his hand back and moved closer to him.

"How long you been workin' in that place?"

"The cantina? Not long. How long have you been a cowboy?"

"All my life, I guess. I started in Texas and then moved up north to New Mexico. How long you been in Texas?"

"Not long. I like New Mexico better."

"You from there?"

"I'm from a lot of places. I just like New Mexico better than Texas."

Their pace was slow and steady. If there was a destination, he'd just as soon they got there as late as possible, as long as he could hold her hand.

"Do you like being a cowboy?"

"I suppose. Not sure what else I'd do, never known anything else. It can get awful lonely sometimes. But I love the range. Especially when we drive the herd. Just me, God, and hundreds of cows. Them days are special."

"You like the cattle drives? Seems like a hardship to me."

"Sure do. When you add it all up, the worst part on the trail is the loss of sleep. Sometimes I have to rub tobacco juice in my eyes to stay awake. You start to see things that probably ain't there."

Her grip on his hand gently tightened. "Is that really the worst part?"

"Well, the rest of it is pretty rewarding. I like riding on the swing best. You know…the fellers on the side of the herd. Trail riders get the dust, and the point makes you feel all alone, with nothin' in front of you. Swing, though, you can see the whole herd spread out, rollin' like a fat snake across the plain."

"I hear the food is terrible."

"I don't know 'bout that. Toward evening Cookie unhitches his wagon and points the wagon tongue north, based on the way he sees the sun, stars, and moon. That way the trail boss knows which way it is without havin' to think about it. Cookie starts up the cook fire, and then we get beans with salt pork and hardtack, sometimes potato and dried fruit, too. Dang near anything tastes better under the stars."

"I bet I'm a better cook than Cookie."

"Is that a fact?"

"My pies are the best. I hear they have peaches around Carlsbad. I make the best peach pie this side of heaven."

"Is that a fact?" That was dumb to say it twice. He struggled with what he should say. "Well, them days on the range are pretty special." He should have kept his mouth shut if that was the best he could do. Why didn't he say he'd like some of that pie?

"Do you have many of those special days?"

He thought harder about his answer this time. He imagined a deep ravine ahead. Jump it, now or never.

"Not like today." He left the ground headed over the ravine.

She looked down a little and gripped his hand tighter.

"I bet you say that to all the pretty girls in Carlsbad."

"Catalina, I never seen a girl as pretty as you." He was mid-air over the ravine now, wondering if he'd make the other side or fall into the abyss.

She pulled his hand behind her back, placing it on her waist. He felt the relief of landing on solid ground.

"What's the Triple X like?"

"The ranch? Wait, who told you I was with the Triple X?"

"I bet there's a lot of things you don't remember telling me at dinner. The way you kept looking at me with those big doe eyes, I wasn't sure you heard half of what I said."

"I suppose you're right. I'm sorry."

She let out a laugh. "I'm teasing, James. Everybody knows who comes and goes in this little town."

He must seem like an idiot. Why couldn't he say the right thing? He didn't need a whole ravine, but maybe there was a small ditch somewhere he could hide in for a while. He felt her gently squeeze his waist. He looked at her face, and the smile she returned brought a rush of blood to his head. He looked away to keep from wobbling.

"Why do you work in a cantina? You're too darn pretty to work there."

She stopped and turned to face him. Closing the distance between them, she pressed her chest against his.

"You don't want to know too much about me, cowboy. I'll make you a deal." She reached up and pulled his face toward hers.

His heart stopped as her mouth touched his. Her lips were the softest thing he'd ever felt. His entire body relaxed as they kissed.

Exactly how long they kissed he wasn't sure. It was as if he melted into her. He didn't want it to ever stop, but it did.

She smiled up at him. Standing on her toes she brought that smile closer to his. Her breath was sweet milk. She stared at him with an unflinching gaze, holding his attention to her brown eyes.

"Here's the deal." The look on her face was one of confidence. She wasn't offering a deal, she was enforcing terms of a surrender. "If you want to know something about me that I'm inclined not to tell you, you have to kiss me first. But it goes both ways. If I want to know something that you're not inclined to tell me, then I have to kiss you. But then you have to tell me, just like I'll tell you."

She pulled his face toward hers again.

The second kiss was as long as the first. His mind was lost in her. He thought of nothing but Catalina and melted again.

She pulled away, holding both his hands and looking him squarely in the face.

"Deal, James?"

"Heck," he stopped for a second to catch his breath. "I'd be dang fool not take that deal."

"Come on, cowboy. Let's walk for a while longer."

She turned and tugged on his hand, and again he followed, thinking of questions to ask, and hoping she'd have some, too. He'd tell her anything.

***

Mary Cunningham held her mug with both hands as she gazed absentmindedly at the flickering flames dancing in the cavernous fireplace of the ranch's main building.

"More tea, my dear?"

"No, thank you, Mrs. Bell. I'm sorry, I got lost in the fire. It feels safe here, at the ranch. I've not felt that in a while. It's a fine feeling."

"I'm glad you feel that way. I understand." Mrs. Bell took a sip from her own mug of tea. "You were saying about Doctor Cunningham?"

Mary breathed deeply over the steaming open end of the mug and turned her attention back to Mrs. Bell, who sat patiently next to her.

"It's that rat. I'm convinced of it. After it bit Sam things began to change. Hardly noticeable at first, little bouts of irritation, disorientation, as if he'd become really lost in thought, but then it became worse. He would shake and get a strange look on his face. Sam fought it. I could tell he was trying to control something, but I don't know what. I held him and stroked his face. That seemed to help, and calm would return.

"Try to get a doctor to see the doctor. Hah!" Mary said at once both bitterly and fearfully. She took a sip of the tea, and then continued quietly. "I did try."

"I know you did."

"He wasn't himself. That's not the Sam I know." She wiped a tear from her cheek.

"We had a fight. He became enraged and shoved me. He actually shoved me. Can you believe it? Even now those words seem so unreal. He cried when he realized what he had done. When he'd dropped to sleep from exhaustion, I went to a suffragette meeting. I never should have gone. When I got back, Sam wasn't there. The room was a mess, ransacked. I don't know if Sam put up a struggle, or maybe, maybe…"

Mrs. Bell put her arms around her. "There, there, Mary. You go on and cry. Let it out. You're safe here."

"I didn't know what else to do. I left town and contacted the inspector. He told me to come here."

"Of course, dear, and I'm so glad you did. It's all right. Here." Mrs. Bell handed her a handkerchief.

"Please forgive me. I'm being so selfish." Mary wiped her eyes and then her nose. "Here I'm worried about a grown man, and you don't know where your daughter is. I'm so sorry. I should be of help here, not a burden."

Mrs. Bell let out a warm chuckle. "You don't know how much you've helped already. Your husband means the world to me. He saved my little Molly many times, first the bouts of asthma and then that bedeviling coma. I can never repay him, but sheltering you in your time of need...I thank God for the chance to do it.

"A blessing, that's what you are to me. Now we can pray together. We'll both pray for Molly and for Doctor Cunningham. We'll double our power of prayer." Mrs. Bell smiled.

"You're quite kind. I wish I knew where they were. It troubles me that there was no note from Sam when I came back to the hotel. If he left on his own accord he would have left a note, at least the Sam I know would have done that. He was so certain that he was bringing danger down on both of us, that it was all his fault. I can see him leaving in order to draw the danger away from me, but not without a note."

Mary took a sip of tea, letting the fire dry her face. "Is there nothing we can do beyond prayer?"

"The inspector says to stay put, so we stay put. Besides, it's been my experience that nothing..." She paused, gently lifting Mary's chin to look directly into her eyes. "Is *beyond* prayer."

Mary closed her eyes, took a deliberate deep breath, then looked again, smiling gratefully at Mrs. Bell as she nodded her assent.

"Mary, God knows where they are, and it is to *Him* we shall address our prayers, steadfast in the knowledge that your arrival here at the ranch has answered one of mine."

The two sat in quiet contemplation before the fireplace with Mrs. Bell holding Mary in her arms like a child.

Mary broke the silence. "They're both alive. I know it. I don't know how, but I know it."

CHAPTER 11
BACK IN ACTION

Sam Cunningham kept his head down, attempting to blend in with the throng of people working their way toward the exit from the pier. The steamer from New York to Liverpool had disgorged its passengers, of which Sam was but one.

Thus far all went according to plan. He had escaped from Dallas on a train headed east without anyone, not even Mary, knowing what he was up to. After Mary left for her suffragette meeting, he woke to find himself alone in their hotel room. He quickly packed a few items that wouldn't be missed, disposed of the rat, and tidied up the room. The rat part was easy, since it was lying limp with no heartbeat when he checked the cage. Before getting rid of it, Sam took a blood sample from the rat. He placed the sample with the packed items, in the hopes that he could analyze it later. He left Mary a note telling her he loved her, not to worry, and that he would return when the danger had passed.

From New York he booked the first passage to England. Other than the occasional bout of what he'd settled on calling his "rage shivers," all of which, fortunately, occurred while locked alone in his cabin, the passage was uneventful. Now he merely needed to work his way to the train station for a trip to London. Then he would report to Inspector Jenkins, who would no doubt be surprised to see him.

He felt hopeful. Mary was safe now that he was no longer near her. The inspector would know what to do next. He always did. It was odd, though, that Jenkins never responded to his urgent cables for help. Time would heal his shivers, he hoped. If not, the medical care in London was the best in the world, even if his American colleagues hated to admit it. Either way, he'd recover and return to Mary a new man, once the inspector calmed the waters and made the world safe again.

The crowd slowed as it neared the pinch point of the pier to the docks. He pushed on, shoulder to shoulder with those around him, clutching his small bag of clothing and personal items he'd purchased in New York before boarding the big liner that sped him across the Atlantic. As he approached the plank crossing over to the docks, it started.

"No, not now," he whispered. His mouth felt dry and his throat began to constrict. He pushed through the crowd toward a railing on the pier. He dropped his bag and grasped the railing with both hands. He closed his eyes and tried to ignore his surroundings. His arms began to quiver. He mustn't lose control, not now in broad daylight in front of hundreds of witnesses. He mustn't draw attention to himself.

"Calm, calm," he thought. He focused on the image of Mary stroking his forehead. He listened for her voice, pushing out the noise of the dockyards. "Calm, Sam, calm. Everything is fine. Stay calm, my love."

His body shook against the rail. Stay in control. "Calm, Sam. It's all right." He focused on her face and tried to let its familiarity fill his mind. Her eyes smiled down on him. Her familiar face filled his mind. He smelled her hair and felt the warmth of her breath. "You're all right, Sam. I love you, and you can make it through this."

He wanted to scream. He wanted to strike. His body pulled hard against the rail, trying to break free, but his hands held fast. Sweat rolled down his temples. His face was on fire.

"Sam, look at me. Look into my eyes. Calm, my kind husband." She ran her fingers through his hair and kissed his cheek. His arms began to relax. The shivering subsided. He opened his eyes and looked out over the water. A slight breeze kicked up, cooling his face.

"I made it. Thank you, darling Mary," he murmured.

She'd pulled him back again.

He gathered himself, straightening his jacket sleeves and picking up his bag, and returned to the mass of passengers pressing toward the dock. Crossing a flat plank, he found himself on the solid ground of the Liverpool port.

The sea of humanity thinned only slightly, but the crowd was now a more diverse mixture of well-dressed passengers, dock workers in greasy, stained clothing, and various supervisors, businessmen, sailors, and government officials. The throng no longer moved in one monolithic procession, but with each individual having a distinct destination that frequently conflicted with others going different directions. The air was filled with a maddening cacophony of horns, shouts, clanging machinery, whistles, clattering wheels, the cry of gulls swooping overhead, and boots and shoes of all sizes striking the ground with different rhythms.

He felt a hand pull on his left arm.

"Doctor Cunningham!"

He turned to see a man with a pockmarked face and bulbous nose. His eyes were half covered by a bowler hat pulled forward on his head.

"Doctor Cunningham, I'm glad to find you."

"I beg your pardon. Who are you?" he shouted back.

Another hand seized his right arm. He turned to see a second man with a bowler cap pulled forward on his face.

"Not to worry, Doctor. We'll take care of you from here," replied the first stranger as the two men began to steer him through the crowd.

"Gentlemen, I insist you identify yourselves!"

"Not to worry," the bulbous-nosed man repeated. "Inspector Jenkins sent us. No time to lose. Just a bit further on."

The two men tightened their grip on his arms and pressed on determinedly.

"Wait just a moment, please!"

Cunningham's plea only seemed cause the two men to push him on harder.

"Not to worry, Doctor. Just a bit further…almost there."

Sam looked about frantically. No one paid attention to the three men roughly working their way toward a side street. His bag dropped to the ground. They had to stop. "I need that bag. There are important medical items in it!"

The two men ignored him and pushed on. He needed to confirm their identity. He tried to hold back, but the pair lifted while they pushed such that his feet had little traction with the brick dockside.

As they rounded a corner a black carriage with drawn, black curtains came into view. Outside the carriage stood another stranger with a bowler pulled down over his eyes.

He had to confirm these were Jenkins's men. "Can any of you tell me where I might find the Saint George's Dragon pub?" Cunningham blurted out.

The two men made no response as they continued to push him toward the waiting coach. The third man opened the carriage door as they approached. The stench of rotten eggs poured forth from the coach's dark interior.

"No! Help!"

A hand covered his mouth. He struggled and kicked, but all three men were on him now. A sack pulled over his head brought darkness as he was thrust into the carriage. He felt more hands pulling him in. The noise of the dockyards muted suddenly with the hard close of the coach's door. He shortened his breath, trying to fight off the sulfuric stench that burned his nostrils.

"Doctor Cunningham, so good of you to drop in. I've been expecting you. How was your trip?"

***

"So this is the inner sanctum, home of the chaplain of Saint George the Martyr Parochial School."

Father Cornish closed his roll-top desk and spun his chair around to face the man standing in his doorway.

"Mr. Aston. Please, have a seat." He pointed at the only other piece of furniture in the diminutive room, a chair set against the wall near the door.

Aston ignored the offer and, leaning his lanky frame into the room, remained standing. "I arrived well before my time, so I inquired if I might come up to your office. I hope you don't mind, Father."

"Not in the slightest. I don't have many visitors."

Aston glanced quickly about the room and then ran his forefinger downward across the bridge of his nose until he squashed the tip of his nose flat against his face.

"You don't approve?" Cornish inquired.

"A bit small for an office, don't you think? More like a broom closet. I would think a priest of your seniority would deserve so much more."

"I'm a school chaplain, not the bishop."

"And perhaps that is what escapes my approval."

"You don't approve of school chaplains?"

"No, I'm sure they have their place. I don't approve of you being relegated to such a role. You don't aspire to a higher calling?"

"I'm not sure there is a higher calling than ministering to young men."

"Do you minister to them here?" Aston waved his hand about the room.

"On occasion."

"Do you take their confession?"

"I listen to them. I hear their concerns. They express their fears."

"Ah!" Aston exclaimed as he pointed at Cornish. "Now that would be interesting. Tell me, what do boys fear?"

"All manner of things. Failure, abandonment, what they see in their dreams."

"Dreams. Do you dream, Father?"

"Of course."

Aston rubbed his chin, appearing momentarily lost in thought. "My mind was once quite imaginative during sleep. My dreams were filled with strange creatures in unfamiliar places when I was a child. As I matured those images slowly left me. Today, as best I can tell, I dream not at all. I fall asleep, I awake, and my mind picks up where it left off with nothing having happened in between. Do you find that odd?"

"There are many things about you that I find odd, Mr. Aston."

James smiled and shook his head. "We need to get you back in the action, don't you think?"

"Meaning what?"

"You were once a rector of a sizable parish. Father Tate felt you were on track for great things in the Church, certainly a bishopric was in the cards."

"If you don't mind, Mr. Aston, I sense that this conversation is heading in a direction that is suppressing my appetite. I'm quite content serving as a chaplain for a boys' school. I take great satisfaction in shepherding this flock. They are fascinating creatures and deserve much more than I can give them, but I try."

"Yes, fascinating creatures, I quite agree. Let's chat about them, shall we?"

"The boys?"

"Do you find them of varying ability, such that you can distinguish the capabilities of one over the other?"

"Certainly, they're no different from any other collection of men. Some are athletically oriented, some are more academically focused, while some are quite artistic, just as one would expect."

"I assume some are bright and some dull?"

"All the boys here are quite accomplished, but some do stand above the others."

"Exactly. I'll wager there are even a few who seem to hold great promise, boys whom you can envision matriculating to greatness, even someone who may be quite influential someday."

"Yes, I'm certain we have a few of those as well."

"Ah! Here is what I'm most interested to learn. How accurate do you think a prediction of such a future might be?"

"You mean a future of great influence or achievement?"

"I'll provide an example to clarify my question. Take the late, great Arthur Wellesley—Duke of Wellington, slayer of Napoleon's empire, Prime Minister. He was born to a modest family. His father had little money and no position to speak of. Yet, he rose to the top of his race and became one of those singular men of history who change the course of the seemingly inevitable. He bent the trajectory of the human experience.

"Was it predictable? During his brief stint at Eton, if you had met the young Arthur Wellesley as a boy, could you have predicted such capacity for greatness?"

Aston's eyes flashed, and he waved his arms about as if conducting the grand climax of a symphony in Cornish's little office.

"And what of Lord Nelson? He was born to a parson in a rectory, sixth of nearly a dozen children. Yet all of England wept at the loss of their naval hero at Trafalgar. Had you been his chaplain at his grammar school in North Walsham, what would you have seen in him? Could you, a mere mortal, predict his importance to a nation?

"What of Oliver Cromwell? Benjamin Disraeli? The Duke of Marlborough? All were men with modest beginnings who rose to great prominence, changing the course of history along the way. Was it predictable?"

"These hypotheticals have stirred my appetite." Cornish glanced at his pocket watch. "I won't be missed if we left a bit early."

"Do you have one among you, here, in this school? Think on it. You may be nurturing the next Marlborough."

"I suppose it's possible."

"Yes, but would you know? Can you know?"

"I doubt one can predict greatness with certainty. There are so many factors that might intervene, so many moments of chance that must be seized or avoided. Some of these young men may not even live to adulthood due to health issues or accidents beyond their control."

Aston's face contorted suddenly. His shoulders trembled and he smiled wildly. Then a look of rehearsed serenity washed over his face, but his body became stiff with tension. It was unsettling. Cornish was at a loss as to what to say next.

"No, I won't be missed." Cornish rose to his feet, stuffing the pocket watch in his waistcoat. "Come now, I believe a bit of supper would do us both good."

A calmness appeared to descend upon Aston. He looked at his hands, settling his gaze in the direction of the two angry moles on the back of the right one.

"Yes, Father, I believe you're right, on both accounts."

***

"Inspector, I beg your pardon, sir."

Jenkins glanced up from the stack of photographs on his desk to the officer standing at his door.

"Fred Miller has arrived. You asked to be notified. Shall I send him in?"

Jenkins nodded, and the officer disappeared down the hall. He looked back at the photographs he'd been studying—hard men all, the worst London had to offer. He wondered which of these villains might have shot Jim Talbot in the arm. Where was the lad? Why couldn't they find him?

Jenkins shook his head as he pushed back from his desk. He hastily retrieved a bottle of scotch, poured two glasses, and set the bottle with the glasses prominently in the center of his desk.

No sooner had he returned to his chair when the familiar jaunty steps of Fred Miller came tapping down the hall.

"Mr. Miller, so good to see you. Please." The inspector pointed to the chair in front of his desk.

"If you only knew, sir. It's marvelous to see you as well." Fred took the offered seat, scooting it closer to the desk. His signature smile filled his weather-beaten face.

"You look tired."

"I am. It is good to see you, sir. I came as quickly as I could."

"I know. May I offer you a drink?"

"I've done a lot of thinking, Inspector. Where are my manners? I'm sorry to barge in on you unannounced. I came straight away, but, may I take a moment of your time? I have much to tell you, but there's something I must know first."

"Certainly, I'm at your disposal. I'm glad you came straightaway. Shall we toast your return?" Jenkins picked up one of the glasses, holding it in midair.

"That's very kind of you. Sorry…and rather rude of me." Fred paused and stared at the other glass sitting on the table before looking back at the inspector. "Perhaps another time."

"Then I'll drink to your health." Jenkins raised the glass and took a satisfying swig. He set the glass back down and smiled. "It's quite good, very smooth. Are you certain you won't join me, Fred?"

"Thank you, perhaps another time."

"As you wish. I have things to tell you as well, but first, what is it you must know?"

Miller sat back and cleared his throat.

"I heard you say just now, 'I know.'" Fred shifted in his chair and again cleared his throat. "How much do you know?"

"About?"

"Starting with me. Where I've been, what I've been through, how I got here, to London, to be sitting now in your office."

"Is that all?"

"No, I need to know why. Why me? And why aren't I dead? And why…? Well, let's start with that."

Jenkins reached for his glass and downed the contents. He let out a satisfied sigh and set the empty glass next to the full one still displayed on his desk. Fred sat staring at him, seeming to take no notice of the full glass before him.

"Very well. Yes, I know where you've been." Jenkins glanced at the full glass. "Do you mind? I'd hate to see it go to waste."

Fred nodded, but continued staring at him with a blank expression giving no indication of what was on his mind, which was quite unusual for Fred.

Jenkins picked up the second glass and took a sip.

"On a night some months past, you were assaulted in Manchester. You were quite drunk at the time, which had become your habit. You were rescued, in the nick of time I might add, and secured to a remote island. Eventually you escaped the island and made *straightaway* to London, and me."

Jenkins took another sip. Fred's hand twitched slightly, but he maintained his quiet stare.

"Now what else was there? Yes, why aren't you dead?"

"What do you mean by 'rescued'?"

"That partially answers the question on the table. A few days before you were assaulted I had a hunch that your 'luck' was about to run out. I sent my best man to wait and watch. Sure enough, two assassins picked you off the street. As they were dragging you to a dark corner of the city, one hit you in the head as a prelude to something more permanent. The head-bashing forced my man to act. He disposed of the assassins and took you under his care."

Jenkins took another relaxed sip and set the glass down on his desk.

"Upon my instructions he transported you to the care of a shepherd, a reliable Welshman."

"Welsh!" Fred's body jerked as if suddenly stabbed by the shepherd's own sharp staff. "No, he was Spanish!"

"He does speak Spanish quite well, that much is true."

Fred sat back in the chair. A look of bewilderment washed over his face, revealing the more familiar Fred once again.

"Then, *you* told him to leave me there alone."

"No, that was his decision, based on his own judgement. He decided it was time."

"Time to test me, like you're testing me now." Fred pointed at the glass on the table.

"You appear to have passed." Jenkins smiled and raised the glass in toast before taking another sip.

Fred lowered his head, shaking it side to side.

"Why? Why aren't I dead? Have you been keeping me alive?"

"Ah, that. No, certainly not...at least not until the last episode with the two assassins."

"I don't understand."

"No, of course, how could you? You were right, though. You were being kept alive. Not by us, but by them."

"You mean the man with the black box?"

"Not exactly, and therein lies the answer. It took some time to solve the puzzle, but the fact that you were kept alive provided the clue."

"He said as much himself. I was to be his witness. I couldn't die. I was to watch mankind destroy itself and testify to his sacrifice. I was to be the 'Mark,' the chronicler for the man with the black box."

"So you were led to believe. Or, more importantly, so I was led to believe."

"I don't understand."

"Let's assume for a moment that the man with the black box is not who we thought he was. What if he answered to another, who actually pulls the strings? Imagine the man with the black box as the puppet. Wouldn't the puppet master be the one we really want?"

"What are you saying?"

"I'm saying the man with the black box was a distraction, a cover for the real villain. As long as the real villain remained hidden, you had to be kept alive to appear to fulfill 'the prophecy,' the prophecy that you were the chronicler of the life and sacrificial death of the man with the black box. Once I determined that the man with the black box was a distraction, you no longer served that purpose. Suddenly you went from being protected to being hunted. When I sensed I had stumbled upon the truth, I also sensed that you were, as a consequence, in mortal danger.

"Nonetheless, now you're here, in my office, and I'm glad for it. Not only that, but I need your help."

"You need *my* help?"

"Indeed. There has been a development relating to your best friend Mr. Aston."

"James? He's alive?"

"Indeed."

"Where is he? Wait. Before you tell me," Fred took a deep breath. "I can't help you."

"And why do you come to that conclusion?"

"You know why, Inspector. Look at me. I'm a failure. I've lost my job, patent agent, a good job. I was on my way to partnership. I've spent the last year mostly in a drunken haze. My funds are gone. My friends cross the street when they see me stumbling toward them."

"Fred, if you don't meet the devil now and again, you're traveling in the same direction. No man is perfect."

"No, you don't want me. You want an honorable man."

"Honorable man?" Jenkins shook his head. "Don't spout that twaddle."

Fred blinked at him with confusion written large on his face.

"Many men do despicable things and believe themselves to be 'honorable,' because they later feel guilty about what they've done. I don't want 'honorable' men helping me. I want righteous men."

Jenkins took another sip and moved around the desk to Fred, looking him square in the eye. "As the blood dripped from Jesus's thorny crown, honorable men felt ashamed and looked away. Righteous men looked into Jesus's face and said 'you are the Son of God, the Messiah.'

"You have looked into the face of both honor and righteousness, Fred, and have made righteousness your cause and choice every time. You belong to the day. And, I say again, I want *your* help."

Fred looked away. His lips trembled.

Jenkins lifted the glass. He held it before Fred's face, turned it upside down, and poured the contents into the wastebasket.

"It is your righteousness that has maintained you, not some contrived notion of honor. You have always been a righteous man, Fred. Drink couldn't take that away from you."

"But, why me?"

Jenkins held up his forefinger and moved to a nearby cabinet. Opening one of its small doors, he retrieved a small item. Turning to Fred, he opened his hand.

"Recognize this?"

"It's a chess piece, of course."

"True, but what else can you tell me about it?" Jenkins asked, motioning Fred to take it.

Fred grasped the piece and turned it over in his hand. He paused, a look of sadness coming into his eyes.

"It's the same style as the pieces from James Aston's office, the board he was playing against Angela Jones before he disappeared."

"And which piece is it?"

"The black queen." Fred's eyes grew wide.

"When I inspected Aston's office after he was reported missing, I noted a chess board near his desk. There was a game played out on the board. The black player had lost. The black king was on its side evidencing surrender, in more ways than one I suspected at the time. There was one piece unaccounted for, however. Someone had removed the black queen."

Fred again took on his not-unfamiliar look of confusion.

"You looked startled upon the realization that you might be holding that very queen. Why?"

"It's James's signature piece. He once explained to me that he used it as bait, since lesser players valued her so. James usually played the black side to give his opponent the slight advantage of going first. At some point he would appear to play his queen recklessly, offering her as a sacrifice for a longer play that would bring the other player down. Wait, you said this piece was missing?"

"I received it in the post last week, mailed from the London General Post Office to me with no indication of who sent it."

Fred seemed to struggle for what to say. He looked quickly about the room and then back at the inspector. "Bait," he whispered.

"And that answers your last question, Fred. No one else but you could have come to that conclusion. Aston is on the loose, somewhere in London. You are just the man I need to help find him."

"But if this piece means 'bait,' then he intends to trap you. He's challenging you, in a sense, to a game."

"Challenge accepted. Care to rejoin me in the game?" Jenkins raised his glass.

Fred stared silently at the wall behind the desk, seemingly lost in thought. "The sheep…"

"Not to worry, the good Welshman is back on the job."

Fred looked back at the chess piece and shook his head. "You said a moment ago you had 'stumbled upon the truth.' What truth?"

"My fault, really, for putting you in danger. I should have been more circumspect. I had a hunch and started making inquiries, inquiries about a specific man. When my inquiries led to violent deaths, I had my answer. I had smoked him out, and he knew it. Thus began the open warfare that put you and many others in danger. I admit that we've not fared very well to date. You." Jenkins poked Fred in the chest with the empty glass he held in his hand. "You are a fortunate survivor."

"Wait. Smoked *who* out?"

"Someone I think your Mr. Aston can lead us to, which is why I need your help."

"But *who* will he lead us to?"

"The puppet master. Charlie."

***

"What do I seek? Freedom."

Aston was quick to answer. Father Cornish set his beer on the table and glanced around the pub before continuing.

"From what?"

"From the customs of the past, from the rules of men long since dead who no longer labor under the rules they set down for all of us to follow, from the dictates of a 'god' whom I can't see, touch or feel, from the shackles of guilt…freedom, sweet and clear and energizing. I asked no man to die for me. Therefore, I owe nothing to no one. I am free, not a slave, but a free man.

"Why are we bound to the past, Father? It's the future that holds the promises. Look at all we've accomplished, not with faith, but with our minds, our wills, our freedom. Superstition and ignorance no longer oversee us. We have reason.

"This mighty island nation lives by the sea. Yet, but two generations past, Britons relied on the wind to propel wooden ships across the waters. If the wind didn't blow, the ship didn't move. Now we burn fuel oil to propel mighty vessels made of steel at incomprehensible speeds. Nature is relevant only as something we've conquered. The wind can blow or not, it matters not to the ship."

"These ships have no rudders, then? And what of anchors? I suppose we have conquered the force of waves and tides as well?"

Aston let out a laugh and raised his glass. "Analogies can be imperfect. Thank you for pointing out the imperfections." He took a long drink and returned the glass to the table with a thud. "Well," he said, raising his eyebrow over a twinkling eye. "Aren't you going to add something about stormy seas?"

"Why raise the obvious point when I can leave it hanging?" Cornish returned the toast, raising his glass and downing the contents.

"You're but one to my two," announced Aston while pointing at the empty glass. "That hardly seems civil." He looked about just in time to flag down the proprietor crossing the room with two plates. "Good sir, another beer for my dear friend here and, I believe by the time you return, I'll need one for myself as well."

The proprietor altered his course and plunked the two plates on their table along with two forks. He then nodded, and turned back toward the bar.

Aston seemed more animated than usual this evening. His eyes flickered back and forth as he spoke. When not speaking, his hand, the one with the two red moles, twitched on the table.

"Bless this food to our use, and us to thy service. Fill our hearts with grateful praise. Amen."

Aston was quick with a forkful of food, not bothering to respond. He took another and washed the bite down with the last of his beer, which was soon replaced by the return of the proprietor.

"I don't think you understand what's coming, Father."

Cornish raised an eyebrow. Aston looked in deadly earnest.

"We humans are sophisticated animals, but we share many traits with other lower species. I tend to think we borrow heavily from three in particular, the rat, the sheep, and the wolf. In fact, you could say that each of us moves between these three species as we navigate life.

"The rat will always survive. He is the master of survival and adaptability. He can live in the sewer just as easily as the garden.

He thrives in darkness, and takes advantage of the smallest of opportunities.

"The wolf is a fierce competitor. Working in packs or alone, he is formidable, and aggressive. He thrives in chaos and culls the weak.

"The future will be dark and chaotic. The weak shall be culled. Men must adapt to live in the sewer. The sheep won't stand a chance." Aston took another bite, smiling as he chewed. "We all must decide. What shall we be? What will you be, Father, the rat, the sheep, or the wolf?"

"I suspect the shepherd will have something to say about that."

"Ah!" James pointed his fork at Cornish. "That's the crux! Man must turn away from the shepherd. The shepherd will lead them to slaughter! The only rational choice is the wolf. But the window of opportunity is closing. One either becomes a wolf, or fate forces you to die or live like a rat.

"You have it in you, Father. That's why I'm here. That's our journey."

Aston took another bite.

"What business brings you here, with me?"

Aston chewed momentarily and pointed his fork at the priest. "Your welfare."

"I can't help thinking that a night of unbroken rest would have been more conducive to that end."

"Your reclamation, then. Take heed."

Father Cornish allowed a laugh. "Then you are an apparition?"

Aston smiled. "Excellent peas tonight."

***

"Edward, why so glum? This last report is a positive one. The change of governments in Constantinople appears to have been pulled off with minimal bloodshed. With the young Turks in control, the vacillations of the Sultan may be a thing of the past. Now we have rational, active men to deal with."

205

Sir Charles Hardinge studied the slumped appearance of the Foreign Secretary for answers to his question.

"It's all so exhausting. Good news...certainly better, that much is true."

"Then?"

"Sherry, that's what I need." Grey opened a cabinet and retrieved a bottle. "What's your poison, Charles?"

"Sherry sounds lovely. Thank you."

Grey poured two glasses, handing one to Hardinge. "To your health."

Hardinge raised his glass and nodded before taking a drink.

Grey lingered with his first sip and sighed before continuing. "Yes, that hit the spot."

"Edward, something bedevils you. May I be of assistance in any way?"

Grey took another sip, sighed again, and set his glass down. "Two Mondays past, when the news first broke that there had been a military revolt overthrowing the Turkish government and that a civil war was imminent, do you know where I was?"

Hardinge shrugged.

"I was at Rosehall on the Cassley. That morning I walked up a lonely glen and lunched by a burn. The air vibrated with the wonderful spring notes of many curlews and from far up the hill came the croaking of ravens."

Grey picked up his glass, but just looked at it, swirling the contents.

"The river conditions were perfect. I had five salmon on the bank by teatime before returning to the post office to check for those damnable red packets. That is when I received news of the revolt. I couldn't resist catching one more fish, but soon knew I had to return to London.

"The next morning I left. The river was still in good order. There was the prospect of a week of good sport if only I could stay. There was the certainty that I must wait a whole year before I could spring salmon fish again. And there wasn't even the compensation of feeling a martyr to duty. If the disturbance in Constantinople became dangerous, British action must be limited to protecting lives and property. The measures necessary for this would be taken by the diplomatic and naval authorities on the spot whether I was here, at the Foreign Office, or not. If I stayed at the Cassley until something dire happened I could be here in London in plenty of time to deal with political complications that might arise later on. The public interest would not suffer if I awaited developments."

He stopped swirling the glass and placed it back down.

"But the fear of what would be said in the House of Commons and in the press, if something did happened and I were absent from my office, destroyed my equanimity. I came back to London feeling cowardly rather than noble, and not at all convinced that the sacrifice was necessary. And now the event has proved it unnecessary."

"You made the right decision. Had events spun further out of control you were here to deal with them. I'm glad you were here. I'm sorry events intruded."

Grey straightened his back and placed his hand on his forehead.

"If you're glad of it, then the trip was not wasted." He rubbed his face and pinched his chin before shaking his head several times. "No, not wasted. I did learn more of the failures of this Jenkins Department."

"Special Department B?"

"Yes. It appears he may have lost all three of his 'box busters.'"

"I'm not sure that has been definitely determined."

"He's lost contact with all three. The girl in New Mexico has been missing now for months. The American doctor has gone silent. The lad in London was last seen jumping into the Thames with blood spurting from his arm. It seems less than promising to me. Not to you, Charles?"

"I wouldn't call them positive developments, but there's been no confirmation that any of the three is dead. In fact, the vigorous pursuit of the girl by a large number of men wanting the bounty on her head would seem to indicate that she is alive, but perhaps driven to ground."

"And what is Jenkins doing to protect her?"

"I don't know the details, but I believe requests have been made of President Roosevelt."

"I think Jenkins is overtasked, outmatched by the situation. The files listed about a dozen subjects of the Crown identified by Jenkins's department for special protection, politicians, military men and so forth. Winston Churchill is on that list, of all people. Neither you nor I, nor the Prime Minister, apparently, is deserving of such protection."

"I'm not aware that anyone has tried to take your life recently, Edward. Three months ago Churchill was attacked at a train station and nearly thrown under an approaching train. A month later a heavy iron bolt was thrown at his moving motorcar, nearly hitting him. The month after that he was assaulted whilst giving a speech."

"My point exactly. Have you read the *Times* this morning?"

Hardinge shook his head. "I haven't yet had time, I'm afraid."

"Winston was staying with cousins at a rented mansion in Rutland. A deadly fire broke out and all the guests retreated to the lawn, all but Churchill, that is. He darted back in. Here," Grey picked up a folded newspaper. "According to the article, when the fire brigades arrived 'the house was almost destroyed, and just as Mr. Churchill left the mansion carrying two marble busts, the roof, which had been blazing furiously, fell in with a crash, Mr. Churchill being just in time to escape injury.' Now, my understanding is that Jenkins's department assigns constant protection to Winston. How could they allow Winston to run such ridiculous risks for two marble busts?"

"He is a difficult customer. I'm certain of that."

"It needs to be shut down, Charles. It's time to end this Special Department B charade. Jenkins is a policeman for this city, not the protector of the Crown, not the savior of mankind."

"You can't be serious?"

"This whole black box thing has gone on too long. The Germans and Austro-Hungarians are clamoring for war. The Serbians are raising armies and the Russians sharpening their bayonets. The masses abroad and here at home demand bloodshed. The world spins madly out of control, and we waste our time with an inspector from Scotland Yard chasing mysterious men with black boxes and squiggly canes."

"And what is your solution for agents with knives buried to the hilt in their throats with 'Charlie' calling cards stuffed in their shirts?"

"I don't know, but the answer certainly isn't Jenkins. For all we know he's behind the whole mess."

"Edward! That's—"

"It's as plausible as any other explanation I've heard of late. All I'm saying is that if what we have tried isn't working, we should try something else."

Hardinge inhaled deeply, holding his breath several seconds before responding.

"And if the tide began to turn, if Jenkins recovers his team intact, would that change your opinion?"

"Perhaps, but those odds seem rather long. Don't you agree?" Grey retrieved his glass and drained the contents. "Another sherry?"

***

Inspector Jenkins stared at the naked body lying on the examination table. It was becoming all too familiar. The hole in the neck surrounded by bruising, the glassy eyes stuck wide open, the lack of any other sign of trauma—this one was like so many others.

He rolled the unlit cigar from one side of his mouth to the other and looked up at the uniformed officer across the table. "Who was he?"

"Economist, sir."

"Economist?"

"Yes, sir, an economist, Cambridge. He was a Fellow of the King's College. His colleagues all considered him a brilliant rising star, the next Adam Smith."

"Inspector Jenkins?"

Jenkins turned to see another uniformed officer with his helmet under his arm standing at the door to the examination room. "Yes?"

"Sorry to interrupt, sir. Constable Dravot, here. I've come to report there is a gentleman out back with a delivery for you. He insists on delivering to you personally."

"What is it he's delivering?"

"A large sack of something he's pushed up in a handcart. He won't say what's inside the sack, and insists you see it. Peachey, that is, Constable Carnehan, stayed with him while I came to fetch you. He insists me and Peachey will be in deep trouble if we try to relieve him of his sack. He says you'll have *us* sacked if I don't go fetch you straight away. 'Inspector Jenkins will nail you to a tree, I promise you that,' says he." Constable Dravot paused seeming to wait for a reaction. When one was not forthcoming, he scratched his head, took a deep breath, and continued. "Just to be safe, sir, I thought it best to interrupt you."

"Did he give you a name?"

"No, sir. He said I was to tell you that the package came from Saint George's Dragon on Brick Lane. But there aren't no Saint George's Dragon on Brick Lane. I told him so myself."

"Good God!" Jenkins spat out the cigar and bounded toward the door, brushing Dravot aside. The inspector sprinted down the hallway toward the back of the building. Racing around a few corners he was soon outside where he spotted another officer with his arms crossed standing in front of a handcart.

"Peachey, I brought the inspector!" shouted Dravot as he came up from behind at a full run.

Peachey snapped to attention as Jenkins skidded to a stop next to the handcart. On the other side of the cart stood not a gentleman, but a small, slight man with long white hair that hung down below his collar. He stood erect with square shoulders under a worn seaman's jacket. His leathery face was tanned and unshaven, and his piercing blue eyes followed the inspector warily.

Jenkins surveyed the lumpy, white sack bundled in the handcart. It was moving, barely, but perceptibly. In fact, he doubted the two officers had noticed at all, but it was slightly moving.

"Gentlemen," he barked at the two officers, "assist this man with getting his cart into the building."

Dravot and Carnehan took charge of the cart, the relief of which the man with the long, white hair obliged, but he continued to keep a keen eye on the inspector. Once inside the building the officers stepped away from the cart and looked quizzically at the inspector for direction.

"Leave! Now!"

"Yes, sir," responded Constable Carnehan. "Shall Daniel, I mean, Constable Dravot and I wait outside where you can call us?"

"Just get out." He took a breath and checked himself. "Thank you, Officers, your service is no longer required."

Constables Dravot and Carnehan shuffled out, closing the door behind them.

The inspector's mind raced with the thought of what was before him. He surveyed the man with the long white hair one last time.

"Who are you?" Jenkins growled.

"A friend, of his." He pointed at the bundle on his cart.

"Where did you find him?"

"I fished him out of the Thames, took him home, and kept him safe."

"Where did you fish him out?"

"Mill Pond Bank."

"Why?"

The man looked amusedly perplexed at the question. "It was the right thing to do. You know, it's not only constables that keeps men safe at night." He smiled, winked, and glanced toward the ceiling.

Jenkins removed a switchblade knife from his pocket. He flicked open the blade, glaring for a moment at the man, and then lunged at the sack. He pierced it at one end and ran the blade along one side, pulling the cloth away from the contents of the sack while creating a slit. He widened the slit and peered inside.

"Well, look what we have here. What a pleasure to see you, lad!"

He pulled back from the bag, and up through the slit popped the familiar, smiling face of Jim Talbot.

"Inspector, I'm sorry, I came as soon as I was able."

"Nonsense, Jim..." He was interrupted by the sound of the door to the room closing. The man with the long white hair was gone.

Jenkins started toward the door, but Talbot grabbed him by the arm.

"Please don't follow him. I promised you wouldn't."

"Promised?"

"He's done many a good turn for me. He pulled me out of the river. He hid me away and nursed me to health." Talbot spoke rapidly in a pleading voice. "I knew I couldn't just walk to Scotland Yard. It was too risky. He said he'd take me here and no one would see me. He made me promise first that you wouldn't follow after him. Please, Inspector, you'll put him in danger too!"

Jenkins leaned back toward the lad so that he wouldn't have to keep pulling on his arm.

"What's his name?"

"I don't know. No, on my word, I don't know. He never told me, and I never asked. I'd be dead without him."

Jenkins looked down at Talbot, who was half-in and half-out of the sack. Jim continued to grip his arm with his left hand. His right arm lay limp at his side.

"You can let go, lad. I'll keep your promise. Now, let's get you out of that sack and up to my office. We need to get you back in action."

CHAPTER 12
THIS SIDE OF HELL

Clayton Spake opened the door to the little cantina on the edge of Toyah, Texas, and peered inside. The smell of tobacco and sweat smacked him in the face as he adjusted his eyes to the gloom. The room went from loud chatter to silence as two full tables of men swung around to watch him make his way to the bar. He ordered a whisky, and the noise gradually returned.

"I'm lookin' for someone."

The bartender didn't bother to look up as he poured a short glass and pushed it in front of Spake, who watched closely taking the measure of the man. The bartender was solid with a barrel chest and bushy sideburns.

"I understand he's a regular in here."

"Everybody's lookin' for someone." The bartender still didn't look up as he corked a bottle and placed it under the bar.

Spake pulled three coins out of his pocket and placed them on the bar. One was silver, the other two were gold. He pushed the silver one with his index finger toward the bartender.

"This is for the drink. He's a cowboy from Carlsbad. Comes to see the gal who works here."

The bartender scooped up the silver coin and stood eyeing the other two with black-as-coal eyes set wide apart above a flat nose that bent to one side.

"This one..." Spake slid one of the gold coins toward the bartender. "Is for tellin' me where I can find him. And this one..." He slid the second gold coin toward the other one. "Is for keeping your mouth shut about tellin' me."

The bartender looked at Spake, then over at a door next to the bar, and then back at Spake. Spake glanced toward the same door. The bartender nodded and scooped up the gold coins.

Spake raised the glass and downed the contents.

"Is there a back door?"

The bartender nodded again without looking up.

Spake eased away from the bar, which caused the chatter in the room to subside. It started up again as he opened the door to the street and stepped outside.

He walked across the street toward the boarding house until he passed some scrub brush that allowed him to turn back to the cantina without being seen by anyone who happened to be looking from that direction. He skirted around an adobe house and was soon joined close on his heels by his dog. The two worked their way around the back of the cantina. The muffled voices from inside were making the same racket as when he'd first opened the front door. Putting his ear to the back door he heard two other voices, a man's and a woman's.

He pointed his right arm at his dog with the palm of his hand open. The dog watched attentively as Spake closed his hand and pointed to the corner of the building. The dog dutifully trotted to his sentinel post and poked his head around the corner, keeping an eye on the street.

Spake swung open the door and strode in as if he owned the place.

"That isn't the front door, cowboy," a young Mexican girl responded with a startled look on her face. "You need to go around the building to the front."

A wiry cowboy stood up from the table at which he and the girl sat. Spake locked eyes with him.

"You Jay White?"

"Who wants to know?"

"You and I need to talk outside."

"What about?" The cowboy looked uneasy and slowly closed the distance between his right hand and a pistol grip protruding from a holster on his right hip.

"I'm here to save your life."

"I don't need savin'. Who are you and what do you want?" The right hand was now nearly on top of the pistol grip.

"Well, if you don't care about your own life, then let's save the life of girl from outside Alamogordo."

"I don't know what you're talkin' about."

"James, don't go outside," the girl urged in a hushed voice. "Stay here with me."

"You ever kept a horned toad in a cage?" Spake paused and reached into his shirt pocket, producing a plug of tobacco. "I believe you could do it if you found the right ant piles and gave it water every now and again." He bit off a piece of the nearly black wad of leaves and slipped it into his mouth, rolling it around on his tongue before shoving the tobacco into his cheek.

"Want some?" Spake held out the remainder of the tobacco plug to White.

"Let's go outside. No, Catalina, stay here." White gestured with his hand as she started to rise from the table. "I'll be back."

Spake led the way. As he emerged the dog turned his head toward him, but seeing no new instructions stayed put. Spake heard the door close behind him and kept walking for an elm tree about ten paces away. He turned and leaned his back against the tree, spitting some brown juice on the ground off to one side.

"You sure you don't want any?" He asked before returning the unused tobacco to his shirt pocket.

"Well, we're outside. What do you want?"

"I want you to tell me where Molly Bell is."

"And why would I do that?"

"Because if you don't, someone other than me will beat it out you, find her, and kill her. I aim to stop all that."

"What makes you think I know anything about Molly Bell?"

"I tracked her to a spot, a spot where her horse met your horse. You done a fair job with the tracks after that, but it's clear as day to me that you were the last person to see her. Since you didn't turn her in for the bounty, you hid her somewhere. Tracks stay in that desert a long time with no rain about. It's just a matter of time."

"I don't know what the heck you're talkin' about."

"Mr. White, I'm not the only tracker out there. I tracked her to you, tracked you to the Triple X Ranch, and then tracked you here. It ain't that hard." He spat out some juice again, hitting the same spot on the ground.

"What's your name?"

"Spake."

"Spake?"

"That's what I said."

"Spake, you strike me as just another bounty hunter. Well, you're barkin' up the wrong tree." White turned and started back toward the Cantina.

"It's a paint."

"What?" Jay spun back around.

"Her horse, it's the same one she left the ranch with before her party was ambushed in the dark. She rides a paint."

"And?"

"You ever heard anyone say what she was ridin'? I didn't think so." He spat out again, enlarging the small, brown puddle.

"And how would you know?"

"Her mother told me. The horned frog is named Joshua."

White stood silently staring in the distance. Then he advanced on Spake, stopping within arm's reach.

"How do I know I can trust you?"

"I done gave you all I can. You're gonna have to decide. You can help me or wait until one of the groups behind me catches you. They won't ask for help, they'll take it. Way I figure it, I'm the only chance you got, and I'm damn sure the only chance Molly Bell's got. So know you're decidin' for the both of you."

White stared hard at him, and then let out a sigh.

"I need to say my goodbyes first. I'll meet you out back of the boarding house."

"Give her a good long kiss. Word's gonna spread pretty quick that you're the key to Molly Bell. You may not make it out of this deal to kiss her again."

White smirked. "I thought you said you were gonna save my life."

"I will, if you don't mess up. I just have my doubts on that account."

***

"There, that's better." Molly pulled the lantern into her lap as she sat cross-legged on the cave floor. She pressed her knees against Job and bent over the lamp, resting her forehead on the damp stalagmite. The stubby flame radiated warmth on her face.

"I know, it's wasteful and I should sleep."

She turned her face side to side, giving each cheek equal time over the lamp.

"Do you dream, Job?"

She waited for an answer she knew wouldn't come.

"I'm there, but I'm just watching. It's like a play. I'm the only one in the audience, but I sit up high somewhere. I can see everything, hear everything, smell everything. I just can't, well, influence. Yep, that's a good word, influence. If I wave my arms, no one can see me. If I yell no one can hear me. I wonder if they can smell me. I don't think so."

The lamp sputtered, but came back to life when she tilted it slightly.

"I don't want to go to sleep. That's all I do in here, eat, sleep, and talk to you. How long, Job?"

Molly's thoughts drifted to the ranch and her mother. She closed her eyes and imagined a warm bowl of stew set before her with gentle hands that would stroke her hair.

A "splat" from somewhere beyond the light of her lamp told her that a stalactite had just given up a drop to its stalagmite partner. They were like opposed teeth, the stalactites and stalagmites, growing larger and closer drop by drop. Surely the growth was imperceptible to her, a mere mortal. But the teeth were growing. They were growing all around her. She was a little warm bug in the cold mouth of a giant creature with thousands of teeth closing in around her.

The lamp sputtered and the darkness jumped forth.

"I want to go home."

Molly pulled a blanket over her shoulders and huddled next to Job.

***

Jay White ripped another bite of jerked beef and eyed his companion, Clayton Spake, doing the same. The big dog sat patiently next to Spake waiting for the occasional piece of dried meat tossed his way.

"So, you never seen a baseball game?"

Spake shook his head and kept on chewing.

"The strange thing was the uniforms these fellas wore. They all had the same baggy suits. They looked like sacks cover them head to toe. One team wore all white and the other all black. Now the fella that throws the ball over the plate for the other team to swing at is called the pitcher. He pitches to both sides, so he don't technically belong to either team. His uniform is the same, except it's all white on the left side and all black on the other side.

"I'm not sure that pitcher was equal parts black and white, though. Seemed to me he favored one side over the other in the way he threw that ball over the plate. But then I can't fault him. Is any man truly impartial? Seems to me you have to tilt somewhat black or white. Livin' right in the middle strikes me as about as easy as balancing with one foot on top of a crooked fencepost."

Spake chewed away without saying a word.

They were traveling light and fast, no fires and short rests to change mounts. Every stop White tried to engage his companion, but Spake wasn't showing any cards. In fact, he hardly spoke at all.

They each had two horses, the extras provided by Spake. Switching mounts periodically increased their speed across the desert.

"That blue roan you got, don't look much like a cattle horse to me."

"Nope, he don't turn quick," Spake replied while casually chewing away.

"Why you favor him, then?"

"He runs hard."

"You always travel with two extra mounts?"

"Nope."

That was more conversation Jay had gotten out of Spake since they left Toyah. He pressed on.

"Why this time?"

Spake stopped chewing, reached in his mouth, and pulled out the remains of a stringy piece of jerky, flicking it toward the dog.

"'Cause I could."

"Those all your horses?"

"They are now."

"What's that mean?"

"Always had the roan."

"Where'd you get the others?"

"Here and there." Spake's jaw stopped momentarily. "You ask a lot a questions."

"I have to. You don't say much."

"Never miss a chance to shut up."

Jay gritted his teeth and suppressed the swear words that came to mind first.

"I'm puttin' a lot of faith in you, mister. I'd like to know if I'm right doin' so." Jay snipped off another bit of jerky and began the task of softening it up in his mouth.

"Fair enough, what do you want to know?" Spake took another chew of meat as well.

"You from these parts?"

"Southeast New Mexico? No, I've been workin' up in Colorado lately, near the town of Steamboat Springs."

"Doin' what?"

Spake chewed for a bit before answering.

"This and that. People hire me to get things done. I like the air in them parts."

"What things?"

"Findin' this or that, sometimes people. Sometimes they want me along to make sure nothin' goes bad."

"You're a hired gun."

"Sometimes the law ain't enough."

Jay swallowed some jerky and washed it down with the warm water that sloshed around in his canteen when he raised it. He studied his companion's face. It was leathered and tan with heavy lines at the corner of his placid, brown eyes. He had a thin hook nose that didn't quite line up straight on his face, a tall but not a big man, hard and lean. He wore a large, black hat with a brim that nearly covered his shoulders.

"I *was* born in New Mexico," Spake volunteered. "Least that's what I'm told. They call the place La Mesa now, outside of Mesilla. Back then they called it Victorio. The Apaches raided the town so often the townsfolks decided to name it after their chief, Victorio. I don't recall. I was too young. I'm told the folks there hated Victorio. Funny you should call your town that if you hated him so much. I can't say. I don't remember him that well."

"You knew Victorio?"

"Not at first, like I said, I was too young."

"Then how did you know him."

Spake let out a sigh and stared off in the distance. "My ma and pa had a homestead not far out of Victorio, about halfway to another little town named San Miguel. My pa weren't there when the Apaches came one night to steal some livestock. Ma didn't cotton to that. She was part Indian herself and weren't one to back down, even to Victorio. She must've put up one hell of a fight. She only had one child, me. I was three or four at the time. I think them Apaches thought they were doin' her an honor by not killin' me. Maybe they thought some of her fight was inside me, and they just wanted to see what I'd become. I don't know. I never asked 'em."

"You lived with the Apaches?"

"For a spell. The Mexican army killed Victorio in 'eighty. I weren't there. I was with another band at the time."

Jay waited for Spake to continue, but he just chewed.

"Spake, it ain't polite the way you talk, leavin' a man hangin' all the time. Can't you tell a story from start to finish without me asking you to keep goin'?"

Spake straightened his back and faced Jay with a blank expression. He cut off another piece of meat and stuck in his mouth.

"When I got big enough I'd go out with small parties, mostly horse thievin' and such. The US pony soldiers never could catch us. One day we're runnin' hard away from about twenty soldiers. We ducked down in an arroyo and watched 'em ride past. They were Buffalo soldiers. I'd never seen a black man up close before. I don't know what come over me. When one rode close by I stood up and stared at him. Someone in the column saw me. Shots came zipping my way. One stung me.

"Them Buffalo soldiers figured out I was a white man, and hauled my carcass over to Fort Selden outside of Las Cruces. An old Buff named Spake nursed me back to health and looked after me for a spell. I was called Spake 'cause of him, like he was my father, which I guess he was at the time.

"I met my natural father later when I was grown. I didn't remember him, but Pa swore he was my father. He told me what my Christian name was. I remembered my Indian name, but not that Christian one. I told him I already had a proper last name, Spake. He said, 'Well, I'll give you my first name, then, so least you'll have a first that's in the family.' So that day it was official. I was Clayton Spake. That's what I told the army when I volunteered. 'Clayton Spake is my name.'"

"You were in the army?"

Spake nodded as he chewed.

"I was with Colonel Roosevelt at San Juan. That's where I met Molly Bell's pa. He was in the Rough Riders like me."

Spake stopped talking as suddenly as he had started. Jay watched him chewing his meal while rolling Clayton Spake's story around in his head.

"Then you're working for Molly Bell's father?"

"I guess I was the closest help to be found in the short run."

Jay looked hard at the man. He hadn't exactly answered the question. Could he trust him? Anyone can make up a tale. How much of it was true?

"The smell of death," Jay pointed at the saddle bag on one of the two horses Spake was riding. A swarm of large black flies buzzed around it. "What's in there that stinks?"

"Scalps."

Jay stopped chewing and sat silently staring at Spake.

"Scalps, you say?"

"Yep."

"Whose?"

"Men trying to find the same thing we're lookin' for."

Jay let his right hand drift toward the pistol dangling from the holster near his hip, a movement that caught the dog's attention, but didn't seem to concern Spake, who continued his rhythmic chewing.

"Bounty hunters, hunting for Molly Bell?"

"Yep."

"You're the scalper."

"That what they call me?"

"Why'd you scalp 'em?"

"Like you said, they were huntin' Molly Bell."

"Why not just kill 'em?"

224

"Discourage the others."

The rumors were true. There was a vigilante spreading terror amongst the bounty hunters, and Clayton Spake had the scalps to prove it. He was the scalper. Jay rocked slightly to his left to improve the angle to his revolver.

"Look, Jay." Spake swallowed, which resulted in a soft whine from the dog. "I confess I'm a hired gun, and I get paid for every scalp I take. But my employer has a different agenda. My employer wants Molly Bell to live. I've been hired to buy him time to find her and protect her. The scalps was my idea. Seems like a good measure of how well I'm doin'."

"So you kill and scalp every bounty hunter you find so that the others will be discouraged and lose their stomach for the pursuit? Is that it?"

"You got a better idea?"

"It ain't Christian!"

"It ain't my cheek to turn."

Jay glared at Spake, who spoke as casually as a seasoned ranch hand explaining how to tie off a calf.

"There's hundreds of mean hombres out there who want to kill that girl. I can't stop 'em by myself, but if I can hold 'em off long enough, I give her a chance. So, I kill 'em when I find 'em and scalp 'em. Ain't been no scalpin' in these parts in near thirty years. Word gets round. Some men go home. Other men get cautious. You can't move so carefree when you think you might be the prey. I figure this side of hell, that's all a man can do to help this girl."

Jay flinched when Spake tossed a piece of dried meat at the dog.

"Jay, that's what they were gonna do to Molly. You haven't heard? The bounty is $100,000 for her scalp. I just turned it around."

"And what are you going to do with me if we find Molly?"

Spake looked at him with a furrowed brow, squinting his brown eyes.

"Nothin'." Spake slowly grinned and tilted his head to one side. "You expecting a wet kiss? Besides, if we find her before help comes, I could use another gun. You know how to use that?" Spake pointed at Jay's revolver over which Jay's right hand hovered.

"It ain't right, I tell you. You can't justify killin' a man and takin' his scalp. It's a sin."

"Maybe I can't, but that's what I done." Spake sat silently for a moment as if contemplating his statement.

White closed the distance from his hand to his revolver until he could feel the cool handle on his palm. What had he gotten himself into? He wanted to scream 'you'll go to hell,' but figured Spake already knew that.

"Catalina was right," he blurted. "I shouldn't have agreed to take you to the cave."

Something changed on Spake's face. It was suddenly tense and focused. The dog stood up and squared his body toward Jay.

"Catalina? The Mexican gal at the bar?"

"She said you were no good. She told me not to tell you about the cave."

"You told her about the cave?" Spake's voice was low and icy. The dog leaned in Jay's direction, watching him intently.

"Who else knows Molly's in the cave."

"No one else, just me and Catalina."

No sooner had the words left Jay's mouth than Spake was up, holding his hand palm out to the dog, and mounting the nearest horse. Jay rose and pulled his revolver. The dog growled but stood his ground glancing between Jay and the hand held palm out.

"Put the gun away, you're makin' the dog nervous."

"Where are you goin'?"

"Back to the cantina."

"You're going to kill her. I won't let you kill her."

"You gonna shoot me? Now Jay, that wouldn't be Christian."

The two men glared at each other as the dog softly growled, a low rattling growl, like a fat stick raked along a picket fence.

"I'll make you a deal. If I go back to that cantina and find your Catalina doing her chores and servin' tables, like nothin' you said matters, I'll leave her be and turn right back around. But if she's gone, I'll track her down and kill her. I won't scalp her, though—no, not a woman."

Jay pulled the hammer back and aimed at Spake's chest.

"Dog!"

Spake's command froze the beast just as it started to lunge. The dog's growling grew louder.

"You been played, Jay. Don't make two mistakes. You shoot me and Molly Bell's dead for sure."

Spake gathered the horses.

"If she's there, I'll leave her be. I promise. If she's gone, you know what I have to do. Either way, you keep headin' for the cave. I'll catch up, but I'm gonna need all the spare horses. Avoid any men you see out there. If you get close to the cave before I catch up, don't go in. Backtrack on your trail. I'll find you. If anyone but me is on your trail coming the other way, you best be ready to use that gun. Save the last bullet for yourself, 'cause they'll make you turn your cheeks until you beg them to follow you to Molly."

With that Spake turned his blue roan and kicked it in the belly with both heels. Soon Spake, the three horses, and the dog were all but small blurry dots at the end of Jay White's pistol barrel.

***

Clayton Spake rode through the night, switching horses every hour. Two hours out of Toyah he gave a wide berth to a large party of men coming toward him from the southeast, the direction he was headed. He found a hidden vantage point to watch them pass. They were just a couple shy of a dozen in all, well-armed and moving steadily forward across the moonlit desert.

He didn't spot any women with them, and stayed concealed long enough to see them come across his own tracks on the trail.

227

The party didn't seem to care that three horses and a dog had suddenly jumped off the trail in front of them. They just kept riding toward New Mexico.

The outskirts of Toyah came into view as the sun rose in the east. He walked the exhausted horses into town. The dog brought up the rear, panting heavily with his head drooped.

He tethered the thirsty horses at a watering trough, and he and the dog shared with them the brackish, brown stuff.

The dog stopped drinking and let out a long burp when Spake stood and headed toward the cantina. He took one more slurp of the water and trotted to catch up to his master.

Spake directed the dog to the back side of the cantina before opening the front door and stepping inside. The room was empty, the tables festooned with dirty bowls, plates, and empty mugs. The bar likewise was stacked with plates and mugs. The smell of meat, beans, beer, sweat, and dust hung in the air.

The door from the back room opened and the bartender appeared, stopping next to bar.

"We're closed."

"I'm here to see Catalina."

"She ain't here. We open in four hours."

"Where'd she go?"

"I didn't ask her."

"I didn't say nothin' about askin' her. Where'd she go?"

"Mister, I said we're closed."

Spake fished a coin out of his pocket and laid it on a nearby table. "Where'd she go?"

The bartender chuckled and shook his head. "You ain't got enough money. Save it for lunch. We'll be open in four hours."

Clayton eyed the bartender, the same man with a barrel chest, bushy sideburns, and black-as-coal eyes who took his money the last time.

"I ain't got time for this. Let me tell you a little secret," said Clayton softly as he advanced on the man, who in turn squinted his right eye and glared at him the whole way.

Once he got within arm's length Spake let loose two sharp whistles which were answered by the sound of the dog growling and scratching at the back door. The bartender turned his head toward the back room, making the mistake Spake anticipated.

Spake lifted his right leg and kicked sideways, landing his boot just below the man's right knee. He raked the boot down the man's leg and stomped on the top of his foot.

The bartender tilted to his right and took swing with his left arm which Clayton blocked with his right. Taking advantage of the bartender's momentum, Spake grabbed the man's sideburns and, using both hands, shoved his face into the corner of the bar. The bartender tried to stand, but Spake still held his head by the sideburns and hair. Spake pulled back on the man's head and then pushed it down, simultaneously bring up his right leg toward his face.

The crack and scream confirmed that the nose was broken. Clayton turned the man around and from behind him pinned his head to the top of the bar with his left forearm. He pulled his revolver and stuck the barrel in the bartender's open mouth.

"See, here's the secret. I ain't gonna ask you again. You either tell me where she went, or I'll blow your jawbone clean outta your mouth. Then I'm gonna scalp you and leave you here to die. I got a whole saddlebag of scalps outside, but I can always make room for one more."

"You, you da capper?" The bartender struggled to get his words out with cold steel in his mouth.

"So I'm told. Now answer me or you get scalped too."

"He, her rode soud," he spat out with his tongue slapping off the gun barrel.

"Goin' where?"

"Her didn' say. Oh! I'm sayin' rue." The man groaned as Spake shoved the barrel against the roof of his mouth. "He head dow de road a Fo Davie."

"Fort Davis? When?"

"He lef abou fo hour ago, righ afer a pary o men came in."

"How many men?"

The bartender did his best to shake his head. Spake pulled the gun barrel out, cocked the hammer back with a convincing click, and pushed the barrel against the man's temple.

"Ten! Ten of 'em! They was all Texans."

"Did she talk with 'em?"

"Yes, I don't know what they said. I was busy gettin' food done. She left me with no help. She seemed to know 'em. It took me two hours to get all them fed."

Clayton let loose of the man who promptly slumped to the floor holding his bloodied nose with one hand and his leg with the other. He walked back to the table, plucked the coin and flipped it at the bartender.

"They said they were gonna kill you. 'Kill the scalper,' they said."

Spake turned his back and stepped outside. He could hear the man whimpering as he closed the cantina door.

He headed back up the street and whistled again for the dog, who came bounding from around the corner of the building. Together they trudged to the trough. Spake untethered the horses.

He glanced down the road to the south and then looked over at the dog, who took advantage of the lull by again slurping up water from the trough.

"Dog." The dog stopped, burped again and looked up expectantly. "She done told already, so no use chasin' and cuttin' her down. We got our work cut out for us now. Come on."

Spake mounted the blue roan, the fresher of the three horses, and rode northwest out of town following the trail of ten riders.

He pushed hard to catch the larger party he had crossed paths with earlier that morning. About an hour beyond the point where the Texans had crossed his trail, he rode down into a depression and found a bewildering set of tracks.

He dismounted the roan and tethered all the horses in order to take a closer look. The dog trotted up panting heavily. Spake poured some water in his black hat and left it for the dog to lap up as he inspected the ground before him.

The party of ten men had come to a stop in the depression before the tracks of two other horses coming from the other direction. The horses all shuffled about for a while indicating some sort of parley between the ten riders and the two. Then the ten riders turned around and headed to the southwest, away from Jay White and the caverns. The two riders turned around and headed northwest, toward Jay White and the caverns.

"It don't make sense," he muttered. He looked at the surrounding terrain. There were several rock outcroppings on either side of the depression as well as a large set of rocks ahead. "Unless..."

Spake retrieved his hat, pouring the last drops of water that remained into his mouth. He mounted the roan, leaving the other horses tethered and guarded by the dog.

He rode to one outcropping and then another, circling around the back of each. Every time he saw the same thing, evidence that a group of men had corralled their horses behind each of the rock features and positioned themselves for a clean shot into the depression where the parley had occurred. Riding northwest out of the depression, Spake made out where all these groups of men had reformed and headed to the northwest with the two parley riders. There had to be about a hundred men in this regrouped party that was now headed in the direction of Carlsbad, straight for Jay White and Molly Bell.

Just when he figured he'd solved one puzzle another more perplexing one caught his eye. Another set of tracks picked up the trail behind the hundred men riding toward Jay White. They weren't horse tracks, though. It made no sense, but the tracks were unmistakably canine. Why would a pack of wolves follow a hundred mounted men?

He spurred the roan and galloped back to the dog and spare horses.

"Dog, you done good for me." He got off the roan and mounted the fresher of the remaining pair. "There's a fair chance both of us ain't gonna make it out of this one. A hundred men just turned back ten bounty hunters. We got to go after them hundred."

The dog looked up at him expectantly, still panting with fresh drool stringing down from his mouth. The dog didn't understand, but Spake felt better having explained the situation to him. He grabbed the reins of the roan and other horse and charged his tiny force toward Carlsbad.

***

Molly held the black box up and peered inside. No explosion this time, but something was going on in the box. She looked harder. There was movement, a commotion of some kind. Her old friends came into focus, the ones who looked like a cross between animal and child. She remembered them vividly, their stooped bodies on skinny legs like dogs walking upright, their short tails and the ridge of hair that ran up their spines. She felt a cold shiver seeing their cat-like faces with the sharp teeth that...no, they eat people! It all came rushing back, the hunger, the poor priest, the businessmen, and the young women with red cheeks and black stockings.

More creatures appeared. She didn't want to see them. The box pressed in on her face no matter how hard she tried to push back.

Now they were swarming. She heard their familiar shrieks. There were hundreds of them, more than she remembered. They were struggling over a mound of something, each one clawing to get to the middle. Yet several were being thrown from the mound in different directions, as if they had assaulted a small hill emitting explosions that kept knocking them off.

There was a hand, a man's hand, emerging from the mound, grasping for a skinny leg and tossing one of the creatures high in the air. A man was under them, a man struggling against a hoard of hundreds! As each creature was thrown from the pile, it scampered back to rejoin the fray, some of them wiping bloody faces with their clawed hands. For a moment a head emerged from the pile, a head topped with curly auburn hair. A man screamed as he was pulled back under.

"Mick! No, stop! It's Mick! Stop! Please, stop!"

Molly woke to darkness. She saw nothing. She blinked but, eyes open or closed, she still saw nothing. The dank smell brought her to her senses.

She was in the cave. It was a dream, or was the cave a dream? No, the box was a dream.

Molly sat up and rubbed her eyes. She still perceived nothing but unassailable blackness. She felt for some matches and struck one. The cave walls flickered into view, the pillars, stalagmites, and stalactites all still standing vigil.

It was a dream…no, a nightmare, but Mick was in danger. He mustn't look into the box! She had to stop him, to warn him, but how? She didn't even know where he was. The image of his hand, his head, and bloody mouths filled her mind. She could hear him scream above the shrieks.

The match flickered one last time as it singed her finger. She dropped the match and was again enveloped in the black nothing.

She sat still in the darkness and tried to think. She *didn't* know where Mick was, but she certainly wouldn't figure that out sitting in a dark cave. She had to find him, somehow, or at least try. How could she bear the thought of Mick being eaten alive by those creatures?

She reached for another match and lit her lantern.

"I have to get out of this cave, find Mick, and warn him."

Job said nothing.

"No, you're not talking me out of it. He needs me. I'd rather die than let them have him."

Job obeyed, remaining silent.

It didn't take long to pack up. She didn't have much to take with her.

"Goodbye, Job. I don't know if I'll be back again. Here, you watch these for me."

She placed the psalm passages Jay had left for her at Job's feet and turned away.

She made for the mouth of the cave, working her way along ledges and steep trails that eventually led her to a faint glow in the distance. As she continued, the increasing brightness of the glow told her that it must be late afternoon or early evening, not yet dusk, though. Perhaps she should wait until morning? No, she must keep pushing forward. Mick was in danger.

Up the wire ladder she scrambled. Coming around the last bend, the cavern's opening floated into view. It was still light. At least she'd have good visibility to survey the approaches to the cave.

The cavern's damp, chilly air gave way to crisp desert smells that tinged her nose far into her nasal passages. The light outside the cave shone bright and beautiful, alive with color and vivid hues.

She scampered out of the mouth of the cave and climbed toward the nearby bluff. The sun's rays warmed her skin. She felt alive and part of the world.

Clambering to the top of the bluff, she peered out at the vast sandy horizon. Her eyes focused on something moving in the distance giving off a substantial cloud of dust.

"No! Please God, no, not now!"

A posse of men and horses like she'd never seen, a hundred men, maybe more, thundered toward her. A man with a large black hat riding out front on a big blue roan pointed at her. As if on command from the man with the black hat, a large dog sprinted ahead of the group and the whole band came charging at a hard gallop. The rumble of hundreds of hooves slamming against the desert floor echoed in her head as she turned to run back toward the cavern. She slipped and skidded, throwing caution to the wind, fear driving her like a panicked animal. She felt her chest tightening, and then she tripped.

She rolled head first down the slope, but managed to flatten out and get her feet oriented downhill as she continued to slide on her back. Her left leg hit hard on something. A stabbing pain radiated from her ankle to her hip. The impact spun her around and her head smacked a hard surface. She rolled onto her stomach and came to a dusty stop in a pile of gravel.

Her head throbbed and her left leg screamed in pain. She couldn't gain her feet. The dust around her cleared to reveal a small space between two large boulders nearby. She crawled toward the space and pulled herself in. She wanted to cry, but gritted her teeth while she worked to bring all her body into the shaded hiding place.

The sound of a galloping horse made her hold her breath. The horse came closer and then stopped. The muffled thunder of the approaching mob rumbled in the background. This must be an outlier, or perhaps someone not with the larger group?

Someone was climbing toward her hiding place.

"Molly, darling. Molly, it's me."

The familiar voice was a rush of cool water on her throbbing head, then a knot formed in her stomach.

"Papa, no! Run while you can. They'll kill us both. Run, Papa!"

A face appeared at the entrance to the hiding place.

"Molly, thank God!"

"Papa, please, they'll kill us both. Run!"

Her father grinned as his eyes began to water. "Don't you worry, darling. They're with me. I've got a whole company of

Colonel Roosevelt's Rough Riders behind me, and there isn't a force this side of hell that will ever lay a hand on my girl again. I promise."

CHAPTER 13
VISIONS

Father Philip Cornish had just finished buttoning his shirt when the bell at his front door chimed. He glanced at his watch. Almost six PM.

"A bit inconvenient," he muttered. He already felt pressed to make the evening's dinner engagement with James Aston.

He hurriedly snapped on his cufflinks while trotting down the hall to the entryway to his apartment. He stopped momentarily and listened at the door for any clue as to who the caller might be at this hour, but the muffled traffic noise from the street outside gave no answer. Opening the door revealed arguably the most beautiful young woman he'd ever laid eyes upon.

"Philip Cornish?"

"Indeed, may I help you?"

"I have a message from your friend, James. May I come in?"

Her strawberry hair streamed down her shoulders with a cascade of curls framing her ivory white face, green eyes, and lips painted a bright red that matched the lighter hue of her rouged cheeks. A short gold necklace bearing a ruby pendant hung around her long, elegant neck. Two earrings with smaller rubies dangled amongst the strawberry curls. The low bust line on her dress revealed a distractingly ample glimpse of what was held tightly below. Her waist narrowed perfectly before broadening to her well-proportioned hips. The scent of lilac, lavender, and spice wafted through the door.

"I said, may I come in?"

"Oh, yes, sorry, please." Cornish stepped aside, timing a deep breath as she entered, savoring the results for as long as discretion would allow.

As she passed he glimpsed her legs, clad in black stockings and ending with red high-heeled shoes, alternately peeking through a slit in the front of her dress running from the bottom to mid-thigh.

"Where is the bedroom?"

"I beg your pardon?"

"James was insistent that I deliver his message in the bedroom. Down this hall then?"

"Um, yes, on the right," he responded meekly.

She sauntered down the hall leaving him momentarily behind. Regaining his senses, he followed.

By the time he caught up she was in his room leaning against the bed, facing back toward the door, with both legs showing through the slit in her dress. This time, though, the dress was hiked slightly, revealing white skin above the mid-thigh stockings.

Cornish stopped abruptly a step inside the doorway. "I beg your pardon. Your name is?"

"How rude of me, wandering into your home without as much as a calling card." She extended the backside of her right hand, beckoning him nearer. "I'm Rose. Pleasure to meet you."

Cornish stepped forward, took her hand, and kissed the warm, soft skin. "The pleasure is all mine, madam. Please, what, pray tell, has James asked that you convey? I was just getting dressed to meet him for dinner."

"Dinner will be delayed, I'm afraid."

"Delayed? For how long."

"As long as you like."

"Pardon?"

"Do you find me attractive, Philip? May I call you Philip?"

"Yes, certainly."

"'Yes' you find me attractive, or 'yes' I may call you Philip?"

"I'm sorry, you mentioned a message of some sort." He paused but she just smiled, showing perfect white teeth. "Yes, on both accounts."

She leaned back further displaying more of the white skin above the black stockings. Her scent filled the room, making him lightheaded.

"James says 'Happy Birthday' and 'I'll see you for dinner upon your convenience.'"

"But..."

"It's dreadfully warm in here. I don't know how you bear it." Rose turned her head and looked toward the ceiling, uncloaking one of the ruby earrings resting against her exposed neck. She looked back at him with her green eyes sparkling. "Do you mind if I get comfortable? You do want me to be comfortable?"

"By all means, madam. Will you excuse me for a moment?"

"Why? Do you not approve?"

"Of course I...I do approve. Only, I'm expecting a delivery shortly. If you'll permit me just a moment, I'd like to leave a note at my door to avoid interruption."

"Do be quick," she replied as she crossed her legs, splitting her dress further. "I detest being alone."

Cornish scrambled back down the hall to a small desk in the entryway. He pulled out two sheets of paper, scrawling out a short messages on both. He placed one sheet in an envelope and darted out the door.

He looked up and down the street frantically until he sighted an empty hansom attended by its driver about forty yards away. He sprinted to the cab, thrusting the note, envelope, and several coins on the driver upon arrival.

"If you please, deliver this envelope to Mister Fred Miller with all due haste. The address is on this note. It's quite urgent."

The driver looked at the coins he'd been handed, stuffed the envelope in his pocket, and reached for the reins. "Right away, sir." With that, the horse bolted forward onto the street.

Cornish trotted back to the front door he hadn't bothered to close and stepped inside, quietly locking the door behind him. He stopped for a moment to catch his breath and rub his right knee, and then proceeded down the hall trying his best to minimize limping on his right leg. The door to his bedroom was closed, so he knocked.

"Come in," came a hushed response from the bedroom.

He took another deep breath, said a short silent prayer, and opened the door.

Rose was roughly in the same position as when he left her, leaning against the bed and facing the doorway. Only now she wore nothing but the ruby draped earrings, the ruby pendant, the black stockings, and red shoes.

"Happy birthday."

Father Philip Cornish shook his head and smiled. "Yes, I believe I shall delay my dinner with James. What a fine present. Two hours should be about right, don't you think?"

"That depends on how hungry you are," she responded coyly.

"Excellent!" He pulled up a nearby chair, turned it around such that the back faced Rose, and mounted it with his legs straddling the seat. He folding his arms over the back of the chair, rested his chin on his folded arms, and gazed at her, making no effort to suppress a grin. "Now, what shall we talk about for two hours?"

"Talk?"

"Madam, you surprise me. You do know I'm a priest?"

"You can't be serious." She stared at him incredulously, her red-lined mouth agape. "You're Father Philip Cornish. Everyone knows about your affair with Lady Brompston and estrangement from your wife. Is this a joke?"

"Ah, Lady Brompston, is that what you would like to chat about? We have two hours, so you pick the topics."

Rose glared at him for several seconds and then pushed off from the bed. "I'm getting dressed. I'll not be humiliated like this."

Cornish rose from his chair and stalked forward, shoving her forcefully back on the bed.

"Madam…Rose, if that is your name, let me make myself perfectly clear. You've been bought and paid for. You're mine, obliged to do my bidding for the next two hours. I expect you to deliver, and so does James Aston." He set his jaw and returned her glare. "I've decided we should chat, that's all. When we're done, you can leave, and you will have fulfilled your contract. And I, I will have had a memorable birthday."

Cornish returned to his straddled seat, again crossing his arms on the back of the chair.

"Now, what shall we discuss?"

She sat for a moment as if working out some puzzle in her head. "May I get dressed first?"

Cornish let out an audible sigh. "If you must. Good heavens! Of course, put on some clothes. Forgive me for thinking aloud. I pray God will forgive me this indulgence in recompense for what I have forgone, but I'd prefer to watch while you dress. I may be a priest, but I am a man, and carrying your image in my mind's eye may provide me with some distraction from the ugliness of life for years to come. I've rarely seen such beauty, and I'm not likely to see it in the flesh again."

She looked confused for a moment, and then sat fully on the bed with her legs crossed. She stared at him, making no move toward dressing herself.

"My name's not Rose, it's Sarah. Talking is not my strong point."

"That's fine, Sarah. I'm an excellent listener as well as speaker. Between the two of us, I'm certain we can fill the next two hours. Are you from London originally?"

"No, I was born in Manchester."

"Manchester, you say. I know it well. In fact, a dear friend of mine is from Manchester. Did you know Mr. Aston once lived there himself?"

***

"Don't take it hard, Mick. The boy's been found, alive and well." Jenkins pointed at the lad sitting to Mick's right. "Would you prefer to have found him drowned in the Thames?"

"Sooner," Mick replied in a hushed tone while glancing about the sparsely attended pub. "That's what I'd have preferred, sir. You'll be letting me go to America now? I promise to do better there."

"That's the second bit of good news. There's no need for you to go to America."

"She's been found?" Mick gripped the table and stared wide-eyed at the inspector. "Tell me Miss Molly is safe!" He sat motionless, holding his breath.

"Yes. She's safe back at the ranch with her parents and crew."

Mick exhaled audibly as his entire body relaxed.

Jenkins smiled. "You needn't always be the savior of the world. Young Talbot here made it back to us with the help of a good Samaritan."

"Well, however he made it, I'm glad of it." Mick grinned sheepishly at Jim, blew off a head of foam from a recently replaced mug, and downed a substantial portion of the dark, nutty brew. Mick's demeanor noticeably changed with the second bit of news. After a hard gulp, he wiped his mouth on his sleeve and turned to face the inspector with a new-found grin.

"You needn't bring us here to celebrate. Not that I object to a free pub meal with young Talbot here." To emphasize the point, Mick elbowed Jim in the ribs hard enough that Jim bounced against the nearby wall from which the table jutted.

"Not a celebration. A reunion of sorts," replied Jenkins before taking a swig of his own brown ale.

"So you say! I've not seen the lad but once or twice since he had his pocket picked near three years ago, though I looked hard and fast for you all over London. What a treat. And now with Miss Molly safe, the world's all put back together. To your health, Master Talbot." Mick raised his glass in Talbot's direction.

"And might I add, Master Talbot, perhaps your health is in need of an alder tree." The Irishman loomed over Jim as he placed his hand on the young man's arm. "See, Inspector? An alder tree, lad, that's what you need."

Mick held up one of Jim's arms, enclosing the biceps between his thumb and pointing finger.

"An alder tree?" Talbot looked first at Mick and then at the inspector.

"Don't get him started, lad. I sense an Irish yarn coming on." Jenkins always marveled at how quickly Mick could flash from morose to giddy, like a big puppy.

"Not a yarn at all, sir! A true story, through and through." Mick let go of Jim's arm and leaned back with an impish smirk on his face.

"But, what has an alder tree have to do with my health?"

"Good question, Master Talbot. You see, I was raised, along with my brother, twins we were, near Cashel. You've heard of the Rock thereabouts, no doubt."

"You have a twin brother?"

"Not just any twin brother, identical we were, from head to toe. Nearby our home was the old Hore Abbey, a finer abbey there never was, but that was six hundred years ago. Now, she lies in ruins with nothin' but sheep to keep the bones company."

Jenkins shook his head. "You were duly warned, Master Talbot."

"When my brother and I were but wee lads, five or six at most, my mother, God rest her soul, showed us two small alder trees, one in each corner of a small courtyard of the abbey ruins. She announced that the two trees would henceforth belong to us, one for each son, and as the trees grew tall and strong, so would her sons. The trees took our names, one Mick the other Danny.

"As the years went by, Danny and I took a keen interest in the progress of our trees. Which one of us would grow to be taller and

243

stronger than the other? Surely the answer lay with those trees. My mother had said so herself, and she was a wise women indeed.

"One year, to my surprise and dismay, the Danny tree branched forth with great vigor. It was clear which tree was taking the lead in this contest, and soon poor Mick was a second to Danny. But weren't just with trees! Danny, the real Danny, he grew stronger every day. When once we would wrestle to exhaustion, now Danny would come out on top. It was an alarming development."

Talbot sat transfixed as he rubbed the biceps Mick had squeezed between his thumb and forefinger.

"Then one day I discovered the secret to the growth of the Danny tree. Danny and I were out doing chores when I noticed he'd snuck away. So I did what any brother would do, I followed him. Into the abbey courtyard he went, straight to the Danny tree. When he arrived at the trunk, he unbuttoned his trousers and proceeded to liberally water the tree, so to speak.

"Desiring to learn the frequency of this behavior, I stalked my brother for several months. Sure enough, three, sometimes five or six times a day, Danny would sneak off, unbutton, and water his tree."

Mick paused long enough to take another swig.

"The mystery was solved. I followed my brother's habits thereafter, and soon the Mick tree was back in the race. And there you have it."

"I'm sorry. I don't follow."

"An alder tree, lad, look at me." Mick flexed his right arm. "We need just find you an alder tree, name it Jim, and water it liberally. Soon you'll be bigger and stronger than you could ever hope for. I'll help you water it! You provide the drink, and I'll take care of the tree. To your health, Master Talbot."

Mick raised his mug again, but stopped shy of his mouth, appearing distracted by something near the front door.

The inspector glanced up at a mirror on the wall near the table that gave him an unobstructed view of the entry to the pub. A familiar form was closing fast on their table, filling the mirror until he stood directly behind Jenkins.

"Fred, glad you could join us. Running a little late, I note. Please, have a seat. I believe you know Mick. This is my assistant, Jim Talbot."

"Gentlemen." Fred nodded in acknowledgment and took a seat next to the inspector.

"A reunion indeed!" Mick exclaimed before taking another drink.

"Sorry, Inspector, I was detained unexpectedly, though fortuitously. And, with this confounded fog, I walked right past the front door twice before I found the place."

Fred placed an envelope on the table and slid it toward Jenkins. "May I mention who it's from?" Fred looked nervously about the room.

Jenkins ignored the question, took up the envelope, and removed a note. There was a message on it, scrawled quickly with a lead pencil, which he read to himself. *6 PM. I'll be found out shortly. Aston at 57 Smith Street this evening. Window will close quickly.*

"As I was leaving to come here, a cab driver knocked on my door and gave me a note instructing me to deliver this envelope to you as soon as possible. I got here as fast as I could."

"And since you've read it, I suspect you'll object strongly to not coming with us." Jenkins tapped the envelope on the table and gave Fred a stern glare.

Fred looked back earnestly. "Inspector, there's no time for reinforcements. You have me and Mick. Surely that's better for the job than Mick alone. It's not far from here, twenty minutes by foot without this fog. Besides, if we find him, perhaps I can persuade him to a nonviolent reaction. I was his best friend."

"'Was' is the operative word." Jenkins rolled the problem around in his head. This was unexpected. The bait he had laid out was all here, but to leave before the scheduled help arrived truly did leave him with no reinforcements. Was *he* being baited for a trap set by another?

"Jim, we can get to 57 Smith Street directly from here in twenty minutes on foot, as Mr. Miller noted, *if* we used the expected direct route. Is there another?"

Talbot looked down at the table appearing lost in thought over an imaginary map. Years as a cab driver in London had no doubt imprinted a detailed bird's eye view of the city in his sharp mind. After a few seconds he swung his face toward the inspector. "Yes...a smuggler's door near an old quay off the Chelsea Embankment. It leads by passage, a hundred yards or so, to a nearby private house. I think I can find it, but it's difficult even if you know where it is."

"Convenient." Jenkins smiled and shook his head as he pondered his predicament. "I suppose that means that we all must go. Mick, where is your collar, and why aren't you wearing it?"

"Go where?" asked the Irishman.

"To find the elusive James Aston. Where is your collar?"

"Oh, that thing, we'll I *am* wearing it." Mick reached inside his jacket and removed the steel contraption from his left forearm, displaying it to the inspector with a schoolboy grin.

"You're supposed to wear it around your neck."

"Why, this thing? It barely fits around my arm, sir!"

Jenkins shook his head in disapproval. He looked at the device, at his watch, and then at Fred and Jim. "Too big for Talbot, give it to Miller."

"What is it?" exclaimed Fred.

Jenkins loosened his scarf, revealing a similar metal collar fitting snuggly around his neck. "It's protection. You put it around your neck, latch it in the back, and then conceal it with a scarf. Unfortunately, a snug fit is required or it's of little use."

Jenkins turned again to Talbot. Was this a trap? He looked at his watch. The window was closing.

"No time to lose. Master Talbot, you'll lead the way. Once we're en route, stick close to Mick no matter what happens."

The inspector brought a mug near his mouth and lowered his voice to a whisper. "Mick, as we are leaving, you'll pass by a man alone at the table nearest the front door in a long grey coat with a bowler pulled nearly over his eyes. There's a set of stairs behind the bar leading to a basement. I want you to fetch the man near the door and deposit him in the basement. The staff will pay no heed. They've been paid to look the other way."

Mick glanced across the room. "Aye, the gent with the pockmarked face and drinker's nose. Dispatched, sir?"

"Only if necessary, restrained will do. I don't want him following us. Quickly, though, we haven't much time." He dropped the mug and announced with a bark, "Gentlemen, we must be off!"

The group jumped from the table, with Fred frantically trying to secure the collar and Mick hurriedly downing his beer while headed toward the door. As Mick passed near the man with the bowler hat, he swooped in with his right arm around the man's neck and pulled him out of his seat in a chokehold. The man's feet scratched at the floor and sputtering noises emanated from his face which was quickly turning bright red.

"Come now, sir, the easier the better." Shuffling hastily behind the bar, Mick disappeared down the stairs with his wriggling cargo.

Jenkins lingered long enough to confirm the room was cleared. He glanced at the bartender, who casually dried a mug with his back to the commotion. Satisfied, he left to join the others.

The group waited outside until Mick emerged, looked at the inspector, and shrugged.

"Dispatched, then?"

"He was quite uncooperative, sir."

"Wait," uttered Fred. "You killed him?"

Mick shrugged again.

"You just killed a man on some suspicion that he might follow us."

Jenkins held his tongue only briefly. "It wasn't suspicion. That's what he intended to do."

"How do you know? Have you never been wrong?"

"Fred, I don't have time for this."

Fred stood his ground in front of Jenkins, blocking the route forward with his jaw set.

Jenkins looked Fred square in the eye. "He followed me to the pub for half a mile in the fog. If you check his right shoe you'll find a badly worn heel with nails exposed, causing a clicking noise when he walks. Realizing this early on while following me, he made a point of walking on his toes with his right foot to avoid the sound of the nails on the sidewalk and street. There is no reason to conceal the sound of the nails unless you're following someone."

"It's impossible to see out here! You committed a man to death based on the sound of steps?"

"When we arrived at the pub he sat at a table that gave him a good view of us. It also gave me a view to confirm the presence of the worn heel on his right shoe. When I caught him looking in our direction he picked up a newspaper and concealed his face. He held the newspaper there for several minutes, upside down.

"I can go on about the information I obtained before tonight leading me to the conclusion that we would certainly be watched and followed. I could explain my recognition of this particular man, pockmarked face and bulbous nose, from pictures I reviewed of various undesirables known to the Yard for having a violent criminal past. Not to mention the critical nature of the journey on which we are embarking, but we are truly running short on time, Mr. Miller."

Fred lowered his head and stepped aside.

"Lead on, Master Talbot." Jenkins pointed down the street, and off they marched.

As expected, Jim displayed the uncanny navigation skills in the London fog that Jenkins was counting on. They made good progress, huddling closely together as the young man walked on briskly. Lamp posts and the occasional pedestrian suddenly appeared from the gloom and then vanished as quickly behind them.

"I told him I only needed to tie him to a pipe, Mr. Miller, but he fought like an animal possessed," Mick whispered.

"It's all right, Mick. I understand."

"Quick it was, in the end. I just twisted his neck till it snapped."

"Quiet, please," hissed Jenkins.

The streets grew murkier as they approached the Thames. The ghostly sound of the occasional mariner or dockside worker calling out in the distance grew more distinct.

At first Jenkins caught a mere hint in the breeze, rotten eggs, maybe? A whiff of sulfur mixed with mold? The smell grew stronger. The inspector glanced at the group. The others all sniffed the air with expressions of concern. Jim Talbot stopped and looked expectantly at Inspector Jenkins.

"Come on lad, press on. Eyes forward, it's rather dark this evening. Show us the way."

Jenkins watched Talbot as the young man peered hesitantly back from where they had come and then at the inspector. The fog was solid now, and the little group huddled in the gloom as Talbot checked his bearing.

"It's hard in this muck, sir. I'm not sure. I think we are almost there." Talbot took an audible sniff, making a nervous show of it. He eyes suddenly widened as he looked frantically about. "No. I've seen this before, in a dream."

"Inspector," Fred Miller interrupted with a whisper. "The smell, I've smelled that many times. We need to turn back."

Jenkins raised his hand, flashing his palm at the group when movement in the darkness caught his eye. A form rushed them. Jenkins drew his gun, but before he could raise it a cloud of stinging dust hit his eyes. He was blind.

He instinctively went to ground and lunged forward hoping to catch the charging assailant below the knees, but his grasping came up empty. A crushing heel came down on his right wrist. He involuntarily released the gun. He felt two powerful hands grab his shoulders and pull him off the ground. A blast of reeking sulfuric stench filled his nostrils. With his left hand he reached for the knife he kept in the pocket of his trousers. He swung the blade hard across his body, but it was deflected downward. A powerful blow hit him squarely in the neck followed by a shriek and more stench.

The force knocked him backwards. Metal clattered on the brick pavestone. He gasped for air. He couldn't breathe. He grasped at his throat. The deformed steel collar was strangling him.

There was the noise of struggling as someone else joined the fray. He rubbed his eyes and blinked, trying to focus. Someone grabbed the knife from his hand, pulling at the blade harder than Jenkins could grasp the handle. He fell to the ground, gasping for air, frantically trying to remove the metal collar that was choking him. The latch wouldn't budge. He heard grunting and feet shuffling. Then Jim Talbot screamed.

"Where are you? Jim!" came Fred Miller's voice. "I can't see!"

Jenkins felt his pistol on the road. He was losing consciousness but regaining his eyesight. He saw two forms struggling. One went down and the other was on him like a cat to a mouse.

"No, Mick! Don't look! No!" Jim screamed at the top of his lungs.

The form on top of the two rose and leapt toward the inspector. Jenkins leveled his pistol and pulled the trigger three times. Three times the gun faithfully answered with three flashes from the short muzzle. Three accompanying bangs echoed through the fog. He felt faint and went down on his hands and knees. His vision darkened. There was a hand on his shoulder. Then the pressure was gone. He gulped in the stinky air, filling his lungs and bringing a rush of blood to his head.

"Are you all right, Inspector?"

He looked up to see Fred Miller rubbing his eyes with one hand and holding the now removed and deformed metal collar with the other.

"Yes, thank you, Fred."

"He bent this steel. He hit you so hard in the neck, the blade on his knife broke. How can a man do that with his hands?"

Jim Talbot came into focus, lying on the road, sobbing. Jenkins and Miller ran to his side.

Jim cried out. "I told him not to look."

"Are you hurt?" asked the inspector.

"He broke my leg, just like the gentlemen with the red packet. The one who sent me to Lord Lansdowne before I met you for the first time. Same leg."

Jenkins pulled back Jim's right trouser leg to see the bone protruding through the skin.

Jim buried his head in his arms and moaned.

"Inspector, over here."

"I told him not to look," Jim cried out again. "He had a black box. I told him not to look."

Jenkins sprinted to join Fred, who was bent over a body lying near the wall of a building. It was Mick, eyes wide open, with a knife, the inspector's knife, embedded in his throat.

"We tried to help him pull the man off you, Inspector." Talbot moaned and rolled on the ground nearby.

"It's all right, Jim. Calm down."

"He broke my leg and then went after Mick. We tried to stop him, but he was too strong. The man grabbed your knife and used it on Mick. I told him not to look!" Talbot was sobbing again.

The inspector felt for Mick's pulse. The big man lay stiffly on the ground, his glassy eyes staring straight ahead. Jenkins pulled the knife from his throat and closed Mick's eyes with his fingers.

Jenkins searched the ground, frantically looking for clues, first noting the knife handle and nearby shattered remnants of the blade that had deformed his steel collar. Then he found what he hoped for, a spot of blood near where he'd last seen the image of their attacker. There was another drop a foot from the first, and then another, and then another, all in a line. He followed the drops for a few yards and then ran back to Fred.

"Do you know how to use this?"

Fred looked down at the pistol Jenkins had thrust into his hand and nodded.

"Stay here with the boy. Shoot anyone who tries to get close to him until I get back. He'll kill Jim if he can."

"Where are you going?"

"I've got to get that box! And I need Talbot to be here when I find it. We've got to get Mick out of that box!"

Jenkins, bloody knife in hand, started along the trail of red dots splattered on the wet street. He moved as quickly as the fog would allow without losing the trail. The stench of rotten eggs lingered over the path he was on, confirming the trail.

The trail led along the edge of the street and then turned down a dark mews. He slowed and bent down to keep the droplets in sight as he entered the mews. The sulfuric scent increased in the mew, mixing with the smell of mildew and stale urine. The walls of the mews seemed to close in around him the deeper he went. The stench grew as did the darkness of the enclosed space.

Out of the fog a wall appeared. The back of the mews was sealed off. He felt around with his left hand keeping the knife pointed forward with the right. Moving laterally along the wall a doorway appeared to his right. He led with the knife and entered the doorway.

He was in the open air again. A barely visible trail of red splatters still lay ahead. He increased his speed as he descended sloping terrain. The sound of water slapping against the shore signaled that the Thames was but a short distance to his front.

His path stopped abruptly at the ledge of a stone wall. Below lay the murky river, rhythmically sloshing against the wall. The bleeding assailant had gone into the water.

"Damn you!" Jenkins exclaimed, but from the river came no reply.

***

"Ah Charles, please sit down and join me. I've good news!"

Sir Edward thrust a champagne flute in Hardinge's hand as he directed him to pair of overstuffed chairs angled toward each other.

"What might we be toasting?"

"World peace!" Grey settled himself into his chair. "I received another of those infernal red packets an hour ago. Only this time…good news. I sent for you straightaway."

"To world peace." Hardinge raised his glass. "Um, excellent stuff, Edward. I take it the Serbians blinked."

Grey frowned. "You knew, then?"

"No…educated guess. When last week the Germans issued their war ultimatum to the Russians and the Russians backed down, it left the Serbs with not much choice."

"Thank God for the Russians." Grey interjected. "They finally saw things clearly. And thanks to you, Charles. You've worked very hard at untangling the Gordian knot of serpents one at a time."

"We…"

"Yes, yes, *we've* worked very hard. First, the settlement brokered between Bulgaria and the Ottomans…that was the beginning. And it was the Russians who stepped forward to pay the compensation the Bulgarians promised and then reneged on. I drink to them. To the Russians."

Hardinge raised his glass in response. "You don't suppose the Russians bailing out the Bulgarians' financial commitment was viewed as a sign of weakness in Berlin, weakness that might have prompted the German ultimatum?"

"It all ended well, did it not? You say a sign of 'weakness.' One could say a sign of 'flexibility' instead. You look skeptical."

Hardinge paused, taking another sip. "I am skeptical. I fear the path to war becomes clearer with each passing crisis. Austria-Hungary, an empire with which we enjoyed long, friendly terms, is now our determined foe and wedded solidly to Germany. Meanwhile, Germany grows more dangerous to us with each new battle cruiser launched. This time she tipped her cards, demonstrating a clear willingness to go to war for matters having nothing to do with her own interests, just to prop up her belligerent ally. Austria is now the tail that wags a very large dog. Russia has been humiliated and may not back down again when Slavic causes are in play. This whole Balkan region is a tinderbox waiting for the match to strike."

Sir Edward slumped in his chair at this assessment, fixating on his champagne glass which he swirled rhythmically with one hand.

"But, we have bought time," Sir Charles added.

"Hardly a 'strike-up-the-band' toast." Grey raised his glass. "To buying time until Armageddon." He swirled away, seemingly lost in thought. "Armageddon…how do you imagine it?" he asked without looking up.

"Pardon?"

"What would it look like, the end of the world?"

"I haven't given it much thought." Hardinge pondered the question without arriving at an immediate answer. "I take it you have."

"Of late, yes, I have."

"And what do you see?"

"It's more than 'see,' I can almost be there." Grey focused on his swirling glass of champagne as if looking into a crystal ball at the future. "The earth is a pulverized mash of mud, blood, and bits and pieces of humanity…no trees, no grass, no structures to be seen, just mounds of bloody mud. And the stench, not of death, but something burning and searing, like some overpowering reaction from a galactic chemistry experiment gone wrong. No noise, though, only silence. Nothing moving, not even flies above the goo."

"Rather grim, Edward."

"Yes, to be avoided at all costs. But, you're right, we have bought time." Grey stopped swirling his glass and raised it high.

Hardinge smiled. "To world peace it is, then. May the time we've bought be used wisely."

"To world peace, and wisdom."

***

"Teddy, you're still up? It's half past one."

Theodore Roosevelt pulled his eyes away from the crackling fire. The yellow glow cast long shadows about his study and shimmered off his wife's white nightgown.

"Edith, my dear. I'm afraid I've kept you up as well."

She pulled a chair next to his and rested her hands in his lap.

"You miss it, don't you, dear husband?"

"Rather chilly for April in New York. I thought I'd warm this old bear up before he came to bed."

"And those?" Edith pointed to a pile of opened letters on nearby table.

"Ah, letters from friends. 'Thank you, Mr. President. I wish you had run again.' 'Job well done, Mr. President. Best of wishes in your retirement.'"

"Do you wish you'd run again?"

"I promised, Edith. America doesn't need a king. You do your job, energetically and honestly, and then you leave. It would be unhealthy for democracy to be saddled with the same president for three or four terms, even a Roosevelt."

He stopped and stared back at the fire.

"And now I've left."

"And you miss it." Edith leaned into her husband and rested her head on his shoulder.

He took her hand in his. "I'm sure Taft will do a fine job. I'm delighted he won the election. And the British Foreign Secretary, Edward Grey, he's calmed the waters once again now that this Bosnia mess has settled down."

"But?"

"Grey worries me, Edith. Can you imagine, a British Foreign Secretary who's never even set foot on the European mainland? He keeps everyone in the dark. One should confront one's enemies and support one's friends. It's hard to tell who is who in his mind. With no one knowing what the British reaction will be to any particular situation, it makes the whole world less stable. I know." The President held up his hand "'Speak softly but carry a big stick.' Yes, that's still my motto, and the British Navy is the biggest stick there is. But I never said 'hold your tongue but carry a big stick.' Well, Taft will handle it now. Yes, I'm sure he'll do a fine job."

"But?"

Theodore shook his head, brushing his cheek against Edith's hair as she still rested on his shoulder.

"I'd sooner find a polar bear in Texas than keep a thought from you." He gave her hand a gentle squeeze. "I can't help anymore. That's the part I miss."

"Help with what?"

He took in a long breath and exhaled slowly. "You worry about *me*, my dear, worry that some assassin might put a bullet in me or throw a bomb in my car. I've had guns fired at me before and bombs tossed in my direction. There's no worry to be had on my behalf. But I have seen war.

"It's not the romantic charging toward the breaking enemy lines that schoolboys imagine. Modern weapons make war a meat grinder of men. It's noisy, messy, smelly, awful work.

"We have sons. There are many families who have sons." He took another long breath, glancing at the picture of the *USS Connecticut*'s football team now hanging in his study. "I worry about guns fired at them and bombs tossed in their direction."

Edith looked her husband square in the face. "You just said this Bosnian mess was over?"

The president took up both her hands. "Europe is seething for a fight. The countries are lining up in one camp or the other. Without one side being obviously superior in arms than the other, neither side is inclined to back down. When both sides think they can win…it's only a matter of time. The Moroccan crisis yesterday, the Bosnian crisis today, there'll be another, and then another, until nothing can hold back the fury. Then…"

"What is it, Teddy? What is it you see?"

"My war was child's play, two small armies skirmishing with each other." He closed his eyes and shook his head. "What do I see? I see a world at war."

CHAPTER 14
THE CALLING CARD

Father Philip Cornish slowed his pace as the address he was looking for came into view. Outside stood a doorman in a top hat, grey jacket with black trim, grey trousers, and a black waistcoat, a uniform that well matched the dreary afternoon hue. The doorman eyed Father Cornish intently as he approached.

"May I be of service, sir?"

Cornish fished for the calling card stowed in an interior pocket of his jacket and, successful in the search, produced it.

"Father Cornish, please wait here. I'll only be a moment."

It *was* but a moment between the doorman retreating behind the large wooden door and returning, just long enough for Cornish to rub his right knee and look up and down the street. Despite the cloudy sky, the day seemed lovely. If anyone had been following him, he hadn't noticed. A motor car rumbled past as the door reopened.

"Please, sir, step inside." The doorman motioned him in and shut the door, leaving the doorman outside and Father Cornish standing in a small anteroom with an impeccably dressed butler sporting long tails and spats.

"Father Cornish, welcome to the club. Please, follow me."

Cornish trailed the butler down a long hall past several sitting rooms, some occupied with men smoking pipes or cigars and chatting in hushed voices, others with men playing cards or chess. An occasional muted chuckle set off mumbled responses.

At the end of the hall they ascended a set of stairs to the floor above. The butler's coat tails wagged slightly with each step. The stairs twisted one hundred and eighty degrees, setting them on a course back down another hallway, evidently directly above the first.

Again they passed several rooms, some occupied and others empty. No noise came from these rooms, though. Men sat in silent contemplation, some reading, some smoking, others sitting and staring at nothing in particular. At the end of the second hallway they came to a door which the butler unlocked.

"Please, wait in here, sir. May I get you something to drink?"

"Yes, I'll have some tea with a splash of scotch. Thank you."

The butler bowed slightly and headed back down the hall. Cornish entered the room and, seeing a comfortable chair near a ceramic heater, took a seat. Soon the butler returned with a tray holding a teapot, two sets of china teacups and saucers, and a glass vial of brown liquid.

"May I get you anything else, sir?"

"No, thank you."

With that, the butler left the room, closing the door behind him. The sound of a key thrust into the door preceded a metallic click as the door was relocked.

Cornish reached for the pot and filled both cups, adding a splash of scotch to each from the glass vial. He picked up one cup and held the warm china piece in his hands, savoring the aroma of the scotch over steaming black tea.

The room had no windows, a few chairs and tables, and a small door in one corner in addition to the larger locked door through which he had entered. Bookcases lined the wall. He wandered over to one, noting the impressive stock of recent publications. He pulled a few off the shelf, one at a time, and flipped through the pages, reading a passage here and there, while sipping his tea.

A noise from behind caught his attention. He turned his gaze to the smaller door. Hearing something again, he placed a book back on the shelf, sat down, and waited calmly. In short order his patience was repaid as the small door opened.

"Father Cornish, good of you to come."

"Inspector Jenkins, my pleasure. It's quite like you, I suppose, appearing magically into a locked room."

"No magic here, Father, this door wasn't locked."

"I assume you'll be staying a while, then. Your tea, a 'Jenkins' as I call it, is ready." Cornish pointed at the other teacup and then to a nearby seat. Jenkins obliged in both instances and was soon holding the cup.

"A 'Jenkins'? I'm honored. To your health, Father." Jenkins raised his cup in toast.

"And to yours, Inspector." Cornish took another long sip, again enjoying the aroma of the scotch over the mellow tea notes. "It is a healthy drink, is it not? The benefits of both tea and scotch, all in one warm dose. What on earth led you to such invention?"

Jenkins chuckled and took another sip. "Quite by accident. Hmm, perhaps it's not an 'invention' but rather a 'discovery.'"

"Do tell."

"Years ago I was having tea with a suspect in his drawing room, a room not unlike this one, but much busier. He was a collector of strange objects, carved rhino horn from Africa, an ancient sword from China, a shrunken human head from New Guinea, a man's scalp from America, an assortment of bizarre and unrelated things." Jenkins pointed about the room, as if placing each object in the location he'd seen them years before.

"My questioning of the gentleman was revealing little, and I contemplated how I might determine more about his character by different means. A shelf behind him held several bottles of scotch of various quality, some rather pedestrian, but some rare and expensive. It was early in the day, and scotch had not been offered. Even if it had been offered I needed my wits about me, and it would be uncivilized if one glass didn't lead to three. Nonetheless, I was curious which bottle the gentleman would offer if asked.

"It then struck me that I might ask for a splash in my tea. He obliged, and I got my answer. It was rather good as well, I decided, the tea fortified with a bit of scotch. I've used the ploy ever since as a means for obtaining information useful to assessing any host who offers tea. What type of scotch do they own? What type do they offer? One can learn much about a man by answering those two questions. Occasionally just the question itself has the added benefit of knocking the host off balance. It is an odd request, scotch in tea. It doesn't take much to throw off a well-rehearsed performance."

Jenkins glanced at his cup. "I've grown rather fond of the concoction over the years. I drink it now even when not in need of the clues it provides."

The inspector took another sip and smiled. "It fortifies me. A 'Jenkins.' Very well, I accept it as a compliment."

"Indeed, as intended." Cornish hoisted his cup in toast. "May I assume by virtue of this meeting that you received my note?"

Jenkins frowned and set his cup down. "Yes, I received it shortly after you sent it."

"Then my cover is indeed blown."

"As to certain quarters, yes."

"Did you find James Aston?"

"I'm afraid not, but he may have found us."

Cornish sensed that all was not right. Jenkins's countenance had turned stoic.

"Do tell, please. I hope my actions…" Cornish's voice trailed off involuntarily as he lost himself in the terrible thoughts that raced through his head. "I pray my actions didn't place you in danger. I've made quite a hash of all this, haven't I?"

"Danger was expected, Father. I knew the odds going in. It is *I* who miscalculated."

Cornish sat silently, contemplating the word "miscalculated."

"I'm sorry, Inspector. Is there anything I can do?"

"Yes, pray for the soul of my man, Mick. He probably saved my life and Fred Miller's as well."

"Fred was with you?"

"He read your note. He would have followed even if I ordered him to stay, and I had little time to argue with him. No need to worry, he escaped unscathed."

"Thank God." Cornish took a long sip. "I suppose he is now compromised as well. I apologize, Inspector. I had but a moment to decide, and I saw our prey slipping away."

"You could have played the role."

"You mean sleep with a whore?"

"Haven't you done worse?"

Cornish diverted his eyes to his teacup and took another sip.

"Or perhaps you haven't."

"I am a sinner, Inspector."

"Aren't we all, Father? You, however, are closer to the saint than the role you play."

Cornish poured a fresh cup of tea, adding a double helping of the scotch as he continued to look away from the inspector.

"Ever wondered why I trusted you in the first place? Why I contacted you three years ago, took you into my confidence, recruited you as an agent, all the while knowing of your past acquaintance with Father Tate, an agent of the enemy?"

"But that is why you recruited me, isn't it? I knew Father Tate. Naturally, you selected me as your agent to infiltrate and monitor the relationship between Tate and Fred Miller. Tate's death shortly after I started meeting with him and Miller was unfortunate, but it appears your plan was sound. It eventually led James Aston to me."

Cornish paused, but continued when Jenkins made no response. "When you recently arranged the renewal of my acquaintance with Fred so that he might act as an intermediary and pass on my information about Aston to you, I saw that the plan might yet bear fruit. As exhausting as Aston could be, I had to play the game. I regret it didn't end well."

"Your relationship with Tate was of some importance, no doubt. That's not why I recruited you."

"Then why? Why trust me?"

"I told you already."

"What? A saint? My reputation is subject to considerable speculation."

"Spare me your sinner act, Father. I know of few men more blameless."

"An act?"

Jenkins paused, fixing Cornish with a penetrating gaze. "Your estranged wife, Judith, she's not 'estranged' at all. The tabloid version makes no hint that Judith may have some connection with your supposed 'mistress,' Lady Brompston."

Father Cornish diverted his eyes again to his teacup.

"Are you married, Inspector?"

"I was once. She passed away."

Cornish looked up at Jenkins but detected no change in expression.

"I'm quite sorry to hear it."

"Thank you. Back to Lady Brompston's paramour," Jenkins continued as if the matter of his wife had never been raised. "The late Sir Reginald, Lady Brompston's deceased husband, was quite well placed in His Majesty's inner circle. It was his passing that permitted Lady Brompston to pursue the dalliance at hand with vigor. But it was her widowed status that in the end caused the real dilemma for her paramour. Shall I continue?"

"Please, you've piqued my interest to be sure."

"As I said, her paramour was faced with a dilemma. Lady Brompston carried his child. His previous conquests, if they had been careless and not practiced their arts with the proper precautions, were persuaded to see a certain physician who could nip the potential scandal in the bud, so to speak. No child, no scandal. Such women who were married might alternatively be persuaded, along with their husbands, to declare the child their own. *Pater est quem nuptiae demonstrate*, again no scandal. Lady Brompston, however, as I mentioned, was widowed.

"She also was not content to go silently into the night. She confronted her lover, but by then she was well into her pregnancy.

Her lover was furious. She had failed to take precautions. She had failed to notify him in time for him to insist that she see that certain trusted doctor. He contemplated having her committed to an asylum, secluded from the press, and he set his most trusted agents on the task. One of them made a startling discovery that offered an elegant solution. Unbeknownst to society, Lady Brompston had a sister, an identical twin."

The inspector paused. He took a deep breath and lowered his chin. Cornish braced himself for the blow that was coming.

"Your wife, Judith. She's not estranged at all. She never left you for America."

Cornish trembled, suppressing the tears that were welling in his eyes. His set down his cup and held his hands to stop them from shaking.

"She is committed. You visit her once a year at the asylum on your wedding anniversary. She was placed there for her own safety. The loss of your first child during a very difficult birth, combined with the unfortunate drugs the doctors used to try to bring her back to health, resulted in the loss of her sanity.

"You sir," Jenkins pointed at him. "You were partly the answer to the paramour's dilemma. Your cooperation was needed to make the plan work."

Jenkins spoke quickly now, as if in a hurry to get through the topic.

"Rumors were planted with the press identifying Lady Brompston's paramour and father of her child as a married priest. Shortly thereafter a public divorce was arranged between you and your wife. The divorce proceedings were held with Judith in *absentia*, the press reporting that she had fled to America upset about an affair you were having with an unnamed lady of some repute. Thereafter, Lady Brompston was declared insane by a royal physician and committed to the asylum, never to be seen or heard of again.

"In fact, it was Lady Brompston who fled to America posing as the estranged Judith Cornish, her identical twin. In turn, Judith Cornish took her place as the woman who to this day resides in the asylum."

Father Cornish produced a handkerchief and wiped his eyes and nose. He gazed at the inspector blinking several times to clear his sight. Jenkins poured himself another cup, adding the customary dollop, and sat back in his chair. He took a sip without taking his eyes off Cornish.

"You never had an affair with Lady Brompston. You were too devoted to her sister, your wife. You merely remained dutifully silent and let the rumors swirl. Your wife didn't run away in shame to perpetual seclusion, she was discreetly admitted to the asylum under a new identity. You played the role and sacrificed your reputation in loyalty to the real paramour.

"The Church of England, never quite sure of the truth, stood by its priest publicly, but punished you with assignments well below your talents and seniority. You'd certainly be much more than a school chaplain by now."

"I enjoy ministering to the boys in my charge."

"Shall I finish the chapter by identifying Lady Brompston's true paramour?"

"No, that won't be necessary." Cornish bowed his head and stared at his lap.

"Good, you are a *loyal* subject. His identity shall remain our secret as well."

Cornish felt dizzy. He raised his head and steadied himself. Jenkins smiled, a smile of concern, and took another sip before setting his cup back in its saucer.

"I never met your wife, but being an identical twin to Lady Brompston, she is no doubt quite beautiful."

"You've met Lady Brompston?"

"Yes, twice. Once in New York a few years ago, and then again, strangely enough, in 'Old' York."

Cornish sat up straight in his chair. "Then the rumors of her return to England are true! Where is she?"

"Dead, I'm afraid."

"And the child she was carrying?"

"A boy, born the 20th day of April 1889."

"Where is he now?"

"I don't know. He was last seen with her on a trip to Austria as a baby. She left Austria without him. He's never been seen since."

"How did she die?"

"When I confronted her in York, she chose a black box over being taken into custody."

Cornish slumped back and rubbed his forehead. It was difficult to focus on the information swirling in his head. "A black box?"

"Interesting, isn't it? You're closer to the mystery I've been trying to solve than you thought."

"I, I don't understand."

"Father Cornish, a man who can make such sacrifice, who can bear such burden and keep it to himself...do you now question why I recruited you?"

"Why are you telling me this now?"

"Excellent question," Jenkins replied softly. "I need you now more than ever. I need not only to trust you fully, but to know that you trust me fully. I need your help, and our relationship can't matriculate with such chasm of truth between us. I had to let *you* know, that *I* know."

Cornish's head was spinning uncontrollably now. He took a long breath and tried to clear his mind with the image of Judith, lovely, lying in their bed in the morning. She was most beautiful when sound asleep, when the worries of the day had long fallen off her brow and the morning light glowed on her relaxed face. When in her deepest sleep her jaw would drop and the last hint of tension would disappear from her skin, giving her the same sublime look of intimate shared marital moments. He closed his eyes and held the image. His heart stung as the image slipped away. He blinked back the moisture welling again in his eyes and looked up at Jenkins.

"I don't blame the Church. How could the bishop ever accept my assertions of innocence when I couldn't adequately explain my divorce? I swore to him that I never had an affair with Lady Brompston and had always remained faithful to my wife. But I remained silent when asked to explain why Judith had left. To defrock me would have confirmed the scandal. He clearly saw my loyalties were elsewhere, and so, after all these years, I'm a chaplain for a small boys' school. Not that I mind tremendously. I think I'm a good chaplain.

"I do have a question, Inspector. I must know. Was Judith poisoned purposely, or was that merely the mistake of a well-meaning physician?"

"You have doubts?"

"Of late, yes. My encounter with James Aston has shaken me. It's made me question assumptions. Then I recalled that I first became involved with Father Tate during Judith's difficulties. You know so much on the matter. Can you address my doubts?"

The inspector sat silently, expressionless. "No, I'm afraid I can't."

The words made Cornish feel hollow. He pushed the thought of Lady Brompston out of his mind and meditated on the silence of the room.

"You mentioned you needed my help. I'm not sure I understand, but of course I'll help you in any way I can. I..."

"Yes, Father?"

"I still struggle with 'why me.' What do I possibly bring to this battle?"

"Another excellent question. There's a powerful member of the present government whose personal situation is in many ways similar to that of the paramour you protect. Such situation makes him vulnerable to influence, which is doubly difficult because he fosters a reputation that is above reproach. I believe he is, in fact, being influenced. If he could learn of the discreet service you provided to a similarly situated gentleman in the past, perhaps he would confide in you. Such a confidence would be very valuable to my understanding the extent of the influence on him."

"I see."

"If I might digress for a moment, Father, I'm curious about your opinion from a theological perspective."

"About?"

"This evil we face, killing men with black boxes, forcing children into unconsciousness and death, knives in throats, what is it, exactly? I find no earthly explanation that works. Do you have an un-earthly one?"

Cornish pondered the questions before answering. "Perhaps Saint Paul gives us a clue. 'For we wrestle not against flesh and blood, but against principalities, against powers, against the rulers of the darkness of this world, against spiritual wickedness in high places.'" He paused to measure the effect on the inspector.

"Quite. Then perhaps we should follow his prescription as well."

"You know the passage then, Inspector?"

"Ephesians six, to wit 'Wherefore take unto you the whole armour of God, that ye may be able to withstand in the evil day, and having done all, to stand. Stand therefore, having your loins girt about with truth, and having the breastplate of righteousness; And your feet shod with the preparation of the gospel of peace; Above all, taking the shield of faith, wherewith ye shall be able to quench all the fiery darts of the wicked.'"

"Well done, Inspector. The shield of faith," Cornish shook his head. "I question why you need my guidance at all."

"It's this point that I find most perplexing—children, why children?" Jenkins set his teacup down and waited patiently for an answer.

Father Cornish started to speak and then lifted a single finger in the air to pause the conversation. He rose from his seat and turned back to a bookcase along the wall behind him. He scanned a row looking for something he remembered seeing earlier while surveying the room. The priest soon confirmed his recollection and pulled out a single book. He started flipping through pages while sitting back down and continued the effort until landing on a page in particular. His lips moved slightly as he read to himself.

"Ah, yes," Cornish said softly. "This is it." He looked up at the inspector. "Do you know of John Henry Newman?"

"One of the original Oxford Movement priests, yes. Very high church, advocate of private confession and such, but then he went Roman, if I recall."

"Let me read something to you from his recently published sermon 'The Mind of Little Children.'

"'The simplicity of a child's ways and notions, his ready belief of everything he is told, his artless love, his frank confidence, his confession of helplessness, his ignorance of evil, his inability to conceal his thoughts, his contentment, his prompt forgetfulness of trouble, his admiring without coveting; and, above all, his reverential spirit, looking at all things about him as wonderful, as tokens and types of the One Invisible, are evidence of his being lately (as it were) a visitant in a higher state of things.'"

"Quite lovely, but your point, Father?"

"The children," Cornish held out his hand as if offering it to a small child. He felt profound concern settle on his face. "The children are closer to God. I see it in the boys at school. I've often thought that if God weeps, he weeps first for the children, for the innocent. You and I, we've made our beds. What happens to us in life, good and bad, is in large part within our control. He will weep not when I meet my fate at this advanced age. But, had I died as an innocent child..."

"Then attacks on children are random, not targeted?"

"All children are equal in the eyes of the Lord."

"True, but are they equal in the eyes of something else?"

"Then you think it's not random?"

"What's your explanation? General revenge?"

"Deeper than that, Inspector. War. Is it possible that we are mortals witnessing the last spasms of a great struggle, a struggle that has gone on for eternity, which seems like thousands of lifetimes of agony to mankind but is but a blink in time to God? Tools we may be, or pawns in the bigger play, but still an integral part of the battle."

Jenkins rubbed his chin and took in a deep, contemplative breath. "Can the pawns influence the game?"

"I don't know, but God demands that we try."

"Then try we must." The inspector smiled.

Cornish thought for a moment. Best to get all the cards on the table.

"He knew. James Aston, he knew. He only played along with the Lady Brompston story to humor...no, to toy with me. But during our first encounter he made it clear that he knew."

Jenkins sat quietly sipping his tea, showing no apparent desire to respond.

"Wait. No, it can't be." The thought struck Cornish like a bolt of lightning. "Random...it's not random at all! James Aston gave it away. He frequently asked me about the accomplishments of the boys under my charge. He lectured me on the possibility that future influential men might be identified when still children. He asked how history might be altered if they never reach adulthood. They're targeting boys, not just any boys, but specific, identified, future influential men!"

Jenkins calmly set down his cup. "And girls too, I might add. Thank you, Father. You've confirmed my opinion on the matter. You see, you've proved quite helpful already."

Cornish pushed the image of James Aston, waving his arms about in the priest's small office, out of his mind.

The two men sat in silence. Jenkins refilled his cup. Cornish tried to sort through all the revelations that bounced around in his head.

"If I may return to our earlier discussion, Inspector, you left me somewhat out on a cliff. Are you at liberty to tell me who this highly placed member of the government is, the one you expect me to assist you with?"

"Yes, the sooner the better. I'm afraid much damage has already been done. There's no telling how much more will come." The inspector set his cup down and leaned in toward Cornish. "I believe you enjoy fly fishing?"

"Very much so, it brings me closer to God."

"Yes, Sir Edward Grey is of the same mind. I think he'd find much comfort in your company."

***

Creaking from the door above woke Dr. Samuel Cunningham. Light from the opening silhouetted the form of a man coming down the stairs that ran along the opposite wall. Cunningham stretched his sore body and pushed up from the cold stone floor, rolling to a sitting position as he watched the image of the man continue downward. At about the halfway point the man stopped, struck a match, and lit a candle stored on a shelf. The candle flickered to life and illuminated the dank room and his prison. As the man descended, the bars between Cunningham and the candle cast a rolling shadow back into his cell.

The man came into focus as he approached. He was tall, lanky with wavy blond hair, a button nose and an otherwise nearly featureless face. He had intense, bird-like eyes and carried a substantial frown on his thin lips.

"I've brought you supper, Doctor Cunningham."

Sam rose as the man produced a loaf of bread from his overcoat. He noted two red moles on the backside of the man's right hand as he passed the loaf through the bars.

"Do you need more water?"

"Who are you?"

"Let's take turns, shall we? Do you need more water?"

Sam looked back at the bucket in the corner of his cell and shook his head.

"You don't know me, then?"

"Should I?"

"I should think so. I certainly know you. Mr. 'Y,' the destroyer of black boxes, the doctor for Molly Bell, another box destroyer. There aren't many of you left, you know. In fact, you may be the last."

Cunningham felt rage well up in his chest at the mention of his young patient.

"Quite inconvenient, the lot of you. I don't know why you bother. It is inevitable. All of mankind will be in the box, someday."

"You still didn't answer my question."

"No, I suppose I haven't. You're quite impertinent for someone locked in a cage. But then you are a doctor. Do you play chess?"

"On occasion."

"Ah, excellent, perhaps we can play sometime. James Aston, does that ring a bell? No? Well, I shouldn't be surprised. Your Inspector Jenkins keeps all of you in the dark. He knows so much more than he tells anyone. I wonder why that is?"

Aston stopped and waited for a reply. Cunningham gave no satisfaction.

"Now, Doctor, we can't carry on a conversation if only one of us speaks. Here, let me help you. Why are you here? Is that a good direction to carry us forward?"

"Why *am* I here?"

"Excellent question! Since you play, chess that is, it makes the explanation easier. If I'm facing a formidable player, I want to keep him off balance, on the defensive, vulnerable. He'll protect his valuable pieces. You, sir, are a rook, second in value only to the king and queen. If I can keep the rook in constant danger, locked away so to speak, my adversary is forced to expend energy on the defensive. That will make him susceptible to mistakes."

Aston paused again and peered intensely at him.

"Then you're keeping me alive as bait."

Aston smiled for the first time, his eyes dancing in the candle light.

"You are indeed a perceptive man, Doctor. 'Bait'? Sounds a bit strong. Besides, I don't fish. Fishing is for simpletons, don't you agree?" Aston continued to smile while he took in a deep breath, seemingly savoring the musty cellar air.

"But you tried to kill me?"

"At first, but when we couldn't bag the lot of you in one swat," Aston's hand swept by revealing the backside. The scarlet moles framing the middle knuckle seemed on fire. "One must remain flexible. If the gambit doesn't succeed, you still have to finish the game."

Aston paused again and rubbed his chin, looking straight back at Cunningham's unflinching glare. The two moles seemed to look at him as well.

"The fire, the substance on the rose bushes, the man with the strange cane—that was all at your bidding."

Aston waved his hand in the air, as if shooing away a fly. "I'd like your thoughts on a matter, Doctor—a hypothesis. You're a man of science, no? Science demands the constant test of a hypothesis, otherwise it's just dogma. Anyone who says the scientific debate is over is hiding something. Perhaps this is outside your area of scientific expertise, but I'd value your opinion, nonetheless.

"For the sake of my hypothesis, let's imagine a contest. The goal is the soul of mankind. Look around any city or town today. Take London, where you're presently being held. God-fearing men abound. Churches and Cathedrals are busy with activity around the clock and bursting at the seams on Sunday. It's hard to find a pub without at least one or two priests in the corner, we employ such an army of them here in England.

"Now, imagine the opposite. Churches empty on Sunday, many even shuttered year-round for lack of attendance, turned into bookstores and cafés, ceremonies in the few active churches attended only by the smattering of clergy still employed. Imagine crowded London streets with not a Christian in sight.

"How do we get from here to there? From east to west? How do we win that contest?"

Aston stopped, but Cunningham declined to fill the silence. Aston ran his tongue across his upper teeth and smiled.

"Ergo, my hypothesis—tragedy and despair, on a massive scale affecting every man, woman and child still left alive, against generation after generation, if necessary. You look confused?" Aston paused again, smiling even more broadly. "Shall I spell it out in more detail?"

"What's become of Molly Bell and Jim Talbot?"

"The other box-busters, funny you should ask."

Cunningham became aware of another presence in the basement, first by the smell, a sulfurous stench. Another man slouched at the base of the stairs. The doctor hadn't heard or seen the newcomer descend the stairs, but there he was.

In the flickering light Sam made out a flabby, unshaven face framing an open mouth full of broken and jagged teeth below a droopy left eye. His clothing looked ragged and dirty.

Aston visibly shuddered upon noticing the man. His face turned white as his lips curled downward into a frightened scowl. He withdrew slightly from the bars before slowly turning to speak to the newcomer. Aston's right hand, the one with the two angry red moles, was shaking, the bravado of the taunting jailer all but gone.

"Charlie, my apologies, I had no idea you were calling this evening."

The man with the droopy left eye reached into a coat pocket and flung the contents toward Aston. Two white cards fluttered across the room, one landing at Aston's feet, the other dropping into Cunningham's cell. Sam looked down at the white card lying on the basement floor near him. It contained a single word, "Charlie."

"You've been compromised," came a breathy and smelly demand from the man with the droopy left eye. "You know what to do." The man abruptly turned, bound up the stairs, and disappeared.

A stench wafted across the cellar strong enough to burn Sam's nostrils and sear his eyes. He looked up at Aston, who was staring at him in horror. Tears ran down his face.

"My God, what have I done?" Aston looked at Cunningham in bewilderment.

"No, I won't," Aston muttered. He turned and fetched something from a shelf in a dark corner. Sam braced himself against the bars as he recognized the rectangular object in Aston's hands.

Aston walked slowly toward Cunningham's cage. He moved close to the cell door. His face lacked any expression as he reached into a pocket, produced a key, and unlocked Sam's cage. Then he slowly raised the black box to his face.

"No, you don't have to do this!" Sam screamed.

Looking into the box, James Aston shouted, "Redeem me!"

Cunningham watched in horror as Aston crumpled to the floor. He swung open his cell door. He had to do it. It didn't matter if the man was evil. The doctor picked up the box and peered inside.

The creatures were there. He turned toward the light and pushed forward. He only needed to reach the light.

They were on him, scratching at his legs. He struggled hard to reach the light. Almost there. Push harder. His mouth began to dry and his throat tightened. His arms quivered.

Suddenly he wanted to turn around and fight, fight the creatures scratching and pulling on his legs. "No, push on to the light!" he screamed. His body shook. Rage welled in his chest. "No, not now. Push on to the light!"

A hand grasped his, a hand that wouldn't let go, a hand with two blazing red moles. James Aston's laughter rose above the din of the shrieking monsters clawing at Sam's legs. The laughter grew louder as Aston's grip grew stronger, pulling him away from the light, pulling him back in.

***

"Molly! What is it? Why are you screaming?"

Molly Bell bolted upright in her bed. It was her mother, holding her now by the shoulders.

"Doctor Cunningham!"

"Molly, what is it child? Calm down. You've had another dream."

"The doctor is in danger. I saw it through his eyes. He can't look into that box. It's a trap. He won't get out this time."

"Dear child, what are you talking about?"

"I saw it all. I felt it all. We must get word to the inspector. He has to save Doctor Cunningham."

"Calm down. It was just a dream."

THE BEGINNING OF THE END

CPSIA information can be obtained
at www.ICGtesting.com
Printed in the USA
JSHW010640080819
1056JS00004B/4